Time was running out for them. . . .

Theirs was a strange affair.
He—an ice-blooded Grand Prix race driver whose emotional shell is being chipped away for the first time.

She—a beautiful and vivacious girl who wants to pack years of love and adventure into one last moment.

Like *LOVE STORY,* a tremendous tale of bittersweet love and haunting passions.

BOBBY DEERFIELD

Originally published as
Heaven Has No Favorites

ERICH MARIA REMARQUE

A FAWCETT CREST BOOK

Fawcett Books, Greenwich, Connecticut

The author has had to take some minor liberties with the procedures and formalities of automobile races. He hopes the race aficionados will forgive him.

BOBBY DEERFIELD
(Originally published as Heaven Has No Favorites)

THIS BOOK CONTAINS THE COMPLETE TEXT OF
THE ORIGINAL HARDCOVER EDITION.

A Fawcett Crest Book reprinted by arrangement with
Harcourt, Brace, Jovanovich

ISBN: 0–449–23367–7

Printed in the United States of America

10 9 8 7 6 5 4 3 2 1

To Paulette Goddard Remarque

Publisher's Note

In the motion picture based on this novel, the name of the character known here as Clerfayt has been changed to Bobby Deerfield.

I

Clerfayt pulled in at a service station where the snow had been cleared away, and blew the horn. Crows were cawing noisily around the telephone poles, and in the small workshop behind the pumps someone was hammering away at sheet metal. The hammering stopped, and a boy of sixteen emerged. He wore a red sweater and steel-rimmed glasses.

"Fill her up," Clerfayt said, getting out.

"High-test?"

"Yes. Any place to eat here?"

The boy jerked his thumb toward the other side of the road. "Over there. They were serving *Berner Platte* for lunch. Want me to take off the chains?"

"Why?"

"The road is even icier farther up."

"All the way up the pass?"

"You can't drive over the pass. It's been closed again since yesterday. Report from the automobile club. With a low sports car like this one, you'd never make it anyhow."

"Really?" Clerfayt said. "You arouse my curiosity."

"And you arouse mine," the boy replied.

The air in the restaurant was stale, smelling of old beer and a long winter. Clerfayt ordered *Bündner Fleisch,* bread, cheese, and a carafe of Aigle. He had the girl bring his meal out to the terrace. It was not very cold outside. The sky was vast and gentian blue.

"Want me to hose down the buggy?" the boy called across from the service station. "It damn well needs it."

"Never mind. Just clean the windshield."

The car had not been washed in a long time, and showed it. A torrential rain beyond Aix had caked the red dust of the Saint-Raphaël coast into a batik pattern on hood and fenders. To that had been added splashed lime from puddles on the roads of central France, and the filth hurled at the chassis by the rear wheels of innumerable trucks. Why have I driven up here at all? Clerfayt thought. It's too late for skiing anyway. And pity? Pity is a poor companion for a journey—and a still worse destination. Why don't I drive to Munich? Or to Milan? But what would I do in Munich? Or Milan? Or anywhere else? I am tired, he thought. Tired of staying places and tired of leaving them. Or am I only tired of decisions? But what do I have to decide that amounts to anything? He finished his wine and went back inside the restaurant.

The girl was standing behind the counter, washing glasses. The stuffed head of a chamois stared out of glassy eyes over her head at the advertisement for a Zurich brewery on the opposite wall. Clerfayt took a flat leather bottle from his pocket. "Can you fill this with cognac for me?"

"Courvoisier, Remy Martin, Martell?"

"Martell."

The girl began measuring out the cognac, glass by glass. A cat came in and rubbed around Clerfayt's legs. He asked for two packs of cigarettes and matches also, and paid his check.

"Are those kilometers?" the gas-station boy in the red sweater asked, pointing to the speedometer.

"No, miles."

The boy whistled sharply. "What are you doing up in the Alps? Why don't you keep a car like this on the *autostrada?*"

Clerfayt looked at him. Glittering eyeglasses, a turned-up nose, a broken-out skin, prominent ears—a creature that had just exchanged the melancholia of childhood for all the faults of semi-adulthood. "We don't always do what's right, son," he said. "Even if we know what it is. Sometimes the whole charm of life is making the wrong choices. Get it?"

"No," the boy replied, snuffing. "But you'll find the SOS telephones all along the pass. If you get stuck, just call. We'll come and get you. Here's our number."

"Don't you have Saint Bernards any more, with little kegs of brandy on their collars?"

"No. Brandy costs too much these days, and the dogs got wise. They drank the stuff themselves. Nowadays we have oxen for rescue work. Big strong oxen to pull the cars out."

The boy met Clerfayt's stare with glittering glasses, and did not flinch.

"You're just about all I needed today," Clerfayt said at last. "An Alpine wise guy at four thousand feet! Is your name by any chance Pestalozzi? Or Lavater?"

"No. My name's Göring."

"What?"

"Göring." The boy grinned, revealing a missing incisor. "But my first name in Hubert."

"Any relation to . . ."

"No," Hubert cut in. "We're Basel Görings. If we belonged to the other family, I wouldn't have to be pumping gas here. We'd be sitting pretty on a fat pension from the German government."

Clerfayt gave the boy a searching look. "A strange day," he said finally. "Who would have expected it? Good luck to you in your future undertakings, son. You've been a big surprise to me."

"You're no surprise to me. You're a racing driver, aren't you?"

"What makes you think so?"

Hubert Göring pointed to an almost-vanished number under the dirt on the hood.

"A detective, too!" Clerfayt got into the car. "Maybe it might be better to lock you up soon, to save humanity another calamity. Once you're premier, it will be too late."

He started the motor. "You've forgotten to pay," Hubert stated. "Forty-two Fränkli."

Clerfayt gave him the money. "Fränkli!" he said. "That reassures me, Hubert. A country that has pet names for its money will never become a dictatorship."

An hour later, the car was struck fast. Several pieces of snow fence had given way on the slope, and a drift had buried the road. Clerfayt could have turned and driven back down, but he did not care to meet Hubert Göring's smug look again so soon. Besides, in general he did not like turning back. So he remained patiently sitting in his car, smoking cigarettes, drinking cognac, listening to the racket of the crows, and waiting for God.

God appeared after a while in the shape of a small snowplow. Clerfayt shared the remainder of his cognac with the driver. Then the man drove on ahead, and his machine began whirling up the snow and tossing it aside. It looked as if it were sawing a huge, white, fallen tree into a sparkling circle of chips which, in the slanting sunlight, showed all the colors of the rainbow.

Two hundred yards farther on, the road was clear again. The snowplow pulled over to the side, and Clerfayt's car glided past it. The driver waved after him. Like Hubert, he was wearing a red sweater and glasses. For that reason, Clerfayt had not ventured any talk with him beyond the safe subjects of snow and liquor; a second Göring so soon after the other would have been a bit too much.

Hubert had been fibbing; the pass was no longer closed. The car mounted rapidly toward the crest, and suddenly, far below, the valley lay outspread before Clerfayt, blue and soft in the early dusk. Scattered over it like toys out of a box were the white roofs of the village, a church spire that seemed to lean, skating rinks, a few hotels, and the first lighted windows of houses. Clerfayt stopped the car for a moment and looked at the view. Then he drove slowly down the serpentine curves. Somewhere down below must be the sanatorium where Hollmann was staying—Hollmann, his co-driver, who had become sick a year ago. The doctor had found it was tuberculosis. Hollmann had laughed at the diagnosis—there was no such disease any more, in this age of antibiotics and miracle molds. And even if there were, the doctors gave you a handful of pills, a few shots, and you were well again. But the wonder drugs had not been quite so wonderful and infallible as they were supposed to be, especially not for people who had grown up during the war and been undernourished for years. During the Mille Miglia in Italy, Hollman had had a hemorrhage just outside Rome, and Clerfayt had had to drop him off at the depot. The doctor had insisted on sending him to the mountains for a few months. Hollmann had raged, and finally yielded; but by now the few months had become a year.

The motor began to sputter. The plugs, Clerfayt thought. Fouled again. That came from not thinking about what you were doing while you drove. He let the car roll down the last part of the slope till it stopped on the level, and opened the hood.

They were, as always, the plugs of the second and fourth cylinders. He unscrewed them, cleaned them, put them back, and started the car again. The motor ran normally, and he pumped the accelerator a few times by hand to rid the cylinders of the superfluous oil. As he straightened up to close the hood, he caught a glimpse of a sleigh and saw the horses shy at the whine of the motor and start to swerve across the road toward the car, the sleigh leaping behind them. He ran toward them, seized the left horse by the bridle, and pulled back for all he was worth.

He was dragged for a few steps. Then the animals stopped. They were quivering, and the steam of their breath was eddying around their heads. Their wild, frightened eyes seemed to belong to primeval creatures. Clerfayt cautiously let go of the leather straps. The horses stood still, snorting and shaking their bells. He could see that they were no ordinary sleigh horses.

A tall man wearing a cap of black fur stood up in the sleigh and spoke reassuringly to the team. He acted as if Clerfayt were not there. Beside him, gripping the arms of her seat hard, sat a young woman. She had a tanned face and very bright eyes.

"I'm sorry to have startled you," Clerfayt said. "It didn't occur to me that horses up here might not be used to cars."

The man occupied himself with the animals a minute longer. Then he let the reins fall slack and turned half around. "Not to cars that make such a racket," he replied in an unfriendly tone. "Still, I would have been able to hold the sleigh. Thank you, though, for wanting to save us."

Clerfayt looked up quickly. The face above him was haughty, with a trace of mockery somewhere in it, as though the man were politely ridiculing him for trying unnecessarily to play the hero. It was a long time since he had so intensely disliked anyone at first sight.

"I did not want to save you," he replied dryly. "Just to save my car from being run into."

"I hope you haven't been too badly splattered for your pains."

The man concerned himself with the horses again. Clerfayt looked at the woman in the sleigh. So that's why, he thought. Wants to be the hero himself. "No, I haven't been splattered," he replied slowly.

The Bella Vista Sanatorium stood on a small height above the village. Clerfayt parked the car in a level square, where a few sleighs stood. He switched off the motor and put a blanket over the hood to keep it warm. "Clerfayt!" someone called from the entrance.

He turned, and was astonished to see Hollmann running toward him. He had expected him to be in bed.

"Clerfayt!" Hollmann called. "Is it really you?"

12

"As real as I'm ever likely to be. And you! You're up and about? I thought you'd be lying in bed."

Hollmann laughed. "That's old-fashioned." He slapped Clerfayt on the back. His eyes devoured the car. "I thought I heard Giuseppe's roar, but figured it must be some kind of hallucination. Then I saw you coming up the rise. What a surprise! Where are you coming from?"

"From Monte Carlo."

"What do you know!" Hollmann was in a state of high excitement. "And with Giuseppe, the old lion! I was beginning to think you two had forgotten me."

He patted the chassis of the car. He had driven it with Clerfayt in half a dozen races, and had been in it when he had his first bad hemorrhage. "It's still Giuseppe, isn't it? Not a younger brother already?"

"It's Giuseppe. But he's not running any more races. I bought him from the factory. He's in retirement now."

"Just like me."

"You're not in retirement; you're on leave."

"A whole year! That's not a leave any more. But come on in. We have to celebrate your coming. What do you drink these days? Still vodka?"

Clerfayt laughed. "Don't tell me you have vodka up here?"

"For visitors, we have everything. This is a modern sanatorium."

"It would seem so. It looks like a hotel."

"That's part of the treatment. Modern therapy. We're guests taking a cure, not patients any longer. The words 'sickness' and 'death' are taboo. They're ignored. Applied psychology. Marvelous for morale, but people die just the same. What were you doing in Monte Carlo? Did you ride in the rally?"

"I did. Don't you read the sport news any more?"

Hollmann gave an embarrassed laugh. "At the beginning, I used to. Then I stopped. Idiotic, isn't it?"

"No, sensible. Read it when you're driving again."

"Right," Hollmann said. "When I'm driving again. And when I win the grand prize in the sweepstakes. Who was your co-driver in the rally?"

"Torriani."

They walked toward the entrance. The snowy slopes glowed pink in the setting sun. Skiers shot like black commas through the glitter. "Pretty up here," Clerfayt said.

"Yes, a pretty prison."

Clerfayt did not reply. He knew other prisons.

"Are you teamed up with Torriani regularly these days?" Hollmann asked.

"No. I keep changing co-drivers. I'm waiting for you."

That was not true. For the past six months, Clerfayt had been driving all the sports-car races with Torriani. But since Hollmann no longer read the sports news, it was a handy lie.

It affected Hollmann like wine. A light dew of perspiration formed on his forehead. "Did you win anything in the rally?" he asked.

"Not a thing. We were too late."

"Where did you drive from?"

"Vienna. It was a crazy idea. We were stopped by every Soviet patrol. They seemed to think we might be kidnaping Stalin. Mostly, I wanted to try out Giuseppe's successor. What roads they have in the Soviet Zone! Like leftovers from the Ice Age!"

Hollmann laughed. "That was Giuseppe's revenge. Where did you start before that?"

Clerftyt raised his hand. "Let's have a drink. And do me a favor—for the first few days let's talk about anything you like, only not about races and cars."

"But Clerfayt—what else should we talk about?"

"Just for a few days."

"What's the matter? Has something happened?"

"Nothing. I'm just tired out. I want to rest a bit and for a few days forget about this crazy business of putting people into machines that go too fast and having them drive like mad. Can't you understand that?"

"Sure I can," Hollmann said. "But what's wrong? What's happened?"

"Nothing," Clerfayt replied impatiently. "I'm just superstitious, like the rest of us. My contract is running out and

14

hasn't been renewed. I don't want to jinx anything, that's all."

"Clerfayt," Hollmann said, "who has cracked up?"

"Ferrer. In a silly, stinking little race on the coast."

"Dead?"

"Not yet. But they've had to amputate one of his legs. And that crazy woman who went around with him, that fake baroness, won't go to see him. She sits in the casino and bawls. Can't stand a cripple. Come on now and give me a drink. The last of my cognac disappeared down the gullet of a snowplow driver who's got more sense than we have. His vehicle can't go more than three miles an hour."

They sat in the lobby, at a small table by the window. Clerfayt looked around. "Are all these people patients?"

"No. There are guests, too, visiting the patients."

"The pale-looking ones are the patients?"

"No, they're the healthy people. They're pale because they've just come here. The others, who look so tanned and athletic, are the patients; they've been here a long time."

A girl brought a glass of orange juice for Hollmann and a small carafe of vodka for Clerfayt. "How long do you intend to stay?" Hollmann asked.

"A few days. Where can I put up?"

"The best place is the Palace Hotel. They have a good bar."

Clerfayt looked at the orange juice. "How do you know?"

"We go over there now and then when we play hooky from here."

"Play hooky?"

"Yes, at night every so often, when we want to feel like normal people. It's against the rules, but when the blues get you, it's better than holding a hopeless discussion with God on why you're sick." Hollmann took a flask from his breast pocket and poured a shot into his glass. "Gin," he said. "It helps, too."

"Aren't you allowed to drink?" Clerfayt asked.

"It isn't absolutely forbidden, but it's simpler this way." Hollmann thrust the flask back into his pocket. "We get to be pretty childish up here."

A sleigh stopped in front of the door. Clerfayt saw that it was the one he had met on the road. The man in the black fur cap got out.

"Do you know who that is?" Clerfayt asked.

"The woman?"

"No, the man."

"A Russian. His name is Boris Volkov."

"White Russian?"

"Yes. But just to vary things, not a former grand duke, and not poor. I gather that his father opened a bank account in London at the right time and was in Moscow at the wrong time. He was shot. The wife and son got out. The story goes that the wife carried emeralds the size of walnuts sewed into her corset. In 1917 women still wore corsets."

Clerfayt laughed. "You're a regular detective agency. How do you know all that?"

"Up here you soon know everything about everyone," Hollmann replied with a trace of bitterness. "In two weeks the skiers leave, and this village goes back to being a gossip society for the rest of the year."

A group of short people pressed by behind them. They were dressed in black and were talking animatedly in Spanish.

"For a small village, you seem to have a pretty international set here," Clerfayt said.

"That we have. Death hasn't got around to being chauvinistic yet."

"I'm no longer so sure of that." Clerfayt looked around toward the door. "Is that the Russian's wife?"

Hollmann glanced around. "No."

The Russian and the woman came in. "Don't tell me those two are also sick," Clerfayt said.

"But they are. They don't look it, do they?"

"No."

"It's this way. For a while, the patients look as though

16

they're brimming over with life. Then that stops; but by then they're no longer running around."

The Russian and the woman lingered near the door. The man was saying something insistently to the woman. She listened, then shook her head vehemently and walked swiftly toward the back of the lobby. The man waited a moment, watching her; then he went outside and climbed into the sleigh.

"They seem to be quarreling," Clerfayt said, not without satisfaction.

"That sort of thing is always happening. After a while everyone here goes a little off his rocker. Prison-camp psychosis. Proportions shift; trivialities become important and important things secondary."

Clerfayt scrutinized Hollmann. "Does that happen to you, too?"

"To me, too. It's this business of forever staring at one point. No one can endure it."

"Do the two of them live in the sanatorium?"

"The woman does; the man lives out."

Clerfayt stood up. "I'll drive over to the hotel now. Where can we have dinner together?"

"Right here. The place has a dining room where guests can come."

"Good. When?"

"Around seven. I must go to bed at nine. Like school."

"Like the army," Clerfayt said. "Or before a race. Remember how our manager in Milan used to come and shoo us up the stairs of the hotel like chickens?"

Hollmann's face brightened. "Gabrielli? Is he still around?"

"Of course. What would happen to him? Managers die in bed—like generals."

The woman who had entered with the Russian came back. At the door she was stopped by a gray-haired matron who seemed to be reprimanding her. Without replying, she turned around. Indecisively, she stood still— then she caught sight of Hollmann and came over to him. "The Crocodile doesn't want to let me out any more," she said softly. "She says I shouldn't have gone for a

17

drive and she'll report me to the Dalai Lama if I do it again. . . ."

She stopped. "This is my friend Clerfayt, Lillian," Hollmann said. "I've told you about him. He's paying me a surprise visit."

The woman nodded absently. She seemed not to have recognized Clerfayt, and turned to Hollmann again. "She wants me to go to bed," she said angrily. "Just because I had a little fever a few days ago. But I'm not letting her keep me locked up. Not tonight! Are you staying up?"

"Yes. We're eating in Limbo."

"I'll come, too."

She nodded to Clerfayt and Hollmann, and left.

"It must sound like Tibetan to you." Hollmann said. "Limbo is our name for the room where guests can eat. The Dalai Lama is the doctor, of course, and the Crocodile the head nurse. . . ."

"And the woman?"

"Her name is Lillian Dunkerque. Half Belgian, half Russian. Lost both her parents in the war."

"She seems awfully worked up about nothing."

Hollmann gave a shrug. Suddenly he looked weary. "I've told you that everybody here is a little off his rocker. Especially when there's been a death in the place."

"There's been a death?"

"Yes, a friend of hers. Just yesterday. It doesn't really concern the rest of us, but something of ours always dies, too. A bit of hope, probably."

"Yes," Clerfayt said. "But that's so everywhere."

Hollmann nodded. "People start dying here as spring approaches. More than in winter. Odd, isn't it?"

were put there because they could then be conveniently carried down in the elevator at night. Like luggage, Lillian thought. And behind them, their last traces were washed away with soap and Lysol.

There was no light burning in Number Seven. Nor were there any candles. The coffin had already been closed, the lid pushed down over the thin face and vivid red hair, and screwed tight. Everything was prepared for removal. The flowers had been taken away from the coffin; they lay in a canvas wrapper on a nearby table. It was a special canvas for this purpose, equipped with rings and cords for bagging up flowers. The wreaths lay alongside, piled one on top of the other, like hats in a millinery shop. The curtains had not been drawn, and the windows were open. It was very cold in the room. The moon shone in.

Lillian had come to see her dead friend once more. It was too late. No one would ever again see the pale face and brilliant hair that had once been Agnes Somerville. Tonight the coffin would be carried down secretly and transported by sled to the crematorium. There, under the assault of the fire, it would begin to burn; the red hair would crackle once and spray sparks; the rigid body would heave up once more in the flames, as though it had come to life—and then everything would collapse into ashes and nothingness and a little faded memory.

Lillian looked at the coffin. Suppose she is still living, she thought suddenly. Could it not be that Agnes had returned to consciousness once more in this inexorable box? Didn't such things happen? Who could say how often it happened? Only a few cases were known, it was true, when the seemingly dead were found to be alive; but how many might not have silently suffocated because no one came to their rescue? Could it not be that now, right now, Agnes Somerville was trying to scream in the narrow darkness of rustling silk, trying with parched throat to scream, incapable of producing a sound?

I'm crazy, Lillian thought; I shouldn't have come into this room. Why did I? Out of sentimentality? Out of confusion? Or out of that horrible curiosity that makes one stare into a dead face as if it were an abyss from which we hope to dredge some kind of answer? Light, she thought; I must turn on the light.

She started back toward the door. Suddenly she stood still and listened. She thought she heard a rustling noise, very low, but quite distinct, like nails scratching on silk. Swiftly, she pressed the light switch. The strong illumination of the bare bulb on the ceiling drove back night, moon, and horror. I'm hearing ghosts, she thought. It was my own dress, my own fingernails. It was not the last feeble flicker of life stirring one last time.

She stared at the coffin. No, this black polished box with the bronze handles, standing there in the glare, contained no life. On the contrary—enclosed within it was the darkest menace known to mankind. It was no longer her friend Agnes Somerville who lay there motionless in her white dress, with halted blood and rotting lungs; nor was it any longer the waxen image of a human being slowly beginning to be destroyed by its own enclosed fluids. No, in this box lurked nothing more than absolute zero, the shadow without shadow, the incomprehensible nothingness with its eternal hunger for that other nothingness that dwelt within all life and grew, that was born with everyone and that was also silently growing in herself, Lillian Dunkerque, consuming her life day after day, until it alone would be all that was left and its shell would be packed into a black box just as this one was, consigned to decay and disposal.

She reached behind her for the door handle. As she touched it, it turned sharply in her hand. She suppressed an outcry. The door opened. An attendant stood there, staring at her as wild-eyed as she stared at him. "What the hell!" he stammered. "Where did you come from?" He looked past her into the room, and at the curtains fluttering in the draft. "The room was locked. How did you get in? Where is the key?"

"It was not locked."

"Then somebody must have—" The attendant glanced at the door. "Oh, the key's still in the lock." He wiped his hand over his face. "You know, for a moment I thought—"

"What?"

He pointed to the coffin. "I thought you were it and—"

"I am," Lillian whispered.

"What do you mean?"

"Nothing."

The man took a step forward into the room. "You didn't get me. I thought you were her in the coffin. Whew! Sure made me jump." He laughed. "That's what I call a scare. What are you doing here, anyway? We've already screwed the lid down on Number Eighteen."

"Who?"

"Number Eighteen. I don't know the name. No need to. When it comes to this, the finest name does no good." The attendant turned off the light and closed the door behind them. "Be glad that you're alive and kicking, Miss," he said genially.

Lillian dug some change out of her bag. "Here's something for the scare I gave you."

The attendant saluted, and rubbed the bristle on his face. "Thank you, Miss. I'll share it with my assistant, Josef. After a little job like this, we can always use a shot with a beer chaser. Don't take it so to heart, Miss. Sooner or later we all have our turn."

"Yes," Lillian said. "That's a comfort. It really is an enormous comfort, isn't it?"

She stood in her room. The central heating hummed. She had all the lamps on, as well as the ceiling light. I'm crazy, she thought. I'm afraid of the night. What shall I do? I can take a sedative and go to sleep with the lights on. I can call up Boris and talk with him. She moved her hand toward the telephone, but did not lift it off the hook. She knew what Boris would say. And she also knew that he would be right; but what good was it being right? The meager rationality of human beings was there to show them that they could not live by reason alone. People lived by feelings—and being right was no help, as far as feelings went.

She crouched in an armchair by the window. I am twenty-four years old, she thought, the same age Agnes was. I've been up here for three years. And before that there were nearly six years of war. What do I know of life? Destruction, the flight from Belgium, tears, terror, my parents' death, hunger, and then this illness caused by malnutrition and homelessness. Before that, I was a child. I scarcely remember what cities used to look like in peacetime. The sparkling lights and the radiant world of the streets—what do I remember of them? All I know are blackouts and the rain of bombs from the merciless dark, and then occupation and dread and hiding and cold. Happiness? That glorious word that once inspired so many splendid dreams—how its meaning had shriveled! Happiness had been a room even without heat, a loaf of bread, a cellar, a place that was not under fire. Then she had come here. She stared out of the window. Below, at the entrance, stood a sled in which supplies were brought to the sanatorium. Or perhaps it was the sled for Agnes Somerville, already come. A year ago, Agnes had arrived at the main entrance to the sanatorium, laughing, wrapped in furs, holding flowers; now she was secretly leaving the building through the delivery entrance, as though she had not paid her bill. Six weeks ago, she had been talking with Lillian about plans for departure. Departure—the phantom, the mirage that never came true.

The telephone rang. She hesitated, then lifted it. "Yes, Boris." She listened. "Yes, Boris. Yes, I am being sensible—Yes, I know it happens everywhere—Yes, I know that many more people die of heart attacks and cancer—I've read the statistics, Boris—Yes, I know that it only seems so to us because we live so close together up here—Yes, many are cured—yes, yes, the new drugs—Yes, Boris, I am being sensible, certainly. No, don't come—yes, I love you, Boris, of course."

She laid down the telephone. "Sensible," she whispered, staring into the mirror. Her face stared back at her, a stranger's face with a stranger's eyes. "Sensible!" Good God, she thought, I've been sensible far too long. What

23

for? To become Number Twenty or Thirty in Room Seven beside the freight elevator? Something in a black box that horrifies people?

She looked at her watch. It was shortly before nine. The night loomed dark and endless before her, filled with panic and boredom, that mixture peculiar to hospitals—the panic in the face of disease, and the boredom of a regimented existence—which together became intolerable because they led to nothing but a feeling of utter helplessness.

Lillian stood up. She couldn't be alone now! There would certainly be a few people downstairs—at least Hollmann and his visitor.

Aside from Hollmann and Clerfayt, three South Americans were still sitting in the dining room: two men and a fat, stocky woman. All three were dressed in black; all three were silent. They sat hunched like dark little mounds in the center of the room, directly under the chandelier.

"They come from Bogotá," Hollmann said. "The sanatorium wired them. The daughter of one of the men—the one with the horn-rimmed glasses—was dying. But since they came, the girl has taken an upturn. Now they don't know what to do—fly back or stay here."

"Why can't the mother stay and the others fly back?"

"The woman isn't her mother. She's the stepmother; she's the one who has the money that pays the sanatorium bills. None of them really wants to stay, not the father either. Back home in Bogotá, they'd almost forgotten Manuela. She wrote them a letter once a month, they sent the check regularly, and that was that. So it went for five years, and as far as they were concerned it could have gone on that way forever. Until Manuela decided to become a nuisance by dying. Then, of course, they had to fly over, or else what would people think? Complications arose; the woman wouldn't let her husband fly over alone. She's older than he, and, as you see, not terribly good-looking. She's jealous and won't let him out of her sight. For reinforcement, she took her

24

brother along. Back in Bogotá, people were saying that she'd forced her stepdaughter out of the house. She wants to show them now that she loves Manuela. So it's not only a question of jealousy, but also one of prestige. If she flew back alone, the talk would begin all over again. So all three sit here and wait."

"And Manuela?"

"They were terribly loving to the girl when they arrived; after all, she might die any moment. Poor Manuela, who had never known love, was so overwhelmed that she actually began to get better. By now, her visitors are impatient. Besides, they suffer from nervous hunger, so they stuff themselves with the famous local confectionery, and get fatter by the day. Another week and they'll be hating Manuela for not dying quickly enough."

"Or else they'll take a fancy to the village, buy the confectioner's shop, and settle down here," Clerfayt said.

Hollmann laughed. "You have a macabre imagination."

"On the contrary. Only macabre experiences. But how do you know all this?"

"I've told you there are no secrets here. Nurse Cornelia Wehrli speaks Spanish, so the stepmother pours out her heart to her."

The three black figures stood up. They had not exchanged a word with one another. With somber dignity, they walked in single file to the door.

They almost collided with Lillian Dunkerque, who came in so quickly that the fat woman was startled and jumped to one side, with a high little cry. Almost running, Lillian went straight to the table where Hollmann and Clerfayt were sitting. Then she turned around and looked at the South Americans. "What made her shriek?" she said. "I'm not a ghost, after all. Or am I? Already?" She fumbled in her handbag for her mirror. "I seem to be frightening everybody tonight."

"Who else?" Hollmann asked.

"The attendant."

"Josef?"

25

"No, the other one, who helps Josef. You know the one I mean—"

Hollmann nodded. "You don't frighten us, Lillian."

She put the mirror away. "Has the Crocodile been here yet?"

"No. But she'll be along any minute and throw us out. She's as strict and on the dot as a Prussian drill sergeant."

"Josef is at the door tonight. I've asked. We could get out. Will you?"

"Where? The Palace bar?"

"Where else?"

"There's nothing doing at the Palace bar," Clerfayt said. "I've just come from there."

Hollmann laughed. "There's always enough doing as far as we're concerned. Even if there's not a soul around. Anything outside the sanatorium is exciting to us. After you've been here a while, you don't ask for much."

"We could slip out now," Lillian Dunkerque said. "Josef is the only one watching. The other attendant is still busy."

Hollmann shrugged. "I have a touch of fever, Lillian. Just this evening, all of a sudden. God knows why. Maybe from seeing that dirty sports car of Clerfayt's."

A cleaning woman came in and began setting the chairs on the tables. "We've slipped out with fever before this," Lillian said.

Hollmann looked at her with some constraint. "I know. Not tonight, Lillian."

"Also on account of the dirty sports car?"

"Possibly. What about Boris? Isn't he going?"

"Boris thinks I'm in bed. I made him take me out for a sleigh ride this afternoon. He wouldn't dissipate twice."

The cleaning woman opened the curtains. The landscape, mighty and hostile, appeared outside the window— moonlit slopes, black woods, snow. Against it, the three people seemed utterly forlorn. The cleaning woman began turning out the lights along the walls. As each successive light was extinguished, the landscape seemed to advance a step further toward the three in the room. "Here comes the Crocodile," Hollmann said.

The head nurse was standing in the doorway. She smiled with prominent teeth and cold eyes. "Night owls, as always. Closing time, Messieurs and Madame!" She made no comment on the fact that Lillian Dunkerque was still up. "Closing time," she repeated. "To bed, to bed! Tomorrow is another day."

Lillian stood up. "Are you so sure of that?"

"Absolutely sure," the head nurse replied with depressing cheerfulness. "There's a sleeping tablet on your night table, Miss Dunkerque. You'll rest in the arms of Morpheus."

"In the arms of Morpheus!" Hollmann said with disgust after she had left. "The Crocodile is the queen of clichés. Tonight she was comparatively gracious. Why in the world must these hygienic policewomen treat everyone who lands in a hospital with that gruesome, patient superiority, as if we were all children or idiots?"

"It's their revenge upon the world for what they are," Lillian replied spitefully. "If waiters and nurses didn't have it, they'd die of inferiority complexes."

They were standing in the lobby in front of the elevator. "Where are you going now?" Lillian asked Clerfayt.

He looked at her. "To the Palace bar."

"Will you take me with you?"

He hesitated for a moment. He had a bit of experience with overexcitable Russian women. With half-Russians, too. But then he recalled the incident with the sleigh, and Volkov's arrogant face. "Why not?" he said.

She gave a rueful smile. "Isn't it dreary? We plead for a little freedom the way a drunkard begs a grudging bartender for one last glass. Isn't it miserable?"

Clerfayt shook his head. "I've done it often enough myself."

For the first time, she looked squarely at him. "You?" she asked. "Why you?"

"Everyone has reasons. Even a clod. Where do you want me to pick you up? Or would you like to come along right now?"

"I'd better not. You must go out through the main entrance. The Crocodile is on watch there. Then go down the first serpentine, hire a sleigh, and drive up to the right, behind the sanatorium, to the delivery entrance. I'll be waiting there."

"Good."

Lillian stepped into the elevator. Hollmann turned to Clerfayt. "You don't mind my not coming along tonight?"

"Of course not. I'm not leaving tomorrow, you know."

Hollmann looked probingly at him. "Would you have preferred to be alone tonight?"

"Not at all. Who wants to be alone?"

Clerfayt went out through the empty lobby. All the lights were out except one small one. Through the big window, the moonlight laid wide rhombuses on the floor. The Crocodile stood beside the door.

"Good night," Clerfayt said.

"Bonne nuit," she replied. He could not imagine why the woman had suddenly decided to speak French.

He walked down the serpentines until he found a sleigh. "Can you put up the top?" he asked the driver.

"Tonight? It's not very cold tonight."

Clerfayt did not feel like arguing. "Not for you. But it is for me," he said. "Can you put it up?"

The driver clambered laboriously down from his seat and pulled and tugged at the leather hood of the sleigh. "That better?"

"Good enough. I want to go up to the sanatorium, to the rear entrance."

Lillian Dunkerque was already there. She had on a thin coat of black fur which she hugged tightly around her. It did not strike Clerfayt as very warm. "Everything's all right," she whispered. "I have Josef's key. He gets a bottle of kirsch for it."

Clerfayt helped her into the sleigh. "Where is your car?" she asked.

"It's being washed."

She leaned back into the darkness of the hood as the sleigh turned and drove past the main entrance. "Did

28

you leave the car down below on account of Hollmann?" she asked.

He looked at her in surprise. "Why on Hollmann's account?"

"So that he won't see it. To spare his feelings."

She had a point there. That afternoon, Clerfayt had seen how the sight of Giuseppe excited Hollmann. It was true, though he had not thought of it.

"That didn't occur to me," he replied. "It was only that the car badly needed washing."

He took out a pack of cigarettes. "Give me one," Lillian said.

"Are you allowed to smoke?"

"Of course," she replied, so sharply that he knew it was not true.

"I have only Gauloises. Strong black Foreign Legion tobacco."

"I know them. We smoked Gauloises during the Occupation."

"In Paris?"

"In a cellar in Paris."

He gave her a light. "Where did you start out from today?" she asked. "Monte Carlo?"

"No, Vienne."

"Vienne? In Austria?"

"Vienne near Lyon. I guess you've never seen it. It's a sleepy little town famous for having the best restaurant in France—the Restaurant de la Pyramide."

"Did you drive by way of Paris?"

Clerfayt smiled. "That would have been quite a detour. Paris is much farther north."

"Which way did you drive?"

He wondered why she was so interested. "The usual route," he said. "Via Basel. I had something to do there."

"What was it like?"

He wondered again why she wanted to know. "Boring," he summarized. "There's nothing but gray sky and flat country until you reach the Alps."

In the darkness he heard her breathing. Then he saw her face as they passed through a lane of light from a shop that sold watches. It held a curious expression of astonishment, mockery, and grief. "Boring?" she said. "Flat country? My God, what I would give not to see these eternal mountains all around."

All at once, he understood why she had been interrogating him. For them, these mountains were walls barring them from real life. The mountains meant easy breathing and hope; yet they could not leave them. Their world had constricted to this mountain valley, and for that reason all news from down below seemed word of a lost paradise.

"How long have you been here?" he asked.

"Three years."

"And when will you be able to go down to the low country?"

"Ask the Dalai Lama," Lillian replied bitterly. "Every few months he promises that it will only be a little while now—the way bankrupt governments promise one four-year plan after another."

The sleigh stopped at the turn into the main street. A group of tourists in ski clothes rollicked past them. An exceedingly blonde woman in a blue sweater laughingly threw her arms around the horse's neck. The horse snorted. "Come Daisy darling," one of the tourists called. Lillian tossed her cigarette into the snow.

"People like that pay a lot of money to come here, and we would give anything to get down again. Isn't it ridiculous?"

"It depends on how you look at it."

The sleigh started forward again. "Give me another cigarette," Lillian said.

Clerfayt held out the pack to her.

"I know it must be incomprehensible to you," she murmured. "That all of us up here feel as if we were in a prison camp. Not in a prison; there you know when you're getting out. But in a camp, where there isn't any sentence."

"I understand," Clerfayt said. "I was in one myself."

"You? In a sanatorium?"

"In a prison camp. During the war. But everything was the reverse for us. Our camp was on a flat moor, and for us the Swiss mountains were the dream of freedom. We could see the mountains from the camp. One of the fellows, who knew the Alps well, used to drive us almost crazy with his stories about them. I think that if they had offered to release us on condition that we just hole up in the mountains for several years, most of us would have snapped at the chance. Ridiculous too, isn't it?"

"Would you have?"

"No. I had a plan of escape."

"Who didn't? Did you escape?"

"Yes."

Lillian leaned forward. "Did you succeed? Or were you recaptured?"

"I succeeded. Otherwise I wouldn't be here. There were no halfway stages about it."

"What about the other man?" she asked after a while. "The one who told stories about the Alps?"

"He died of typhus. A week before the camp was liberated."

The sleigh stopped in front of the hotel. Clerfayt noticed that Lillian was wearing no overshoes. He lifted her out, carried her across the stretch of snow, and set her down on the threshold. "Satin shoes weren't made for wading through snow," he said. "Shall we go into the bar?"

"Yes. I need a drink."

In the bar, skiers were clumping about the dance floor in their heavy footgear. The waiter arranged the chairs at a corner table for them. "Vodka?" he asked Clerfayt.

"I think not. Something hot. Mulled wine or grog." Clerfayt looked at Lillian. "Which would you like?"

"Vodka. Isn't that what you've been drinking?"

"Yes. But that was before dinner. How about something that the French call God in velvet trousers? A Bordeaux."

He saw that she was scrutinizing him mistrustfully. She seemed to think he was treating her like a sick person

31

who had to take precautions with what she drank. "I'm not trying to put anything over on you," he said. "I would order the wine if I were by myself. We can drink all the vodka you like tomorrow before dinner. We'll smuggle a bottle into the sanatorium."

"All right. Let's drink wine. Could we have the kind you drank down in the plains in France last night—in the Hôtel de la Pyramide in Vienne?"

It surprised Clerfayt that she had retained the name. Have to be careful with her, he thought; anyone who notices names so well will notice other things too. "It was a Bordeaux," he said. "A Lafite-Rothschild."

This was not strictly true. He had had a regional wine in Vienne, one that was not exported; but there was no need to explain that. "Bring us a Château Lafite 1937, if you have it," he said to the waiter. "And don't warm it with a hot napkin. Let's, rather, have it as it comes from the cellar."

"We have it *chambré,* sir."

"What luck!"

The waiter went over to the bar, and returned. "You are wanted on the telephone, sir."

"By whom?"

"I don't know, sir. Shall I ask?"

"The sanatorium," Lillian said nervously. "The Crocodile."

"We'll soon find out." Clerfayt stood up. "Where is the booth?"

"Outside in the corridor, to the right."

"Bring the wine meanwhile. Open the bottle and let it breathe."

"Was it the Crocodile?" Lillian asked when he returned.

"No. It was a call from Monte Carlo." Clerfayt hesitated a moment, but when he saw her face light up, he thought that it could do her no harm to hear that people died in other places too. "From the hospital in Monte Carlo," he added. "Someone I knew has died."

"Do you have to go back?"

32

"No. There's nothing to be done. I almost think it's lucky for him that he did die."

"Lucky?"

"Yes. He had a smashup in the race. He would have been a cripple for the rest of his life."

Lillian stared at him. She thought she had not heard correctly. What kind of barbarous nonsense was this healthy intruder talking? "Don't you think cripples also like to live?" she asked softly, suddenly filled with hatred.

Clerfayt did not reply at once. The harsh, metallic, demanding voice of the woman who had telephoned him was still ringing in his ears: "What am I to do? Ferrer hasn't left a penny. Come! Help me! I'm stuck here. It's your fault. You're all to blame. You with your damned races."

He shook it off. "It depends," he said to Lillian. "This man was madly in love with a woman who cheated on him with every mechanic. He was also wild about racing, but he would never have risen above the average. All he wanted from life was to win in the big races and be with that woman. He died before he found out the truth about both—and he also died without knowing that the woman wouldn't even come to his bedside after he was amputated. That's why I call it luck."

"Even so, he might have wanted to live," Lillian said stubbornly.

"I don't know about that," Clerfayt replied, irritated. "But I've seen people die more miserable deaths. Haven't you?"

"Yes. But in every case, they would have liked to live."

Clerfayt remained silent. What am I saying? he thought. And what for? Am I talking to convince myself of something I don't believe? That harsh, cold, demanding voice of Ferrer's woman on the telephone!

"Nobody escapes," he said at last, impatiently. "And nobody knows when and how it will catch up with him. What's the use of haggling over time? What is a long life, anyhow? A long past. And the future always extends only to the next breath. Or to the next race. Beyond that, we know nothing." He raised his glass. "Shall we drink to that?"

"To what?"

"To nothing. To a bit of courage, perhaps."

"I am tired of courage," Lillian said. "And of consolations, too. Just tell me what things look like down there, beyond the mountains."

"Desolate. It's been raining for weeks."

She set her glass down on the table. "Up here, it hasn't rained since October. Only snowed. I've almost forgotten what rain looks like."

It was snowing when they came out. Clerfayt whistled for a sleigh.

They were drawn up the serpentines. The bells on the horse's harness jingled. The darkness was full of white flakes, and they had the road to themselves. After a while, they heard the jingling of other bells farther up the mountain. The driver turned into a bypass, beside a street lamp, to make room for the other sleigh. The horse stamped and puffed. In the sifting snow, the other sleigh glided past them almost without a sound. It was a low goods sleigh on which stood a long box wrapped in black oilcloth. Beside the box lay a piece of canvas protecting flowers, and another that covered a heap of wreaths.

The driver of their sleigh crossed himself, and urged his horse on again. In silence, they drove up the last curves and stopped at the side entrance to the sanatorium. An electric bulb under a frosted shade cast a circle of yellow light on the snow, in which lay a few scattered green leaves. Lillian got out. "Nothing helps," she said, and smiled with an effort. "You forget it for a while—but you don't escape it."

She opened the door. "Thank you," she murmured. "And forgive me—I was bad company. But I couldn't be alone tonight."

"Neither could I."

"You? Why you?"

"For the same reason as yours. I told you about it. The telephone call from Monte Carlo."

"But you said he was lucky."

"There are all kinds of luck. And we say all sorts of things." Clerfayt reached into his coat pocket. "Here's the kirsch you were going to give the attendant. And here's that bottle of vodka for you. Good night."

III

Clerfayt awoke to an overcast sky. The wind was shaking the windows.

"Föhn," the waiter said. "The warm wind that makes everyone tired. You feel it in your bones beforehand. Old fractures ache."

"Are you a skier?"

"Not me. With me, they're war wounds."

"How would a Swiss—?"

"I happen to be Austrian," the waiter said. "My skiing days are over. I have only one foot left. But you wouldn't believe how the missing one hurts in this weather."

"How is the snow?"

"Strictly between ourselves, sticky as honey. According to the hotel bulletin: good, powder snow in the higher elevations."

Clerfayt decided to put off skiing. He did not feel up to it; the waiter seemed to be right about the effect of the wind. He had a headache, besides. The cognac last night, he thought. Why had he gone on drinking after taking the girl back to the sanatorium—that odd girl with her mixture of *Weltschmerz* and craving for life? Curious people up here—people without skins. I used to be a

36

little like that, he thought. A thousand years ago. I have changed from the bottom up. Had to. But what was left? What besides a measure of cynicism, irony, and false superiority? And what was there to look forward to? How much longer could he go on racing? Wasn't he already overdue? And then what followed? What awaited him? A job as auto salesman in some provincial town— and old age slowly creeping up with endless evenings, diminishing forces, with the pain of memory and the wear and tear of resignation, the empty pattern and the pretense of an existence that seeped away in stale repetitions?

Weltschmerz is contagious, he thought, and got up. There he was in the midst of life, without goal and without support. He put on his coat, and discovered a black velvet glove in the pocket. He had found it on the table when he returned to the bar alone last night. It must belong to Lillian Dunkerque. He replaced it in his pocket, so that he could leave it at the sanatorium later.

He had been tramping through the snow for about an hour when he came on a small, squarish building off the street, close to the woods. It had a round dome from which black smoke rose. An ugly memory came up in him of something he had wanted to forget; he had invested several years of wild and foolish living in the effort to forget it. "What's that over there?" he asked a young fellow who was shoveling snow away in front of a shop.

"Over there? The crematorium, sir."

Clerfayt swallowed. So he had not been wrong. "Here?" he said. "Why do you have a crematorium here?"

"For the hospitals, of course. For the bodies."

"You mean to say you need a crematorium? Do so many die?"

The boy leaned on his shovel. "Not so many any more, sir. But in the old days—before the war, before the first war, I mean, and after it, too—there were an awful lot that died. We have long winters here, and in winter it's hard to hack open the ground. It's all frozen hard as stone, meters deep. It's a lot more practical to cremate the bodies than bury them. We've had this one for almost thirty years."

"Thirty years? So you had one before crematoriums became really modern. Long before they were used for mass production."

The boy did not follow Clerfayt's reference. "We've always been right up front when it comes to practical things, sir. Besides, it's cheaper. People don't want to spend too much money nowadays. It used to be different. Lots of times the families used to want the bodies shipped home in sealed zinc coffins. Times were different then!"

"I suppose so."

"And how! You ought to hear my father tell about it. He's been all over the world."

"How so?"

"Going along with the bodies," the boy said, with amazement at such ignorance. "In those days, people had a certain amount of respect, sir. They didn't let their dead travel alone. Especially not overseas. For instance, my father knows South America like the inside of his own pocket. People there are rolling in dough, and they always wanted their dead brought back. That was before airplanes were all the rage. The bodies went by railroad and by ship, in a dignified way, as it ought to be. Naturally, the trip took weeks. It was a real experience for the undertaker's man who went along. The meals they serve on those ships! My father collected the menus and had them bound, you know, like an album. On one trip, with a high-class Chilean lady, my father put on more than thirty pounds. Everything was free, even the beer, and besides there was a big tip for him when the coffin was delivered. Then—" the young fellow cast an unfriendly glance at the small squarish building whose dome now expelled only a wisp of smoke—"then they installed the crematorium. At first it was only for people without religion, but now it's become the modern thing to use."

"That's so," Clerfayt agreed. "Not only here."

The boy nodded. "People no longer have any respect for death, my father says. Two world wars did that; too many corpses all over the place. Millions of them. That

38

ruined his job, my father says. Now even people in South America who can afford better have their dead cremated and the ashes sent by plane."

"With no one to go along?"

"That's right, sir."

The smoke from the crematorium had stopped. Clerfayt lit a cigarette and held out his pack to the talkative young man. "You ought to have heard about the cigars my father used to bring back," the boy said, scrutinizing his cigarette. "Havanas, sir, the best cigars in the world. Boxes of them. Dad always felt they were too good for him to smoke; he used to sell them to the hotels here."

"What does your father do now?"

"Now we have this florist shop." The boy indicated the shop in front of which they stood. "If you need any flowers, sir, we're cheaper than the robbers in the village. And we often have some really fine things. Just this morning a fresh shipment came in. Couldn't you use some?"

Clerfayt reflected. Flowers? Why not? He could send some over to the sanatorium to the rebellious young woman. It would cheer her up. And if that Russian friend of hers found out about it, so much the better. He stepped into the shop.

A thin, high-pitched bell tinkled. A man appeared from behind a curtain; he looked a cross between a waiter and a sexton. He was dressed in a dark suit, and was surprisingly small. Clerfayt studied him with some curiosity. He had visualized a more muscular person—but then it occurred to him that the man had not had to carry the coffins himself.

The shop looked miserable, and the flowers were ordinary, except for a few which were far too beautiful for the place. Clerfayt noted a container full of white lilac and, in another vase, one long spray of white orchids. "Fresh as the dew," the little man said. "Just came in today. Something special, this orchid. It lasts at least three weeks. A rare type."

"You know orchids?"

"Yes, sir. I'm something of an orchid fancier. I've seen many varieties. In their native habitat, too."

In South America, Clerfayt thought. Perhaps, after delivering his coffins, the man had made little expeditions into the wilds, so that he would have stories to tell about the jungle to gaping children and children's children. "I'll take them," he said. He drew Lillian's black velvet glove from his pocket. "And would you put this in the box along with them. Have you an envelope and a card?"

He went back to the village. As he walked, he had the feeling that he could still smell the repulsively sweetish smoke of the crematorium. He knew that this was impossible; even though the föhn had pressed the smoke down, he was now much too far away to be able to smell any of it. It was only the recollection of furnaces that had burned day and night—furnaces not far from the camp where he had been kept. Furnaces he wanted to forget.

He stepped into a bar. "A double kirsch."

"Why don't you try a pflümli," the bartender said. "We have really good stuff. The kirsch you get nowadays is mostly adulterated."

"Plum brandy isn't?"

"It's less well known and isn't exported. Why don't you try it?"

"All right. Give me a double."

The bartender filled the glass to the brim. Clerfayt drained it. "Pretty good," the bartender declared. "But can you taste anything that way?"

"I wasn't interested in tasting anything; I was interested in driving away a taste. Give me another, this time for the taste."

"Double?"

"Double."

"Then I'll take one along with you," the bartender said. "Drinking is a contagious disease."

"In bartenders, too?"

"I'm only half bartender; I'm half artist. I paint in my free time. I learned how from a painter who was up here for a while."

"Good," Clerfayt said. "Then let's drink to art. It's one of the few things one can safely drink to nowadays. Landscapes don't take pot shots at you. Cheers!"

He went to the garage to see about Giuseppe. The car stood far at the back of the big, dimly lighted place, its hood facing the wall.

Clerfayt paused at the entrance. In the semi-darkness he could make out someone sitting at the wheel. "Do your mechanics play racing driver?" he asked the owner of the garage, who had come up to him.

"That isn't one of my mechanics. It's someone who says he's a friend of yours."

Clerfayt peered, and recognized Hollmann.

"Isn't he?" the owner asked.

"He is, all right. How long has he been here?"

"Not over five minutes."

"Is this the first time?"

"No. He was over earlier this morning, but only for a moment."

Hollmann was sitting at Giuseppe's wheel, his back to Clerfayt. There could be no doubt that he was dreaming he was racing. The soft click of gears as he shifted could be heard. Clerfayt stood for a moment; then he went out, signing to the garageman to follow him. "Don't tell him I saw him."

The man nodded.

"Let him do whatever he likes with the car. Here . . ." Clerfayt took the keys from his pocket. "Give these to him if he asks for them. If he doesn't ask, leave them in the ignition after he leaves. For next time. Understand?"

"You want me to let him do as he likes. Even take the car out?"

"If he wants to," Clerfayt said.

Clerfayt met him at the sanatorium for lunch. Hollmann looked tired. "Föhn," he said. "Everyone feels rotten in this weather. Hard to get to sleep, and when you do, you sleep like you're drugged and have crazy dreams. How do you feel?"

41

"Normal hangover. Drank too much."

"With Lillian?"

"Afterward. It must be the altitude up here—the liquor doesn't affect you while you're drinking, but apparently you pay for it next morning."

Clerfayt looked around the dining room. There were not many people there. The South Americans were seated in a corner. Lillian was missing.

"In weather like this, most of us stay in bed," Hollmann said.

"Have you been outside today?"

"No. Heard any news of Ferrer?"

"He's dead."

They remained silent for a while. There was nothing to say about it. "What are you doing this afternoon?" Hollmann asked at last.

"I'll sleep and tramp around a bit. Don't worry about me. I just enjoy being in a place where there are hardly any cars, aside from Giuseppe."

The door opened. Boris Volkov looked in, and nodded to Hollmann. He ignored Clerfayt, and shut the door again without entering the dining room.

"He's looking for Lillian," Hollmann said. "Heaven knows where she is. She ought to be in her room."

Clerfayt stood up. "I'll take a nap. You're right about the air here being tiring. Can you stay up tonight? Have dinner with me again?"

"Of course. I don't have any fever today, and I didn't put yesterday's down on the chart. I'm a real trusty around here: the nurse lets me take my own temperature. That's making the grade! How I hate thermometers."

"See you at eight, then, right here."

"Seven. Unless you want to eat somewhere else? This place must begin to bore you."

"Don't be silly. I've seldom had a chance for a good solid stretch of prewar boredom. A pity. Boredom's become the rare luxury of our time. Only the Swiss can afford it, at least in Europe—not even the Swedes, ever since their currency went to pot. Shall I smuggle anything up from the village for you?"

"No, I can't think of anything I need. There's going to be a party here tonight. An Italian woman is giving it, Maria Savini. Secret, of course."

"Are you going?"

Hollmann shook his head. "They always throw this kind of party after somebody's left. Meaning: died. The idea is to have a good time to work up fresh courage." He yawned. "Time for the prescribed siesta. Lie flat and no talking. For me, too. See you tonight."

The coughing had stopped. Lillian Dunkerque lay back exhausted. She had offered her morning sacrifice; the day was paid for, and last night as well. She waited for the nurse to come for her. It was time for the weekly fluoroscopy. She knew the routine to the point of nausea; nevertheless, it made her nervous every time.

She hated the intimacy of the X-ray room. She hated standing there naked to the waist, feeling the assistant doctor's eyes on her. She did not mind the Dalai Lama. To him, she was a case; to the assistant, she was a woman. It did not bother her so much that she was naked; it bothered her that she was more than naked when she stepped behind the screen. Then, she was naked beneath her skin, naked to the bones and to her moving and pulsating organs. To the eyeglasses twinkling in the reddish dusk, she was more naked than she had even seen herself, or ever could.

For a while, she and Agnes Somerville had come to the examinations together. There she had seen Agnes Somerville converted from a beautiful young woman to a living skeleton in which lungs and stomach crouched like ghostly animals, expanding as if they were consuming her life. She had seen the skeleton moving, to the side, forward, seen how it drew breath and spoke, and she knew that she must look the same. Hence her feeling that it was more than obscenity to be looked at by the assistant doctor through the fluoroscope.

The nurse came. "Who is ahead of me?" Lillian asked.

"Miss Savini."

Lillian put on her housecoat and followed the nurse to

the elevator. Through the window, she saw the gray day. "Is it cold?" she asked.

"No. Forty degrees."

Spring will be here soon, she thought. The sick wind, the föhn, the wet, splashy weather, the heavy air, semi-suffocation in the mornings. Maria Savini came out of the X-ray room. She shook her black hair back. "How was it?" Lillian asked.

"He won't say a thing. He's in one of his vile humors. What do you think of my new negligee?"

"Wonderful silk!"

"You really like it? It's from Lizio in Florence." Maria made a comic grimace. It looked odd, with her wasted face. "What the hell! We can't go out in the evenings, so we concentrate on our negligees. Are you coming over tonight?"

"I don't know yet."

"Miss Dunkerque, the doctor is waiting," the nurse admonished her from the door.

"Come," Maria said. "Everyone else is coming. I have new records from America. Fabulous!"

Lillian entered the dusky room. "At last!" the Dalai Lama said. "Will you ever learn to be punctual, Miss Dunkerque?"

"I'm sorry."

"All right. Temperature chart."

The nurse handed it to him. He studied it, and murmured with the assistant. Lillian tried to catch what he was saying. She could not. "Light out," the Dalai Lama said at last. "Turn right, please—left—once more—"

The phosphorescent glow of the screen glimmered on his bald head and the assistant's glasses. Following the orders to breathe and not to breathe, Lillian felt somewhat nauseated; it was like being on the verge of fainting.

The examination took longer than usual. "Let's see that case history again," the Dalai Lama said.

The nurse switched on the light. Lillian stood beside the screen and waited. "You've had two bouts of pleurisy, haven't you?" the Dalai Lama asked. "One through not being careful?"

Lillian did not answer at once. Why had he asked? It was right there in the case history. Or had the Crocodile complained about her, and was he warming over this old business in order to give her a new lecture? "Is that right, Miss Dunkerque?" the doctor persisted.

"Yes."

"You were lucky. Almost no adhesions. But what's this—?"

The Dalai Lama looked up. "You can go into the next room. Get yourself ready for refilling the pneumo, please."

Lillian followed the nurse. "What is it?" she asked. "Fluid?"

The nurse shook her head. "Perhaps the temperature variations—"

"But that has nothing to do with my lungs! It's only emotional. Miss Somerville's departure. The föhn. I am negative! You know I'm not positive! Or am I?"

"No, no. Come, lie down. You want to be ready when the doctor comes."

The nurse moved the machine closer. It's no use, Lillian thought. For weeks I've done everything they wanted, and instead of getting better, it's certainly gotten worse. Nothing to do with yesterday. After all, I don't have any fever today; more likely I'd have fever if I'd just gone to bed on time last night. You never know. What is he going to do with me now? Is he going to poke around in me and puncture me, or only fill me up like a tired balloon?

The doctor came in. "I have no fever," Lillian said quickly. "It's just a little emotional upset. I haven't had any fever for a week, and even then I only had it when I was upset. That isn't organic. . . ."

The Dalai Lama sat down beside her and felt for a point for the needle. "You'd better stay in for the next few days."

"I can't just stay in bed all the time. That's what gives me fever. It drives me crazy."

"You need only remain in your room. For today, though, bed rest. Iodine, nurse, right here."

Lillian studied the brown spot of iodine while she was

changing her clothes in her room. Then she drew out the vodka from under her lingerie and poured a glass. She listened toward the corridor. The nurse would be coming with her supper any minute, and she did not want to be caught drinking.

I'm not too thin, she thought, posting herself in front of the mirror. I've gained half a pound. A great achievement. She drank ironically to her mirror image, and hid the bottle again. She heard the cart with her supper outside. She reached for a dress.

"Are you getting dressed?" the nurse asked. "You're not allowed out, you know."

"I'm dressing because it makes me feel better."

The nurse shook her head. "Why don't you get into bed? I'd love to have my meals served in bed once in a while!"

"Lie down in the snow and catch pneumonia," Lillian said. "Then you could take to your bed and let others serve you."

"Not me. All I'd do would be to catch a cold. Here's a package for you. It looks like flowers."

Boris, Lillian thought. He often sent her flowers after she had been pumped up.

"Aren't you going to open it?" the nurse asked curiously.

"Later."

Lillian dabbled at her food for a while, then had it taken away. The nurse made her bed. "Don't you want to turn your radio on?" she asked.

"If you want to hear it, turn it on."

The nurse experimented with the knobs. She got Zurich with a talk on Conrad Ferdinand Meyer, and Lausanne with news. She turned the dial farther, and suddenly she had Paris. Someone was playing a Debussy piano piece. Lillian went to the window and waited for the nurse to finish and leave the room. She stared out into the evening mist, and listened to the music from Paris, and it was unendurable.

"Do you know Paris?" the nurse asked.

"Yes."

"I've never seen it. It must be wonderful."

"When I was there, it was cold and dark and dreary and occupied by the Germans."

The nurse laughed. "But that's over now. It hasn't been like that for several years. By now it must be just as it was before the war. Wouldn't you like to go again?"

"No," Lillian replied harshly. "Who would want to go to Paris in winter? Are you through?"

"I will be in a moment. What's the hurry? There's nothing in particular to do here."

The nurse left at last. Lillian turned off the radio. Yes, she thought, there was nothing in particular to do here. You could only wait. Wait for what? For life to continue to consist of waiting?

She undid the blue ribbon around the white box. Boris —he had come to terms with the idea of staying up here, she thought. Or at least that was what he said. But could she ever?

She parted the tissue paper that wrapped the flowers, and instantly let the box drop as if there were a snake inside.

She stared at the orchids on the floor. She knew those flowers. Coincidence, she thought, a ghastly coincidence; they are other flowers, not the same ones, others like them. But something in her knew, even as she thought this, that such coincidences did not occur. This kind of orchid was not kept in stock in the village. She had tried to buy some, and not found them, and at last had ordered hers from Zurich. She counted the blossoms on the spray. The very same number. Then she saw that a petal was missing from the lowest blossom. She remembered having noticed that when the package arrived from Zurich. There could no longer be the slightest doubt: the flowers lying on the rug at her feet were the very ones she had placed upon Agnes Somerville's coffin.

I am having a fit of nerves, she thought. There must be an explanation for all this; these aren't ghost flowers that have manifested themselves again. Someone is playing a gruesome joke on me. But why? And how? How could this spray of orchids possibly have come back to me?

47

And what is the meaning of this glove beside them, looking like a dead, blackened hand reaching out in menace, like the symbol of a ghostly mafia?

She walked around the spray on the floor as though it were really a snake. The blossoms no longer seemed to be flowers; contact with death had made them sinister, and their whiteness was whiter than anything she had ever seen before. Quickly, she opened the glass door to her balcony, warily picked up the tissue paper, and with it the spray of flowers, and threw both over the railing. She sent the box flying after it.

She listened into the mist. Distant voices and the bells of sleighs wafted through it. She went back into her room and saw the glove on the floor. Now she recognized it, and recalled having worn it in the Palace bar with Clerfayt. Clerfayt, she thought—what had he to do with it? She must find out. At once!

It was some time before he answered the telephone.

"Did you send my glove back to me?" she asked.

"Yes. You forgot it at the bar."

"Are the flowers from you, too? The orchids?"

"Yes. Wasn't my card along?"

"Your card?"

"You didn't find it?"

"No." Lillian swallowed. "Not yet. Where did you get those flowers?"

"In a flower shop," Clerfayt replied in a tone of surprise. "Why?"

"Here in the village?"

"Yes, but why? Were they stolen?"

"No. Or perhaps they were. I don't know—"
Lillian fell silent.

"Shall I come up?" Clerfayt asked.

"Yes."

"When?"

"In an hour—it's quiet then."

"All right, in an hour. At the delivery entrance."

"Yes."

With a sigh, Lillian set the telephone back on the hook. Thank God, she thought, here was someone you did not have to give explanations to. Someone who simply came, and did not pester you with questions. Someone who did not care about you and was not worrying over you, like Boris.

Clerfayt stood at the side door. "Can't you stand orchids?" he said, pointing to the snow.

There lay the flowers and the box. "Where did you get them?" Lillian asked.

"In a small flower shop down below—on the outskirts of the village. Why? Is there something wrong with them?"

"These flowers—" Lillian said with an effort—"these are the very same flowers I put on my friend's coffin yesterday. I saw them once again before the coffin was taken away. The sanatorium doesn't keep any of the flowers. Everything is taken away. I've just asked the attendant. Everything was sent to the crematorium. I don't know how—"

"To the crematorium?" Clerfayt asked.

"Yes."

"Good Lord! The shop where I bought the flowers is right near the crematorium. It's a poor little place, and I wondered that they had flowers like these. This explains it. . . ."

"What do you mean?"

"Instead of burning the flowers with the coffin, one of the workers at the crematorium must have kept them out and sold them to the shop."

"How could that be?"

"Couldn't be anything else. Flowers are flowers, and one spray of orchids looks like another. Hardly likely that a little trick like that would be found out. Who would count on the crazy coincidence that a rare type of orchid would come back to the very person who sent it."

Clerfayt took Lillian's arm. "What shall we do about it?" he asked. "Shall we be shocked, or shall we laugh at mankind's deep-seated money-making instinct? I propose we laugh; if we didn't laugh now and then, we'd die of grief at all the things that happen in this glorious century of ours."

Lillian stared at the flowers with abhorrence. "How

repulsive," she said under her breath. "Stealing from a dead woman."

"Neither more nor less repulsive than many other things," Clerfayt replied. "I never would have thought I would search corpses for cigarettes and bread, and yet I did just that. In the war. It's terrible at first, but you get used to it, especially when you're hungry and haven't had a smoke in a long time. Come, let's go out for a drink."

She looked at the flowers. "What shall we do with them?"

"Leave them there. They have nothing to do with you, with your dead friend, or with me. I'll send you other flowers tomorrow. From a different shop."

He opened the door of the sleigh. As he did so, he noticed the driver's face. The man's eyes were resting upon the orchids with calm interest, and he knew that the driver would be back after the orchids just as soon as he had taken Lillian and himself to the hotel. God only knew what would happen to the orchids then. He thought of trampling on them. But why should he choose to play God? That never worked out well.

The sleigh stopped. Some planks had been laid down on the wet snow to make a path to the hotel entrance. Lillian got out. She suddenly struck Clerfayt as somehow exotic, as, slender, bending forward a little and holding her coat wrapped close across her chest, she made her way in her evening shoes through the clumping, heavy-shod crowd of winter-sports people, amid all that noisy health strangely radiating the dark fascination of her illness.

He followed her. What am I letting myself in for? he thought. And with whom? Isn't she one of those people whose emotions stick out like the legs of a young girl in a much too short dress? Still, she was quite a bit different from Lydia Morelli, with whom he had talked over the telephone an hour ago, Lydia Morelli, who had learned all the tricks and never forgot a single one.

He caught up to Lillian at the door. "This evening," he said, "we are going to talk about nothing but the most superficial things in the world."

An hour later the bar was packed. Lillian looked toward the door. "Here comes Boris," she said. "I might have known it."

Clerfayt had already seen the Russian pushing his way slowly through the crowd clustered at the bar.

Boris ignored Clerfayt. "Your sleigh is waiting outside, Lillian," he said.

"Send the sleigh away, Boris," she replied. "I don't need it. This is Mr. Clerfayt. You've already met him."

Clerfayt rose, a shade too negligently.

"Really?" Volkov said. "Oh, so I have. I beg your pardon." He glanced at Clerfayt, and past him. "You had that sports car that made the horses shy, hadn't you?"

Clerfayt felt the hidden disdain. He did not reply, and remained standing.

"I suppose you have forgotten you're due to be X-rayed tomorrow," Volkov said to Lillian.

"I have not forgotten, Boris."

"You must be rested and well-slept."

"I know that. I have time enough."

She spoke slowly, as if answering a child who did not understand. Clerfayt realized that this was her only way of restraining her irritation. He felt almost sorry for the Russian; the man was in a hopeless situation. "Won't you sit down?" he asked, not entirely with benevolent intent.

"No thanks," Volkov replied coldly, as if he were speaking to a waiter who had asked whether he wished to order anything. Like Clerfayt a moment before, he sensed the other man's disdain.

"I am waiting for someone," he said to Lillian. "If you want the sleigh meanwhile—"

"No, Boris! I am going to stay."

Clerfayt had had enough. "I brought Miss Dunkerque here," he said quietly. "And I think I am capable of taking her back."

Volkov looked fully at him for the first time. His expression changed. He almost smiled. "I am afraid you misunderstand me," he said. "But there would be no point in explaining."

He bowed to Lillian, and for a moment it seemed as if the mask of superiority were falling away, and there was nothing he could do to preserve it. Then he composed himself and went to the bar.

Clerfayt sat down. He was dissatisfied with himself. What am I up to? he thought. After all, I'm no longer twenty years old. "Why don't you go back with him?" he asked.

"Do you want to get rid of me?"

He looked at her. She seemed really helpless, but he knew that helplessness was the most dangerous attribute a woman could have—for no woman was really helpless. "Of course not," he said. "Then we'll stay."

She craned a bit to see the bar. "He isn't going," she said softly. "He's watching me. He thinks I'll give in."

Clerfayt took the bottle and filled their glasses. "Good. Let's see who holds out longest."

"You don't understand him," Lillian countered sharply. "He isn't jealous."

"Isn't he?"

"No. He's unhappy and sick and concerned about me. It's easy to be superior when you're healthy."

Clerfayt set the bottle down on the table. This damn loyal little bird! No sooner was she saved, than she pecked at the rescuing hand. "Possibly," he said evenly. "But is it a crime to be well?"

The expression in Lillian's eyes changed. "Of course not," she murmured. "I don't know what I'm saying. I had better go."

She reached for her handbag, but did not get up. Clerfayt had had enough of her for the day, but not for anything in the world would he have let her go as long as Volkov stood at the bar waiting for her. He was not yet that old, he thought. "You don't have to be careful about my feelings," he said. "I'm not very sensitive."

"Everybody here is sensitive."

"I'm not from here."

"Yes," Lillian said. "I suppose that's it!"

"What?"

She smiled. "That's what gets on all our nerves. Haven't you noticed? Even your friend Hollmann's."

Clerfayt looked at her in surprise. "That could be true. I probably shouldn't have come." He nodded toward the bar. "Do I get on Volkov's nerves, too?"

"Haven't you noticed?"

"I suppose so. He certainly doesn't try to hide it."

"He's leaving," Lillian said.

Clerfayt could see that. "And what about you?" he asked. "Shouldn't you be in the sanatorium too—rather than here?"

"Who knows? The Dalai Lama? I myself? The Crocodile? God?" She picked up her glass. "And who is responsible? Who?" she asked hopelessly. "Myself? God? And who is responsible for whom? Come, let's dance."

Clerfayt remained in his seat.

She stared at him. "Are you worried about me, also? Do you think I shouldn't—"

"I don't think anything," Clerfayt replied. "Only, I cannot dance. One of my legs isn't up to it any more. But if you want to, we can try."

They moved to the dance floor. "Agnes Somerville always did what the Dalai Lama told her to—" Lillian said as the noise of the tramping tourists closed around them. "To the letter—"

IV

The sanatorium was quiet. The patients were taking their rest cure. Silently, they lay in their beds and deck chairs, stretched out like sacrificial victims, the weary air fighting a silent battle with the enemy nibbling at them in the warm darkness of the lungs.

Lillian Dunkerque, in blue slacks, sat curled in the chair on her balcony. The night was far away, forgotten. That was how it always was up here—once the morning was reached, the panic of the night dwindled to a shadow on the horizon and you could hardly understand it any longer. Lillian sat up and stretched in the light of the late forenoon. It was a soft, shimmering curtain that veiled yesterdays and made tomorrows unreal. In front of her, packed around with snow which had blown upon the balcony during the night, was the bottle of vodka Clerfayt had given her.

The telephone rang. She went to it, lifted it. "Yes, Boris—No, of course not—where would we end if we did that?—Let's not talk about it—Of course you can come up—Yes, I'm alone, naturally—"

She returned to the balcony. For a moment, she considered whether she ought to hide the vodka; but then she went for a glass and uncapped the bottle. The vodka was very cold and very good.

"Good morning, Boris," she said when she heard the door. "I'm drinking vodka. Would you care for some, too? Then get yourself a glass."

She stretched out in the deck chair and waited. Volkov came out on the balcony, a glass in his hand. Lillian breathed a sigh of relief. Thank God, no sermon, she thought. Volkov poured himself a glass. She held out hers. He filled it to the brim. "Why, Dusha?" he asked. "X-ray panic?"

She shook her head.

"Fever?"

"Not that either. Subnormal temperature, rather."

"Has the Dalai Lama said anything about your pictures?"

"No. What would he say? I don't want to know what he thinks, anyhow."

"Good," Volkov replied. "Let's drink to that."

He drank his vodka down in one swallow and put the bottle at a distance from him. "Let me have another glass," Lillian said.

"As much as you like."

She observed him. She knew that he hated her to drink; but she knew also that he would not say a word to dissuade her from drinking. Not now. He was too diplomatic for that; he knew her moods. "Another?" he asked. "The glasses are small."

"No." She set her glass down beside her without having drunk. "Boris," she said, drawing her legs in their blue slacks up on to the chair, "we understand each other too well."

"Really?"

"Yes. You understand me too well and I you, and that's our misery."

"Especially in föhn weather," Volkov replied, laughing.

"Not only in föhn weather."

"Or when there are strangers around."

"You see," Lillian said, "you already know the reason. You can explain everything. I can't explain anything. You know everything about me in advance. How wearisome that is. Is that the föhn, too?"

"The föhn and springtime."

Lillian closed her eyes. She felt the oppressive, disturbing air. "Why aren't you jealous?" she asked.

"I am. All the time."

She opened her eyes. "Of whom? Of Clerfayt?"

He shook his head.

"I thought not. Then of what?"

Volkov did not answer. Why was she asking? he thought. What did she know about it? Jealousy did not begin with another person, nor end with that. It began with the air that the beloved breathed, and never ended. Not even with the other's death.

"Of what, Boris?" Lillian asked. "Of Clerfayt, after all?"

"I don't know. Perhaps of the thing that has come up here with him."

"What has come up?" Lillian stretched, and closed her eyes again. "You don't have to be jealous. Clerfayt will drive away again in a few days, and will forget us and we him."

For a while, she lay still in her deck chair. Volkov sat behind her, reading. The sun advanced until the edge of its shifting rectangle of light reached her eyes, filling them under her closed lids with warm orange and golden light. "Sometimes I would like to do something utterly crazy, Boris," she said. "Something that would shatter the glass ring here. Let myself go—let the chips fall where they may."

"Everyone would like to do that."

"You, too?"

"Me, too."

"Then why don't we do it?"

"It would not change anything. We would only feel the glass ring that surrounds us more keenly. Or else shatter it, cut ourselves on its sharp edges, and bleed to death."

"You, too?"

Boris looked at the thin figure before him. How little she knew about him, for all she thought she understood him! "I have accepted it," he said, knowing that this was not true. "It's simpler, Dusha. Before we consume ourselves with pointless hatred of it, we ought to try to see whether we can't live with it."

Lillian felt a wave of weariness coming over her. Here they were, at it again, the everlasting discussion in which you entangled yourself as in a spider web. It was all perfectly true, but how did that help you?

"Accepting is resignation," she murmured after a while. "I'm not yet old enough for that."

Why doesn't he go? she thought. And why do I insult him even when I don't want to? Why should I despise him for being here longer than I have and for having the good fortune to think differently about it? Why does it drive me wild that he is like the man in prison who thanks God for not having been executed—and I like the one who curses God because he isn't free.

"Don't mind me, Boris," she said. "I'm just talking. It's noon and the vodka and the föhn. And perhaps X-ray panic, too—only I don't want to admit it. Up here, no news is bad news."

The bells of the church down in the village began to ring. Volkov stood up and lowered the awning somewhat to shut out the sun. "Eva Moser is being discharged tomorrow," he said. "Well."

"I know. She's been discharged twice before."

"This time she really is well. The Crocodile told me so."

Through the fading clangor of the bells, Lillian suddenly heard Giuseppe's roar. The car sped up the serpentines and stopped. She wondered why Clerfayt was bringing it up; this was the first time since the day of his arrival.

"I hope he doesn't intend to go skiing with the car," Volkov said.

"Certainly not. Why?"

"He's parked it on the slope behind the fir trees. By the practice field for novices, not in front of the hotel."

"He must have his reasons. Tell me, why can't you bear him, really?"

"I don't know. Perhaps because I was once much like him."

"You?" Lillian replied sleepily. "That must have been a long time ago."

"Yes," Volkov said. "That was long ago."

Half an hour later, Lillian heard Clerfayt's car drive off. Boris had already left. She continued to lie for a while, eyes closed, looking at the flickering brightness under her eyelids. Then she stood up and went downstairs.

To her surprise, she saw Clerfayt sitting on a bench in front of the sanatorium. "I thought you drove down just before," she said, sitting down beside him.

He blinked into the strong light. "That was Hollmann."

"Hollmann?"

"Yes. I sent him to the village to buy a bottle of vodka."

"With the car?"

"Yes," Clerfayt said. "With the car. It was high time for him to be getting his hands on the wheel of that buggy."

They heard the motor again. Clerfayt stood up and listened. "Now we'll see what he does—whether he comes right back up here like a good little boy, or whether he tears off in Giuseppe."

"Tears off? Where?"

"Wherever he likes. There's plenty of gas in the tank —enough to take him practically to Zurich."

"What?" Lillian asked. "What's that you're saying?"

Clerfayt was listening again. "He's not coming back. He's driving along the village street toward the lake and the highway. See, there he is already—beyond the Palace Hotel. Thank God!"

Lillian had sprung to her feet. "Thank God? Are you crazy? You've sent him off in an open sports car? To Zurich if he likes? Don't you realize that he's sick?"

"That's just the reason. He already had the idea he'd forgotten how to drive."

"And suppose he catches cold?"

Clerfayt laughed. "He's warmly dressed. And cars have the same effect on racing drivers as evening dresses on women—if they're having fun, they never catch cold in the one or the other."

Lillian stared at him. "And suppose he does catch cold just the same? Do you know what that means up here? Water on the lungs, adhesions, dangerous relapses. Up here a cold can mean the end of you."

Clerfayt looked at her. He thought her considerably more attractive than she had seemed last night. "You ought to keep that in mind when you play hooky and go to the Palace bar at night, instead of staying in bed," he said. "In a skimpy evening dress and satin shoes."

"That has nothing to do with Hollmann!"

"Of course not. But I believe in the therapy of the forbidden. I thought you did, too."

Lillian was perplexed for a moment. Then she said: "Not for others."

"Good. Most people believe in it only for others." Clerfayt looked down toward the lake. "There he is. See him? Just listen to the way he's taking the curves. He hasn't forgotten how to shift yet. Tonight he'll be a different man."

"Where? In Zurich?"

"Anywhere. Here too."

"Tonight he'll be in bed with a fever."

"I don't think so. And even so! Better a little fever than for him to go skulking around the car and thinking he's a cripple."

Lillian turned sharply. It was as though he had slapped her. Cripple, she thought. Because Hollmann is sick? How dare he, this ignorant lout! Did he by any chance think of her as a cripple too? She recalled the first evening in the Palace bar when he had talked on the telephone with Monte Carlo. Hadn't he also spoken of cripples then? "Up here a little fever can quickly turn into fatal pneumonia," she said angrily. "But I suppose that wouldn't bother you. All you'd say was that Hollmann was lucky to die after after having sat in a sports car once more and imagined he was a great racing driver."

At once she was sorry she had said that. She did not understand why she was so furious.

"You have a good memory," Clerfayt said, amused. "I've noticed that before. But calm down; the car isn't as fast as it sounds. With chains on the wheels, you can't exactly drive at racing speeds."

He put his arm around her shoulders. She did not speak or move. She saw Giuseppe emerge from the woods behind the lake, small and black. Compact as a buzzing bumblebee, it shot through the white glare that hung above the snow, in the sunlight. She heard the pounding of the motor and the echo tossed back by the mountains. The car headed for the road that led over the pass to the other side of the mountains, and suddenly she knew what it was that had so excited her. She saw the car vanish behind a curve. Only the sound of the motor remained, a furious, imperative drumbeat that called to some unknown departure and that she felt as deeper than mere noise.

"I hope he really isn't skipping out," Clerfayt said.

Lillian did not reply at once. Her lips were dry. "Why should he skip out?" she said with an effort. "He's almost cured, you know. Why should he risk everything?"

"That's the time people often do take risks."

"Would you risk it if you were in his place?"

"I don't know."

Lillian took a deep breath. "Would you do it if you knew you would never get well again?" she asked.

"Instead of staying here?"

"Instead of vegetating here for a few months longer."

Clerfayt smiled. He knew other kinds of vegetating. "It depends on what you mean by that," he said.

"Living cautiously," Lillian replied quickly.

He laughed. "That's hardly the sort of thing you ask a racing driver."

"Would you do it?"

"I have no idea. One never knows what one will do beforehand. Perhaps I would—to make one last effort to seize hold of everything that means life, without considering time. But I might also live by the clock and scrimp on every day and every hour. One never knows. I've experienced some odd reactions."

Lillian drew her shoulder away from under Clerfayt's arm. "Don't you have to settle that with yourself before every race?"

"It seems more dramatic than it is. I don't drive for romantic reasons. I drive for money and because I can't do anything else—not because I'm so adventurous. I've had enough adventures in this damned age of ours without wanting any more. Probably you have, too."

"Yes," Lillian replied. "But not the right ones."

They suddenly heard the motor again. "He's coming back," Clerfayt said.

"Yes," she repeated, taking a deep breath. "He's coming back. Are you disappointed?"

"No. I only wanted him to have a chance to drive the car. The last time he was in it, he had his first hemorrhage."

Lillian saw Giuseppe zooming toward them on the highway. All at once she could not endure the prospect of seeing Hollmann's radiant face. "I have to go in," she said hastily. "The Crocodile is already looking for me." She turned toward the entrance. "And when are you driving over the pass?" she asked.

"Whenever you like," Clerfayt replied.

It was Sunday, and Lillian always found Sundays in the sanatorium harder to get through than weekdays. The Sundays had a false peacefulness, and lacked the routine of weekdays. The doctors paid no calls, unless it was essential, so there was one reminder the less that you were ill. On the other hand, for this reason the patients were all the more restless, and at night the Crocodile often had to collect bedpatients from rooms where they did not belong.

Lillian came down to dinner in defiance of orders; the Crocodile did not usually check up on Sundays. She had had two glasses of vodka to defend herself against the dreariness of dusk; but it did not do any good. Then she had put on her best dress—clothes sometimes gave one more of a lift than any philosophic comforting. But this time, even that had been useless. There was no throwing off the blues, the sudden attack of melancholia, the contending with God that everyone up here was prey to, and that came and went without visible cause. It had come fluttering upon her like a dark moth.

Not until she stepped into the dining room did she realize where it came from. The room was almost full, and at a table in the center, surrounded by half a dozen of her friends, sat Eva Moser, a cake, a bottle of champagne, and a pile of gaily wrapped gifts in front of her. This was her last evening. She was due to leave tomorrow afternoon.

At first, Lillian wanted to turn back. Then she saw Hollmann, sitting alone next to the table of the three black-clad South Americans who were waiting for Manuela's death. Hollmann beckoned to her.

"I drove Giuseppe," he said. "Did you see?"

"Yes. Did anyone else see you?"

"Who?"

"The Crocodile? Or the Dalai Lama?"

"Nobody. And what if they did! I feel great. I was beginning to think I couldn't drive the damned buggy any more."

"Everyone seems to be feeling great this evening," Lillian replied bitterly. "What do you think of that?"

She gestured toward Eva Moser. The girl sat with plump and overheated face, the center of attention for all her sympathetic and gloomily envious friends, who exaggerated their good will because it could not entirely dispel their envy. Eva Moser was like someone who has drawn the grand prize at a lottery and cannot understand why everyone else is so interested in her.

"Have you taken your temperature?" Lillian asked Hollmann.

He laughed. "That can wait till tomorrow. I don't want to think about it today."

"Don't you think you have fever?"

"I don't care. And I don't think so."

Why am I asking him? Lillian thought. Am I envious

of him? "Isn't Clerfayt eating with you tonight?" she asked.

"No. He had an unexpected visitor this afternoon. And why should he be coming up here all the time, anyhow? It must get dull for him."

"Then why doesn't he leave?" Lillian asked with hostility.

"He is leaving, but not for a few days. Wednesday or Thursday."

"This week?"

"Yes. I suppose he'll be driving down with his visitor."

Lillian did not answer. She did not know for certain whether Hollmann was supplying this information intentionally, and since she did not know, she assumed that it was intentional and therefore did not ask anything further. "Have you anything to drink with you?" she said.

"Not a drop. I gave the rest of my gin to Charles Ney this afternoon."

"Didn't you buy a bottle of vodka this morning?"

"I gave that to Dolores Palmer."

"Why? Have you decided to become a model patient?"

"Something like that," Hollmann replied with a touch of embarrassment.

"This morning you were anything but."

"This morning is a long time ago."

Lillian pushed back her plate. "Who will I go out with at night from now on?"

"There are plenty of others. And Clerfayt is still around for the time being."

"All right. But what about afterward?"

"Isn't Boris coming tonight?" Hollmann asked.

"No, not tonight. And you can't play hooky with Boris. I told him I had a headache."

"Do you?"

"Yes," Lillian said, and stood up. "I'm even going to make the Crocodile happy tonight, so that there won't be one unhappy soul in the place. I'm going to sleep. Good night, Hollmann."

"Is something the matter, Lillian?"

"Just the usual thing. The panic of boredom. A sign of

good health, the Dalai Lama would say. I hear that when you're really badly off, there's no more panic. You're too weak for it. How kind God is, wouldn't you say?"

The night nurse had completed her evening round. Lillian lay on her bed, trying to read. After a while, she dropped the book. Once again the long night stretched before her, the waiting for sleep—sleep and then the sudden starting out of sleep and that weightless moment when you recognized nothing, neither the room nor yourself, when you hung in soughing darkness and nothing but fear, nebulous fear of death, for unending seconds—until the window slowly became familiar again and its frame was no longer a shadowy cross in an unknown cosmos, but once more a window, and the room a room, and the coil of primordial terror and soundless screaming became yourself once more, a being called Lillian Dunkerque for its brief time on earth.

There was a knock at the door. Charles Ney stood outside in a red bathrobe and slippers. "The coast is clear," he whispered as he came in. "Come on over to Dolores' good-by party for Eva Moser."

"What for? Why doesn't she just go? Why does she have to have a good-by party?"

"We want one, not she."

"You've already had one in the dining room."

"That was only to fool the Crocodile. Come on, don't be a wet blanket."

"I don't feel like going to a party."

Charles Ney smiled a perfectly lovely smile. "Come, columbine of moonlight, silver, and smoky fire! If you stay here, you'll be mad at yourself for being alone, and when you're there, you'll be mad at yourself for having come. It's all the same—so come!" He listened toward the corridor, and opened the door. The clicking of crutches could be heard. A gaunt, elderly woman hobbled by. "Everybody's coming. Here's Streptomycin Lilly already. And here comes Schirmer with André."

A graybeard in a wheel chair was rolled past them by a young man who pranced along behind the chair, doing a

Charleston step. "You see, even the dead rise to offer Miss Moser an *Ave Eva, morituri te salutant,*" Charles Ney said. "Forget your Russian blood for one evening and remember your life-loving Walloon father. Get dressed and come."

"I won't dress. I'll come in pajamas."

"Come in pajamas, but come!"

Dolores Palmer lived a floor below Lillian's. She had been there for three years, occupying a suite that consisted of bedroom, living room, and bath. It was the most expensive unit in the sanatorium, and Dolores took care to claim every privilege to which this entitled her.

"We have two whole bottles of vodka for you in the bathroom," she said to Lillian. "I hope that's enough. Where do you want to sit? Next to our debutante, who's sailing forth into the real world, or among the feverish stay-behinds? Pick your place."

Lillian looked around. It was a scene familiar to her: the lamps were draped with cloths; the graybeard was in charge of the record player; Streptomycin Lilly sat in a corner, on the floor, because the drug had affected her sense of balance and she tended to topple. The others sat around with the half-hearted, artificial Bohemian air of overage children secretly staying up too late. Dolores Palmer was wearing a Chinese gown, long and straight, with slit skirt. She had a tragic beauty of which she had not the slightest awareness. Her lovers were deceived by it, as travelers in the desert are deceived by a mirage. While they wore themselves out trying to be interesting to her, Dolores really wanted something far simpler: a petty-bourgeois existence, but with a maximum of luxury. Grand emotions bored her, but she inspired them and was constantly having to contend with them.

Eva Moser sat by the window, looking out. Her mood had shifted violently. "She's bawling," Maria Savini said to Lillian. "Would you believe it?"

"Whatever for?"

"Ask her yourself. The craziest thing. She says this place is her home."

"It *is* my home," Eva Moser sobbed. "I've been happy here. I have friends here. Down there I won't know anybody."

There was a general silence for a moment. "You can stay on if you want to, Eva," Charles Ney said finally. "There's no one stopping you."

"Yes there is! My father! It costs a lot of money for me to stay here. He wants me to get a job. What sort of job? I can't do anything! Whatever I used to know, I've forgotten here."

"We all forget everything here," Streptomycin Lilly offered mildly from her corner. "Anyone who stays here for a few years is no longer good for anything down below."

Lilly was the Dalai Lama's guinea pig for new cures. At this time, he was trying streptomycin on her. She could not tolerate the drug very well; but even if the Dalai Lama were to discharge her, she would not have Eva Moser's problem. She was the only patient in the sanatorium who had been born in the village, and could easily find a job anywhere. She was an excellent cook.

"What kind of job can I get?" Eva Moser was whipping herself up into a frenzy. "Stenographer? Who would take me? I'm a rotten typist. Besides, people are leery of stenographers who come from a sanatorium."

"Be secretary to a man with t.b.," the graybeard croaked.

Lillian looked at Eva as if she were a prehistoric animal which had crawled out of a crack in the floor. There had been other discharged patients who had said that they would like to stay—but they had only done so out of consideration for the others, to play down the curious feeling of desertion that often accompanied discharge. But Eva Moser was a different case; she meant what she was saying. She was genuinely in despair. She had become used to the sanatorium, and was afraid of life down below.

Dolores Palmer brought Lillian a glass of vodka. "That woman!" she said, throwing a look of disgust at Eva

Moser. "No self-control! How she's carrying on! It's absolutely obscene, isn't it?"

"I'm going," Lillian declared. "I can't stand it."

"Don't go," Charles Ney said, leaning toward her. "Beautiful, flickering light in the uncertain darkness, stay a while. The night is full of shadows and platitudes, and we need you and Dolores as figureheads to bear before our tattered sails, lest we be trampled mercilessly under Eva Moser's dreadful brogans. Sing something, Lillian!"

"What shall I sing! A lullaby for children who will never be born?"

"Eva will have children. Heaps of them. You can be sure of that. No, sing the song of the clouds that do not return and of the snow that buries the heart. The song of the exiles of the mountains. Sing it for us. Not for that strapping wench Eva. We need the dark wine of self-glorification tonight. It's better to wallow in sentimentality than to weep."

"Charles got hold of half a bottle of cognac somewhere," Dolores commented matter-of-factly. She strolled long-leggedly over to the phonograph. "Play the new American records, Schirmer."

"That monster," Charles Ney sighed to her retreating back. "She looks like the most poetical being on earth and has a brain like an almanac. I love her as one loves the jungle, and she answers like a vegetable garden. What's to be done about it?"

"Suffer and be happy."

Lillian stood up. As she did so, the door opened, framing the Crocodile. "Just as I thought! Cigarettes! Alcohol in the room! An orgy! And you here, too, Miss Ruesch!" she snapped at Streptomycin Lilly. "Creeping in here on crutches! And Mr. Schirmer, you, too! You ought to be in bed."

"I ought to have been dead long ago," the graybeard replied cheerfully. "Theoretically, I am." He switched off the phonograph, pulled the nylon underclothes out of the loudspeaker and waved them in the air. "I'm living on borrowed time. When you do that, you live by special rules."

"Is that so? And what are these rules, if I may ask?"

"To get as much as possible out of what life you have left. How you do that is up to you."

"I must request you to go to bed at once. Who brought you here, may I ask?"

"My good sense."

The graybeard got back into his wheel chair. André was chary of taking over the pushing of it. Lillian stepped forward. "Come on, Schirmer. I'll wheel you back." She pushed the chair to the door.

"So it was you who brought him!" the Crocodile said. "I might have guessed it."

Lillian pushed the chair out into the corridor. Charles Ney and the others followed, giggling like children caught in mischief. "One moment," Schirmer said, swiveling his chair so that he was facing the door. The Crocodile stood squarely in the doorway. "Three sick people could lead happy existences on the amount of life you've missed," Schirmer pronounced. "I wish you a blissful night with your wrought-iron conscience."

He swiveled the chair again. Charles Ney took over the pushing. He laughed. "What's the point, Schirmer? She's only doing her job."

"I know. Only she does it with such a damned superior air. But I'll outlive her! I've already outlived her predecessor; she was only forty-four and died in four weeks of cancer. I'll outlive this bitch—how old is she, anyway? Must be over sixty. Or almost seventy."

"What wonderful people we are," Charles grinned.

"No," the graybeard replied with fierce satisfaction. "We're just people condemned to death. But we're not the only ones. So are the others. Only we know it. They don't."

Half an hour later, Eva Moser came to Lillian's room. "Have they brought my bed in here?" she asked.

"No."

"Where can it be? My room has been emptied out. All my clothes are gone, too. I have to sleep somewhere. Where can my things be?"

It was one of the usual jokes, when someone was discharged from the sanatorium, to hide his things on the last night. Eva Moser was in a state. "I had everything dry-cleaned. Suppose they get my clothes all messed up. I'll have to be careful about money, now that I'm going down."

"Doesn't your father look after you?"

"Oh him! He wants me off his hands. I think he wants to marry again."

Lillian felt that she could not stand the girl around a minute longer. "Go into the hall," she said. "Hide near the elevator until Charles Ney comes out. He'll be coming to me. Go straight to his room—he won't have locked it. Telephone me from there. Say you'll throw his dinner jacket into the bathtub and pour ink on his shirts if your things aren't brought back at once. Clear?"

"Yes, but—"

"They've hidden them somewhere. I bet Charles Ney knows all about it."

Lillian lifted the telephone. "Charles?"

She signaled to Eva Moser to leave. "Charles," she said, "could you drop in at my room? Yes? Fine."

He came a few minutes later. "What happened with the Crocodile?" Lillian asked.

"Everything's fixed up. Dolores handles her beautifully. She's wonderful with people like that. She simply told the truth—that we wanted to drown our sorrow at having to stay here. An inspired idea. The Crocodile almost dropped a tear before she left."

The telephone rang. Eva Moser's voice was so loud that Charles could hear what she was saying. "She's in your bathroom," Lillian reported. "She's filled the tub with hot water. In her left hand she's holding your new dinner jacket and in her right a bottle of turquoise-colored ink. Don't try to catch her by surprise. The moment you open the door, she'll take action. Here, talk to her."

She handed the telephone to Charles and went to the window. The Palace Hotel in the village still showed many lighted windows. In two or three weeks, that would be over. The tourists would fly away like birds of passage, and the long, monotonous year would wear on through spring, summer, and fall to next winter.

The telephone clicked behind her. "That slut!" Charles Ney said suspiciously. "That idea didn't pop into her head just like that. Why did you ask me to come here?"

"I wanted to know about the Crocodile."

"You're not usually that curious about her," Charles grinned. "We'll talk about it tomorrow. Now I have to go to the rescue of my dinner jacket. It would be just like that idiot to boil it. Good night. It was a wonderful evening!"

He closed the door behind him. Lillian heard his slippers padding rapidly down the corridor. His dinner jacket, she thought—that was his dream of freedom, his symbol of hope, of nights in cities—his mascot, just as her two evening dresses were hers, useless up here, but she would not give them up; she clung to them as if her life depended on them. If she were to give them up, she would be giving up hope as well. She went to the window again and looked at the lights down below. A wonderful evening! How many such hopeless wonderful evenings she had known!

She drew the curtains. There was the panic again. She looked for her cache of sleeping pills. For a moment, she thought she heard Clerfayt's motor. She looked at the clock. He could save her from the long night; but she could not telephone him. Hollmann had said that he had someone with him. Who? Some healthy woman from Paris or Milan or Monte Carlo! To hell with Clerfayt; he would be driving away in a few days anyhow. She swallowed the pills. I ought to submit, she thought; I ought to do as Boris says; I ought to live with it; I ought to stop fighting against it; I ought to submit, but if I do submit, I'm lost.

She sat down at her table and took a sheet of letter paper. "Beloved," she wrote, "you with the indistinct face, unknown, who have never come and are always expected, don't you feel that the time is running out . . ." And then she stopped writing, pushed off the table the box in which lay many letters she had never sent because she had no address to send them to, and looked down at the white sheet in front of her. Why am I crying? she thought. That doesn't change anything—

V

The old man lay as flat under his blanket as though there were no longer a body there. His face was gaunt, his eyes deep-sunken, but of a strong blue; the veins bulged under the skin, which looked like crumpled tissue paper. He lay in a narrow bed in a narrow room. On the night table beside the bed stood a chessboard.

His name was Richter. He was eighty years old and had been living in the sanatorium for twenty years. At first he had occupied a double room on the first floor, then a single room with balcony on the second—and now that he no longer had any money, he had this narrow room. He was the prize exhibit of the sanatorium. The Dalai Lama always cited his case when patients became downhearted, and Richter showed his gratitude. He did not and did not die.

Lillian sat beside his bed. "Look at that, will you!" Richter said, pointing to the chessboard. "The man plays like a night watchman. He ought to know that this knight move will give me a mate inside the next ten moves. What's the matter with Régnier nowadays? He used to play good chess. Were you here during the war?"

"No," Lillian said.

"He came during the war, in 1944, I think. What a relief that was! Before that, my dear young lady, before Régnier came, I had to play against a chess club in Zurich for a whole year. We had nobody up here. It was terribly dull."

Chess was Richter's sole passion. During the war, the various chess players in the sanatorium had left or died, and no new ones arrived. Two German friends with whom he had played by correspondence had been killed in Russia; another was taken prisoner at Stalingrad. For a few months, Richter was entirely without partners; he grew tired of life and lost weight. Then the head doctor made arrangements for him to play against members of a Zurich chess club. Most of the people were not strong enough for him; with the others, the games took too long. In the beginning, Richter impatiently made his moves by telephone; but that became too expensive, and he was compelled to resort to post cards back and forth. That meant that he could make a move only every other day. After a while, his partners had abandoned these correspondence games, and Richter was once again forced to play over old games out of books.

Then Régnier had come. He played one game with Richter, and Richter was ecstatic: at last he had found an opponent worthy of him. But Régnier was a Frenchman who had been liberated from a German concentration camp. When he heard that Richter was German, he refused to play with him. National enmities did not stop at the sanatorium.

Richter began pining away again, and Régnier, too, was confined to his bed. Both men were bored; but neither wanted to give in. A Negro from Jamaica, a believer in brotherly love, finally found a solution. He, too, was a bed-patient. He wrote a letter to Richter and one to Régnier, inviting them to a game of chess from bed to bed, via telephone. Both men were overjoyed. The only difficulty was that the Negro had only the faintest notion of the game; but he solved that problem simply. He played white against Richter, black against Régnier. Since white had the first move, Régnier made it on the board that stood beside his bed, and telephoned it to the Negro. The latter telephoned the move to Richter. Then he waited for Richter's move, and telephoned that to Régnier. He telephoned Régnier's second move back to Richter, and Richter's response to Régnier. He himself did not even have a board, since he was only having Régnier and Richter play against one another without their knowledge. The trick was to play white against one man, black against the other; had he played white or black in both games, he would not have been able to pass on the moves.

Shortly after the end of the war, the Negro died. Régnier and Richter had by then been compelled to take rooms without telephones, for reasons of economy. Régnier was on the third, Richter on the second floor. The Crocodile now assumed the Negro's part, and the nurses transmitted the moves to the two opponents, who still thought they were playing against the Negro. They were given to believe that he could no longer talk because of advanced tuberculosis of the larynx. All went well until Régnier was able to get up again. His first thought was to visit his Negro friend, and so the whole story came out.

By this time, his nationalistic feelings had somewhat subsided. When he heard that Richter's family in Germany had been killed in air raids, he made peace, and henceforth the men played harmoniously with one another. After a while, Régnier was confined to his bed again, and various patients did messenger service for the two. Lillian was among them. Then, three weeks ago, Régnier had died. Richter had been so weak at this time that he was not expected to live, and no one wanted to tell him that Régnier was dead. To deceive him, the Crocodile had leaped into the breach as partner; she had recently learned the game, but was, of course, no opponent for Richter. The result was that Richter, who still believed he was playing against Régnier, was stunned to see how his friend's game had degenerated.

"Don't you want to learn chess?" he asked Lillian, who had just brought him the Crocodile's last move. "I can teach you quickly."

Lillian shook her head. She saw the fear in the blue eyes. The old man took it as a bad sign that Régnier was playing so miserably; he was afraid he would soon be again without a partner. He put the same question to everyone who visited him.

"It doesn't take long to learn. I'll show you all the tricks. I played against Lasker."

"I have no talent for it. And no patience."

"Everyone has talent. And you have to have patience when you can't sleep at night. What else is there to do? Pray? A lot of good praying does. I'm an atheist. Philosophy isn't any help either. And detective stories only for a short time. I've tried everything, my girl. Only two things are any use. One is to have someone else with you; that's why I married. But my wife died years ago—"

"And the other?"

"Solving chess problems. Chess is so far removed from everything human—from doubts and anxiety—so abstract —that it gives peace of mind. At least for one night— and that's all we ask for, isn't it? Just to hold out until next morning—"

"Yes. That's all we ask for here."

Through the room's window, nothing could be seen but clouds and a snow-covered slope. The clouds were yellow and gold and turbulent now, in late afternoon. "Wouldn't you like me to teach you?" the old man asked. "We could start right now."

The strong eyes flickered in the cadaverous head. Hungering for company, Lillian thought, not for chess games. Hungering for someone to be there when the door suddenly opened and in came the hot and icy wind that made the blood rush from the throat and fill the lungs, until there was an end to breathing.

"How long have you been here?" she asked.

"Twenty years. A lifetime, eh?"

"Yes, a lifetime."

A lifetime, she thought, and every day was like every

other, the endless routine, day after day, and at the end of the year the days coalesced as if they had been only a single day, so much were they alike, and, similarly, the years coalesced as if they had only been a single year, so everlastingly the same were they.

"Shall we start today?" Richter asked.

"No," Lillian replied absently. "There wouldn't be any point. I won't be staying here long."

"You are leaving?" Richter croaked.

"Yes, I'm leaving. In a few days."

What am I saying? she thought in profound astonishment. It isn't true. Yet the words lingered in her ears as though they could not be retracted. Confused, she stood up.

"Are you cured?"

The hoarse voice sounded vexed, as if Lillian had committed a breach of trust. "I'm not going for long," she said hastily. "Just for a short time. I'll be coming back."

"Everyone comes back," Richter croaked, reassured. "Everyone."

"Do you want me to take your move to Régnier?"

"There's no point." Richter knocked over the chess pieces on his board. "He's as good as mate. Tell him to start a new game."

"A new game. All right."

Lillian's restlessness stayed with her. In the afternoon, she cajoled a young nurse, assistant in the operating room, into showing her the last X rays that had been taken of her. The nurse thought Lillian would not understand them, and brought her the prints.

"Can I keep them here for a few minutes?" Lillian asked.

The nurse hesitated. "It's against the regulations. I'm really not supposed even to show them to you."

"But the doctor usually shows them to me himself, and explains them to me. This time he forgot to." Lillian went to her wardrobe and took out a yellow dress. "Here is the dress I promised you last week. You can take it with you."

The nurse flushed. "The dress? Did you really mean it?"

"Why not? I don't ever wear it myself. I've become too thin for it."

"You could have it taken in."

Lillian shook her head. "No, no, you have it."

The nurse picked up the dress as if it were made of glass, and held it up against herself. "I think it's just my size," she murmured, looking in the mirror. Then she laid it over a chair. "May I come back for it in a few minutes? I have to go into Number Twenty-six for a moment. She's left."

"Left?"

"Yes. An hour ago."

"Who is Number Twenty-six?"

"The little South American girl from Bogotá."

"The one with the three relatives visiting? Manuela?"

"Yes. It happened quickly, but it was to be expected."

"Why are we talking all around it?" Lillian said, embittered by the euphemisms of the sanatorium. "She hasn't left! She's dead, dead, done for!"

"Yes, of course," the nurse replied, intimidated and eyeing the dress, which hung over the chair like a yellow quarantine flag. Lillian saw the look. "Go along," she said more calmly. "When you come back, you can take the X rays right with you."

"Good."

Quickly, Lillian drew the dark, smooth prints out of the envelope and went to the window with them. She could not really read them. The Dalai Lama had sometimes pointed out the crucial shadows and discolorations. For several months, he had not been doing so.

She looked at the shiny grays and blacks that decreed life or death for her. There were her shoulder bones, her spinal column, her ribs; there was her skeleton—and in between the bones the uncanny, shadowy something that meant health or illness. She recalled the earlier pictures, the nebulous gray spots, and tried to find them again. She thought she could see them, and it seemed to her that they had become bigger. Going away from the window, she carried the pictures close to the lamp. She took off the lamp shade, for more light, and suddenly it seemed to her that she was seeing herself after death, after years in the grave, the flesh already decayed to gray earth, and only the bones withstanding dissolution. She laid the films on the table. I'm being a fool again, she thought—but nevertheless she went to the mirror and looked in; she studied her face, the face that was hers and not hers, alien, and nevertheless hers. I don't know it, not as it really looks, she thought; I don't know the face that others see; I know only this mirror phantom which is inverted, shows the right side where others see the left; I know only this lie, just as I know only the other lie, while I do not recognize the reality, the skeleton that labors quietly away within me in order to come to the surface. This, she thought, looking at the black glossy film, this is the only real mirror.

She felt her forehead and cheek; she felt the bones underneath, and it seemed to her that they were closer to the skin than they used to be. The flesh is already melting away, she thought; the Unbribable, the Nameless One is already peering out of my eye sockets, or else he is peering invisibly over my shoulder, and his eyes and mine are meeting in the mirror.

"Why, what ever are you doing?" the young nurse asked from behind her. She had returned on her noiseless rubber soles, to collect the dress and the X rays.

"I'm looking in the mirror. I've lost three pounds in the last two months."

"Just recently you gained half a pound."

"I've lost that again."

"You're too restless. And you must eat more. It seems to me you've been recuperating very well."

Lillian whirled around. "Why do you nurses always treat us like children?" she said, vastly irritated. "Do you think we believe everything you tell us? Here." She held the X-ray pictures out to the nurse. "Look at them! I know enough about it. You know the pictures look bad."

The nurse stared at her in alarm. "Can you read X rays? Have you learned how?"

"Yes, I've learned how. I've had time enough to."

That was not true. But all at once Lillian could not retreat. It was as though she were standing on a high tightrope, her hands still clutching the rail of the support at the moment before she would have to let go of it and start walking the rope across the gulf. She could still avoid everything if she kept silent now, and she really wanted to; but something that was stronger than fear impelled her forward. "It's no secret," she said quietly. "The doctor himself has told me that I'm not getting any better. I only wanted to see for myself; that's why I asked you for the prints. I don't understand why there's so much play acting in front of the patients. After all, it's much better to know the score."

"Most patients can't bear it."

"Is that why you didn't tell me? I can bear it."

Lillian had the sense of an infinite circus tent below her, all hushed with expectation.

"But you say you already know," she nurse replied uncertainly.

"What?" Lillian asked breathlessly.

"Your X rays—since you can read them."

The stillness of expectation was no longer a stillness. It was a high, strange ringing in her ears. "Of course I know the cavities aren't getting any smaller," Lillian said with effort. "That happens often enough."

"Of course." Relieved, the nurse began to chatter. "There are always fluctuations. Ups and downs. Little relapses happen all the time. Especially in winter."

"And in spring," Lillian said. "And in summer. And in fall."

The nurse laughed. "You have a sense of humor. If only you'd take things a bit easier. And follow the doctor's orders. He knows best, after all."

"I will, from now on. Don't forget your dress."

Lillian could hardly wait for the nurse to leave. It seemed to her that a whiff of death had come into the room with her, carried from Manuela's room in the folds of the white uniform. How little she suspects, Lillian thought. How little the whole lot of them suspect. Why doesn't she go? How slowly and with what disgusting pleasure she is laying the dress over her arm!

"You'll pick up a few pounds quickly enough," the nurse said. "The thing is to eat all the good things on the menu. Tonight, for example. There's a wonderful chocolate pudding with vanilla sauce for dessert."

I provoked it, Lillian thought. Not because I'm courageous, but because I'm afraid. I lied. I wanted to hear the opposite; in spite of everything, we always want to hear the opposite.

There was a knock, and Hollmann came in. "Clerfayt is leaving tomorrow. Tonight is full moon. The usual party up at the ski lodge. How about the two of us slipping out and driving up there with him?"

"You slipping out again?"

"For the last time. And this is different."

"Manuela has died."

"So I've heard. It's a blessing for everyone concerned. For those three relations—and probably for Manuela, too."

"You talk like Clerfayt," Lillian said angrily.

"I imagine that after a while we'll all have to talk like Clerfayt," Hollmann replied quietly. "In his case, the perspective is shorter, which is why what he says sounds harsher. He lives from one race to the next. And every year the chances get to be more and more against him. Shall we go out with him tonight?"

"I don't know."

"It's his last evening. And whatever we do is not going to bring Manuela back."

"You're talking like him again."

"Why shouldn't I?"

"When is he leaving?"

"Tomorrow afternoon. He wants to get down out of the mountains before it starts snowing. The weather forecast says a big snowstorm by tomorrow night."

"Is he going alone?" Lillian asked, with effort.

"Yes. You coming tonight?"

Lillian did not answer. So many things were tumbling down upon her all at once. She must think everything over. But what was there to think over, really? What else had she been doing for months but think things over? All that was left was to make a decision.

"Didn't you say you were going to be more careful from now on?" she asked.

"Not tonight. Dolores, Maria, and Charles are coming, too. Josef is at the door. If we sneak out of here at ten o'clock, we'll make the cable car in time. It's running till one o'clock tonight. I'll come for you." Hollmann laughed. "Then from tomorrow on, I'm going to be the goddamdest most-careful patient in the sanatorium. But tonight we're celebrating."

"What?"

"Anything. That there's a full moon. That Giuseppe has come. That we're alive. Or celebrating farewells."

"Or that we're going to be model patients from tomorrow on?"

"That, too. I'll come for you. It's a costume party—you haven't forgotten?"

"No."

Hollmann closed the door behind him. Tomorrow, Lillian thought. Tomorrow—what had suddenly happened to it? It was a tomorrow different from all yesterday's tomorrows. By tomorrow evening, Clerfayt would have left and the sanatorium routine would again spread over everything—like the wet snow which came in on the sickly wind—soft, gentle, covering everything, slowly smothering everything. Not me, she thought. Not me!

The ski lodge was perched high above the village, and once a month in winter, at full moon, it was kept open at night for a torchlight ski run. The Palace Hotel had sent a small gypsy band up for the party, two violinists and a cembalo player. They brought the cembalo up with them; there was no piano in the lodge.

The guests came in ski clothes or costumes. Charles

Ney and Hollmann wore pasted-on mustaches for disguise. Charles Ney was in evening dress, which he wore as a costume; he had no opportunity to use it normally. Dolores Palmer wore a dress of Spanish lace and a mantilla embroidered with sequins. Lillian Dunkerque had on her light-blue slacks and a short fur jacket.

The lodge was jammed, but Clerfayt had managed to reserve a table at the window; the headwaiter of the Palace Hotel, which also managed the lodge, was a racing fan.

Lillian was very excited. She stared out into the dramatic night. Somewhere high above the mountains a storm was raging, though there were no signs of it down below. The moon slipped out from behind the tattered clouds and plunged back into them, and the shadows of the clouds brought the white slopes to life, as though gigantic phantom flamingos were flying over the landscape with monstrous wings.

A big fire was blazing in the fireplace of the lodge. There was punch and wine to drink. "What would you like?" Clerfayt asked. "It's all hot drinks, punch and mulled wine, but the waiter has put in some vodka and cognac for us if we want it. I let him take Giuseppe on a drive through the village this afternoon. He fouled two plugs and felt marvelous. Would you care for cognac? Though this is a night for mulled wine."

"Good," Lillian said. "Mulled wine."

The waiter brought the glasses. "When are you going tomorrow?" Lillian asked.

"Before dark."

"Where?"

"To Paris. Are you coming along?"

"Yes," Lillian replied.

Clerfayt laughed; he did not believe her. "All right," he said. "But you'd better not take much baggage with you. Giuseppe isn't built for it."

"I'd only need one suitcase. The rest could be sent. Where will we be making our first stop?"

"We'll drive out of the snow country, because you hate

it so much. Not very far. Over the mountains to the Ticino. To Lake Maggiore. It's already spring there."

"And then?"

"To Geneva."

"And then?"

"To Paris."

"Can't we drive straight to Paris?"

"We would have to leave tonight. It's too far for one day."

"Can you make it there in one day from Lake Maggiore?"

Clerfayt began looking at her more closely. Up to this moment, he had thought it all a game; but these questions were too specific for a game. "One long day's driving will get you there," he said. "But why? Don't you want to see the meadows of flowering narcissus around Geneva? Everyone wants to see them."

"I can see them as we drive past."

On the terrace, fireworks were being shot off. Rockets streaked up, Catherine wheels dashed sparks, and then came big rockets that rose high and red and then, when they seemed to have exhausted themselves in their solitary flight, suddenly burst into sheaves of gold and green and blue and dropped back to earth again in a shower of glittering stars.

"Good Lord!" Hollmann whispered. "The Dalai Lama!"

"Where?"

"At the door. He's just come in."

Sure enough, there was the doctor, standing pale and baldheaded in the doorway, surveying the racket in the lodge. He was wearing a gray suit. Someone plumped a paper hat on his head. He knocked it off and moved toward a table fairly close to the door.

"Who would have figured on that!" Hollmann said. "What are we going to do now?"

"Not a thing," Lillian said.

"Shouldn't we kind of try to disappear into the crowd and slip out?"

"No."

"He won't recognize you with your mustache," Dolores Palmer said.

"But he'll recognize you. And Lillian. Especially Lillian."

"We can sit so that he doesn't see their faces," Charles Ney said, standing up. Dolores changed places with him, and Maria Savini took Hollmann's chair. Clerfayt smiled with amusement and looked across at Lillian, to see whether she wished to change with him. She shook her head.

"You change, too, Lillian," Charles said. "Otherwise he'll spot you, and tomorrow there'll be hell to pay."

Lillian looked across at the Dalai Lama's pale face and colorless eyes; it floated above the tables like a moon, sometimes obscured by the crowd and then appearing again like the real moon emerging from between clouds.

"No," she said. "I'll sit right here."

The skiers were preparing to set out. "Aren't you going with them?" Dolores asked Clerfayt. He was in ski clothes.

"I wouldn't dream of it. It's much too dangerous for me."

Dolores laughed. "He really means it," Hollmann said. "Whatever you can't do perfectly is dangerous."

"And if you can do it perfectly?" Lillian asked.

"Then it's even more dangerous," Clerfayt said. "You get careless."

They went out to see the descent. Hollmann, Charles Ney, Maria, and Dolores slipped through in the confusion of everyone's leaving; Lillian walked without haste, at Clerfayt's side, past the doctor's colorless eyes.

They tramped across the firmly trod path in the snow to the starting point. The fiery smoke of the torches cast shifting shadows across faces and snow. The first skiers shot down the moonlit slope, torches held high in their hands. They rapidly became glowing dots and vanished behind other, lower slopes. Lillian watched the skiers go, plunging down the slope as if plunging into life—the way the rockets that had reached the highest point of their flight had dropped back to earth in a rain of stars.

"When are we leaving tomorrow?" she asked Clerfayt.

He looked up. And understood her at once. "Whenever you like," he replied. "At any time. Even after dark. Or earlier. Or later, if you can't be ready."

"No need to delay. I can pack fast. When do you want to go?"

"Around four o'clock."

"I can be ready by four."

"Good. I'll come for you."

Clerfayt looked down again, following the track of the skiers.

"You don't have to worry about me," Lillian said. "You can just drop me off in Paris. I'll go along like—" She fumbled for a word.

"Like a hitchhiker?" Clerfayt suggested.

"Yes. Exactly."

"All right."

She felt that she was trembling. She studied Clerfayt. He asked no questions. I don't have to explain anything to him, she thought. He takes me at my word. What to me is the decision of my life is to him only the kind of ordinary decision people make every day. Perhaps he doesn't even think me particularly sick; I suppose it takes an auto smashup to convince him that someone is really incapacitated. She felt to her surprise as if a burden she had borne for years were sliding from her shoulders. Here was the first person in years who was not concerned about her illness. It made her happy in a strange way. It was as if she had crossed a frontier hitherto impassable to her. Her sickness, which had always been like an opaque window between herself and the world, no longer existed, at least for the moment. Instead, life lay outspread before her, breathtakingly clear and wide, flooded with moonlight; life with clouds and valleys and happenings. And she belonged to it, she was no longer excluded from it; she stood like all the others, the healthy people, at the starting point, a burning, crackling torch in her hand,

VI

Volkov found her next morning occupied with her suitcases. "Packing, Dusha? This early?"

"Yes, Boris, I'm packing."

"What for? You'll unpack everything again in a few days."

He had seen her packing this way several times. It came over her every year, like the impulse of migratory birds to fly away in spring and in fall. Then the suitcases would stand around for a few days, sometimes even for a few weeks, until Lillian lost courage and gave up.

"I'm going, Boris," she said. She dreaded this conversation. "This time I really am going."

He leaned against the door and watched her. Dresses and coats were lying on the bed, sweaters and nightgowns hanging from the curtain rod and the knob of the bathroom door. High-heeled shoes stood on the dressing table and the chairs, and a pile of ski things had been dumped on the floor near the balcony.

"I really am going," Lillian repeated, irritated because he did not believe her.

He nodded. "You're going tomorrow. And the day

after tomorrow or in a week we'll unpack again. Why do you put yourself through this for nothing?"

"Boris!" she cried. "Stop it. It's no use any more. I'm going."

"Tomorrow?"

"No, today."

She felt his gentleness and his disbelief; there again were the spider webs that were to entangle her and hold her fast. "I am going," she said resolutely. "Today. With Clerfayt!"

She saw the change in his eyes. "With Clerfayt?"

"Yes." She looked squarely at him. She wanted to get it over with quickly. "I'm going away by myself. But I will be riding with Clerfayt because he is leaving today and I don't have the courage to take the train. I'm not going with him for any other reason. Alone, I'm not strong enough to fight clear of everything up here."

"To fight clear of me?"

"Of you, too—but not in the way you think."

Volkov took a step forward into the room. "You cannot go," he said.

"Yes, Boris, I can. I wanted to write to you. Look there—" She gestured toward a small brass wastepaper basket near her table. "It's no use. I couldn't. It's hopeless to try to explain it."

Hopeless, he thought. What does that mean? Why is something that didn't even exist yesterday hopeless today? He looked down at the clothes and the shoes. A second ago they had still represented a sweet disorder; now they suddenly glittered with the bitter light of parting and were weapons aimed at his heart. He no longer saw them as charming frivolities; he looked at them with the pain one feels coming from the funeral of a loved person and unexpectedly seeing some of his personal possessions—a hat, a shirt, a pair of shoes. "You cannot go!" he said.

She shook her head. "I know that I can't explain it. That's why I thought of going away without seeing you, and of writing to you from down below. But I couldn't have done that either. Don't make it hard for me!"

Don't make it hard for me, he thought. They always say that, these little packets of grace, egotism, and helplessness; they always say it when they set about tearing your heart to pieces. Don't make it hard for me. Did they ever wonder whether they were making it hard for the man? But wouldn't it be even worse if they really thought of that side of it? Wouldn't that have the fatal quality of pity: like giving caresses while you held nettles in your hand?

"You're going with Clerfayt?"

"I'm riding down with Clerfayt," Lillian replied tormentedly. "He's taking me with him like a man picking up a hitchhiker. We'll go our separate ways in Paris. I'm staying there and he's going on. My uncle lives there. He's in charge of that little trust fund I have. So I will stay there."

"At your uncle's?"

"In Paris."

She knew that she was not telling the truth, but at the moment it seemed to her to be the truth. "Please understand me, Boris!" she pleaded.

He looked at the suitcases. "Why do you want to be understood? It's enough that you're going."

She bowed her head. "You're right. Go on hitting me."

Go on hitting, he thought. If you as much as twitched for a moment, they said, "Go on hitting," as though you were the one who was leaving. Their logic never extended beyond the last reply; everything before that was immediately stricken off the record. Not what caused the cry, but the cry itself counted. "I'm not hitting you," he said.

"You want me to stay with you."

"I want you to stay here. That's different."

I, too, am already lying, he thought. Of course I only want her to stay with me; she's all I have, the last I have. The planet earth has shrunk for me to this village; I can count its inhabitants, know almost every one of them; this has become my world and she is what I want in this world; I cannot lose her, I must not lose her, but I have already lost her. "I don't want you to throw your life away like worthless money," he said.

"These are words, Boris. If someone in prison has the choice of living free for a year and then dying, or of rotting in prison—what choice should he make?"

"You are not in prison, Dusha! You have a frightfully false conception of what life is like down below."

"I realize that. I don't know what it's like, after all. I only know the part that consisted of war, betrayal, and misery, and even though the rest may also be full of disappointments, it couldn't be worse than the part I know and that, I know, cannot be the whole of it. There must be something else, too; the other parts that I don't know, that speak out of books and pictures and music and make me restless and call me—" She stopped abruptly. "Let's not talk any more, Boris. Everything I say is false; it becomes false while I am saying it; the words become false and sentimental and don't convey it. They turn into knives, and I don't want to hurt you. Yet every word must be a stab if I try to be honest, and even when I think I'm being honest, I'm still not—don't you see that I don't know myself?"

She looked at him with a mixture of pity, hostility, and love grown powerless. Why did he force her to go over everything she had told herself a thousand times and already wanted to forget?

"Let Clerfayt go off by himself. In a few days you'll realize how wrong it would have been to follow that Pied Piper," Volkov said.

"Boris," Lillian replied hopelessly, "it isn't Clerfayt. Does it always have to be another man?"

He did not answer. Why am I saying these things to her? he thought. I'm a fool; I'm doing everything to drive her away. Why don't I smile and tell her she's doing perfectly right? Why don't I make use of the old trick? Don't I know that a man who wants to hold on to a woman loses her, while women run after the man who smilingly lets them go? Have I forgotten that? "No," he said, "it need not always be another man. But if it isn't, why don't you ask me whether I want to come with you?"

90

"You?"

Wrong, he thought, wrong again! Why am I forcing myself on her? She wants to escape from illness—why should she take a sick man with her? I'm the last man she would like to travel with.

"I don't want to take anything with me, Boris," she replied. "I love you, but I want to take nothing with me."

"You want to forget everything?"

Wrong again, he thought in desperation.

"I don't know," Lillian said, downcast. "I don't want to take anything with me from here. I can't. Don't torture me."

For a moment, he stood very still. He knew that it was better to say no more; but at the same time it seemed to him frightfully important to explain to her that both of them no longer had long to live and that the thing she now so detested in her life—all the time that hung so heavy for her—would some day be the most important thing of all, when only hours and days were left, and that she would bitterly repent that she had thrown time away, the time that now seemed to her nothing but interminable boredom. But he knew also that as soon as he attempted to say this, every word would be transformed into sentimentality, which was no more bearable for being the truth, and which could never reach to her.

It was too late. From one breath to the next, it was suddenly too late. What moment had he let slip? He did not know. Yesterday, all had been closeness and familiarity, and now a wall of glass had slid between them like that between the driver's seat and the rear in a limousine. They could still see one another, but mutual understanding had ceased; they heard one another, but theirs were different languages that floated past each other's ears and did not reach the mind. There was no longer anything to be done. The estrangement that had grown up overnight filled everything. It was there in every look and every gesture. There was no longer anything to be done.

"Good-by, Lillian," he said.

"Forgive me, Boris."

"In love there is never anything to forgive."

She had no time to think. A nurse came with a summons from the Dalai Lama.

The doctor smelled of good soap and antiseptic linen. "I saw you in the ski lodge last night," he said stiffly.

Lillian nodded.

"You know that you are not supposed to go out."

"Yes, I know."

A flush passed over the Dalai Lama's pale face. "It seems to be a matter of indifference to you whether or not you follow these orders. I must ask you to leave the sanatorium. Perhaps elsewhere you will find a place that better suits your wishes."

Lillian did not reply; the irony was too sharp.

"I have spoken with the head nurse," the Dalai Lama continued, interpreting her silence as fright. "She tells me that this is not the first time she has warned you. You have disregarded the warnings. This sort of thing destroys the morale of the sanatorium. We cannot tolerate someone who—"

"I realize that," Lillian interrupted him. "I will leave the sanatorium this afternoon."

The Dalai Lama looked at her in surprise. "There's not that much of a hurry," he replied at last. "Take your time, until you've found another place. Or have you already done so?"

"No."

The doctor was thrown somewhat off course. He had expected tears and appeals to be given another chance. "Why are you working so determinedly against your own health, Miss Dunkerque?" he asked finally.

"It didn't improve when I did everything that was prescribed."

"But that is certainly no reason to stop doing the right things when your condition takes a turn for the worse," the doctor exclaimed irritably. "On the contrary. That is the time to be particularly careful."

When it takes a turn for the worse, Lillian thought.

The news did not strike her as hard as it had done yesterday, when the nurse had let it slip out. "Self-destructive nonsense," the Dalai Lama went on thundering. He was firmly convinced that he had a heart of gold under a rough exterior. "Put that nonsense out of your pretty head."

He gripped her shoulder and shook her gently. "Oh, well, go back to your room, and from now on obey the regulations one hundred per cent."

Lillian slid her shoulder out from under his hand. "I would only go on breaking the rules," she said quietly. "That's why it would be better for me to leave the sanatorium."

Far from frightening her, what the Dalai Lama had said about her condition had made her coolly sure of herself. It also made her feel better about Boris, since freedom of choice now seemed to have been taken from her, in a strange fashion. She felt like a soldier who after long waiting has received his marching orders. Now there was nothing more to do than to obey. The new situation had already taken possession of her, just as the soldier's marching orders were already part of the uniform and the battle—and perhaps also of the end.

"Don't drive things to extremes," the Dalai Lama thundered. "The sanatoriums up here are pretty filled up. Where would you go? To a pension?"

There he stood, the big, good-natured god of the sanatorium, fuming because this intransigent chit was taking him at his word about dismissal, and was forcing him to take it back. "The few rules we have are in your own interest, after all," he growled. "Where would we be if we let people do just what they liked? As for the rest— we're not running a prison here. Or do you think we are?"

Lillian smiled. "Not any more," she said. "And I am not a patient any longer. You can speak to me now as you would to a woman. Not as if I were a child or a convict."

She saw the flush rise to the Dalai Lama's face again. Then she was outside.

She finished packing her clothes. By this evening I shall have left the mountains, she thought. For the first time in years, she felt an expectation that gave promise of fulfillment; not the expectation of a mirage that was years away and always receded further. Here was something that would be fulfilled during the next few hours. Past and future hung in a quivering balance, and her first feeling was not of loneliness, but of high, tense solitude. She was taking nothing with her and she did not know where she was going.

She was afraid that Volkov would appear again, and longed to see him once more. As she closed her suitcases, her eyes were blind with tears. She waited until she had calmed down a bit. Then she paid her bill and fended off two assaults by the Crocodile—the second in the Dalai Lama's name. She said good-by to Dolores Palmer, Maria Savini, and Charles Ney, who stared at her as the Japanese during the war might have looked at their suicide pilots. Then she returned to her room and waited. She heard a scratching and barking at the door. When she opened it, Volkov's shepherd dog came in. The animal loved her and had often come by himself to visit her. She thought Boris had sent it, and that he would be along in a moment. But he did not come. Instead, the room nurse appeared with the information that Manuela's relatives were going to send the dead girl to Bogotá in a zinc casket.

"When?" Lillian asked, for the sake of saying something.

"Today. They want to get out of here as quickly as possible. The sleigh is already waiting outside. Usually the caskets are sent out at night, but this time it has to make a ship. The family are traveling by plane."

"I must go now," Lillian murmured. She had heard Clerfayt's car. "Good-by."

She closed the door behind her and went down the long corridor like an escaping thief. She hoped to get through the lobby unnoticed, but the Crocodile was waiting beside the elevator.

"The chief asked me to tell you again that you can stay. And that you ought to stay."

"Thank you," Lillian said, and walked on.

"Be reasonable, Miss Dunkerque. You don't understand your situation. You must not leave the mountains now. You would not live out the year."

"That's just why I must go."

Lillian went on. At the bridge tables a few heads turned toward her; otherwise the lobby was deserted. The patients were taking their rest cures. Boris was not there. Hollmann stood at the front door.

"If you're absolutely determined to leave, at least go by train," the Crocodile said.

Mutely, Lillian showed the head nurse her fur coat and warm clothes. The Crocodile made a contemptuous gesture. "A lot of good that does. Do you insist on committing suicide?"

"Everyone does that—some faster than others. We will be driving carefully. And not far."

The front door was very close now. The sun blazed in from outside. A few more steps, Lillian thought, and she would have run this gantlet.

One more step! "You have been warned," the even cold voice at her side said. "We wash our hands."

Lillian did not feel in a humorous mood, but she could not help smiling. The Crocodile had saved the situation with a last cliché. "Wash them and sterilize them," Lillian said. "Good-by! Thanks for everything."

She was outside. The snow blazed back the light so strongly that she could barely see. *"Au revoir, Hollmann!"*

"Au revoir, Lillian. I'll be following you soon."

She looked up. He was laughing. Thank God, she thought, at last someone who doesn't behave like a schoolmaster. Hollmann wrapped her in her woolen stole and her fur coat. "We'll drive slowly," Clerfayt said. "When the sun goes down, we'll close the top. Now the sides protect you against the wind."

"Yes," she replied. "Can we go?"

"You haven't forgotten anything?"

"No."

"If you have, it can be sent later."

She had not thought of that. It came as a sudden comfort. She had imagined that all ties would be cut off, once she left. "Yes, that's true; things can be sent later," she said.

A small man who looked like a cross between a waiter and a sexton came hurrying across the square. Clerfayt started. "Why, that's—"

The man passed close by the car as he entered the sanatorium, and Clerfayt recognized him. He was wearing a dark suit, a black hat, and carried a suitcase. It was the man who used to go along with the coffins. He seemed transformed, was no longer seedy and morose looking, but merry and authoritative. He was on the way to Bogotá.

"Who?" Lillian asked.

"Nothing. I thought it was someone I knew. Ready?"

"Yes," Lillian said. "Ready."

The car started. Hollmann waved. There was no sign of Boris. The dog ran after the car for a while, then dropped back. Lillian looked around. On the sun terraces, which had been empty a moment before, a long row of people had appeared. The patients, who had been resting in their deck chairs, had all stood up. They had learned the news via the sanatorium grapevine and now, hearing the motor, they were standing in a thin row, dark against the stark blue sky, looking down.

"Like the top row in a bullfighting arena," Clerfayt said.

"Yes," Lillian replied. "But what are we? The bulls or the matadors?"

"Always the bulls. But we think we're the matadors."

VII

The car glided slowly through a white gorge above which the gentian-blue sky flowed like a mirrored brook. They were already over the pass, but the snow was still piled almost six feet high on both sides of the road. They could not yet see over it. Nothing existed but the walls of snow and the blue ribbon of sky. If you leaned back long enough, you no longer knew which was above and which below, the blueness or the whiteness.

Then came the smell of resin and firs, and a village came into view, brown and flat. Clerfayt stopped. "We can take the chains off, I think," he said. "How is it farther down?" he asked the gas-station attendant.

"Rugged."

"What?"

Clerfayt looked at the boy. He was wearing a red sweater, a new leather jacket, steel-rimmed glasses, and had acne and protruding ears. "Why, I know you! Herbert or Helmut or——"

"Hubert."

The boy pointed to a wooden signboard that hung between the pumps: H. GÖRING, SERVICE STATION AND GARAGE.

"That sign's new, isn't it?" Clerfayt asked.

"Brand new."

"Why only the first initial?"

"More practical that way. Lots of people think the name's Hermann."

"With a family name like that, I should think you'd want to change it, not have it painted big as life."

"We'd be dopes to do that," the boy explained. "Now that the German cars are coming again! You ought to see the tips I get. No, sir, that name is worth a mint of money."

Clerfayt looked at the leather jacket. "Has that already come from your tips?"

"Half. But before the season is over, I'll have a pair of ski boots and a coat out of them, that's for sure."

"Maybe you've miscalculated. A lot of people won't give you a tip just because of your name."

The boy grinned, and tossed the chains into the car. "Those who can afford to come for winter sports will, sir. Besides, I get it coming or going—some give because they're glad he's gone, and others because they have pleasant memories, but the tips keep coming. Some funny things have happened since the sign's been hanging there. Gas, sir?"

"I can use seventeen gallons," Clerfayt said. "But I'll not take them from you. I'd rather buy my gas from somebody who's not as good a businessman as you are, Hubert. It's time your views were given a bit of a shake, boy."

An hour later, the snow was behind them. Cataracts leaped from the sides of the slopes along the road; water dripped from the roofs of houses, and the trunks of the trees gleamed with moisture. The sunset was reflected redly from the windows. In the streets of villages, children were playing. The fields were black and wet, and last year's grass lay yellow and gray-green upon the meadows. "Shall we stop off somewhere?" Clerfayt asked.

"Not yet."

"Are you afraid that the snow will catch up to us?"

Lillian nodded. "I never want to see it again."

"Not before next winter."

Lillian did not answer. Next winter, she thought—that was as far as Sirius or the Pleiades. She would never see it.

"How about something to drink?" Clerfayt asked. "Coffee with kirsch? We still have a good way to drive."

"That sounds good," Lillian said. "When will we be at Lake Maggiore?"

"In a few hours. Late this evening."

Clerfayt stopped the car in front of a restaurant. They went in. A waitress turned on the lights. On the walls hung prints of stags and heath cocks. "Are you hungry?" Clerfayt asked. "What did you have for lunch?"

"Nothing."

"I thought as much." He turned to the waitress. "What do you have in the way of food?"

"Salami, *Landjäger*, *Schüblig*. The *Schüblig* are hot."

"Two *Schüblig* and some of that dark bread there. With butter and open wine. Do you have Fendant?"

"Fendant and Valpolicella."

"Fendant. And what would you like for yourself?"

"A pflümli, if it's all right with you," the waitress said.

"It's all right."

Lillian sat in the corner next to the window. She listened to the talk between Clerfayt and the waitress. The light of the lamp caught on the bottles of the little bar. Outside the window, the village trees towered blackly into the high, green-tinted evening sky, and the first lights were on in the houses. Everything was intensely peaceful and normal; here was an evening without fear and rebellion, and she belonged to it, with the same normality and peacefulness. She had escaped into life. The feeling of it almost choked her.

"*Schüblig* are fatty peasant sausages," Clerfayt said. "They're very good, but perhaps you don't like them."

"I like everything," Lillian said. "Everything down here!"

Clerfayt regarded her thoughtfully. "I'm afraid that's true."

"Why are you afraid?"

He laughed. "Nothing is more dangerous than a woman who likes everything. How is a man to arrange matters so that she likes him alone?"

"By doing nothing."

"Right."

The waitress brought the clear, white wine. She poured it into small water glasses. Then she raised her own glass of plum brandy. "Your health!"

They drank. Clerfayt looked around the shabby restaurant.

"This is not yet Paris," he said, smiling.

"Yes it is," Lillian replied. "It is the first suburb of Paris. Paris starts from here on."

At Göschenen they had stars and a clear night sky. Clerfayt drove the car up the ramp to one of the flatcars that stood waiting. Aside from his car, two sedans and a red sports car were taking the tunnel. "Would you rather stay in the car or sit in the train?"

"Won't we get very dirty if we stay in the car?"

"No. The train is electric. And we'll close the top."

The railroad officials placed chocks under the wheels. The other drivers also remained in their cars. In the two sedans, the ceiling lights were turned on. The train went through a switch and entered the Gotthard tunnel.

The walls of the tunnel were damp. Signal lights flew by. After a few moments, Lillian had the feeling that she was riding down a shaft into the center of the earth. The air was stale and old. The noise of the train was re-echoed a thousandfold. In front of her, Lillian saw the two illuminated sedans rocking like two cabins in a boat on the way to Hades. "Will this ever end?" she said.

"In fifteen minutes. The Gotthard is one of the longest tunnels in Europe." Clerfayt handed her his flask, which he had had refilled in the restaurant. "It's a good idea to get used to tunnels," he said. "Judging by the way things are going, we'll all be living like this soon, in air-raid shelters and underground cities."

"Where do we come out?"

"At Airolo. There the South begins."

Lillian had feared the first night. She had expected memories and regrets to come creeping at her out of the darkness like rats. But now the noisy ride through the stone bowels of the earth routed all other thoughts. The remote fear of every creature that lives upon the ground and not in it, the fear of being buried alive, made her wait so passionately for light and sky that everything else was wiped out. The whole thing's going almost too fast, she thought. A few hours ago, I was stuck on the peaks of the mountains and wanted to come down; now I'm rushing through the earth and want to go up again.

A piece of paper fluttered out of one of the sedans and slapped into the windshield. There it remained stuck, pressed flat, like a crushed pigeon. "There are characters who have to eat always and everywhere," Clerfayt said. "They would take sandwiches with them to hell itself." He reached around to the outside of the windshield and pulled the paper away.

A second piece of wax paper flew through the center of the earth. Lillian laughed. A missile followed, slamming into the windshield frame. Lillian laughed. "A roll," Clerfayt said. "The good people in front of us are now eating only the sandwich meat, not the bread. A small bourgeois pandemonium in the bowels of the earth."

Lillian stretched. The tunnel seemed to strip her free of all the elements of the past which had been fluttering around her. It seemed as if the sharp bristles of the noise were brushing her clean of everything. The old planet on which the sanatorium stood remained behind her forever; she could not go back, any more than you could cross the Styx twice. She would rise from the depths to a new planet, cast out upon the earth, falling and at the same time hurled forward, clinging only to a single thought: to come out of this and to breathe. It seemed to her that she was being pulled at the last moment through a narrow trench whose walls were collapsing close behind her; she was being dragged toward the light which rose like a milky monstrance in front of her, and raced toward her, and she was there.

The Acheronian roars became a normal rattling, and then ceased altogether. The train stopped in a soft ambiance of gray and gold and mild air. It was the air of life after the vault-like, cold, dead air of the tunnel. It took Lillian a while before she realized that it was raining. She listened to the drops that pattered gently down upon the top of the car; she breathed the soft air, and held her hand out into the rain. Saved, she thought. Cast across the Styx and saved.

"It ought to be the other way round," Clerfayt said. "It should have been raining over there, and on this side we should have clear skies. Are you disappointed?"

She shook her head. "I haven't seen rain since last October."

"And you haven't been down below for four years? It must seem almost like being reborn. Reborn with memories."

Clerfayt drove to the gasoline station by the road, to fill the tank. "I could envy you," he said. "You're beginning from the beginning again. With the passionateness of youth, but without the weakness of youth."

The train rode off, its red lights vanishing in the rain. The gas-station attendant brought back the car key. The car rolled backward onto the road. Clerfayt stopped it, to turn. For a moment, by the quiet light of the instrument board, he saw Lillian in the small compartment under the top, while outside the rain shimmered and chattered. There was something different about her; he had never before seen her looking quite like this. Her face was illuminated by the glow of the speedometer, the clock and the other instruments for measuring times and speeds. In contrast to these, her face seemed, for the span of a heartbeat, utterly timeless and untouched by all that —timeless, Clerfayt felt, as Death, with whom that face was beginning a race beside which all automobile races were childish sports. I will set her down in Paris and lose her, he thought. No, I must try to hold her. I would be an idiot if I did not try.

"Have you any idea what you will do in Paris?" he asked.

"I have an uncle there. He's in charge of my money. Up to now, he has sent it to me in monthly installments. I'm going to get it all away from him. It will be something of a drama. He still thinks I'm fourteen years old."

"And how old are you really?"

"Twenty-four and eighty."

Clerfayt laughed. "A good combination. I was once thirty-six and eighty—when I came back from the war."

"And what happened?"

"I became forty," Clerfayt said, shifting into first gear. "It was very sad."

The car climbed the ascent from the railroad to the highway, and began the long downhill stretch. At the same moment, another motor howled behind them. It was the red sports car that had been hurtled through the tunnel with them. The driver had been lying in wait behind a shed. Now he roared up behind them with his four cylinders as if there were sixteen of them.

"You always run into that kind," Clerfayt said. "He wants to race us. Shall we give him a lesson? Or let him keep his illusion that he has the fastest car in the world?"

"Let's let everyone keep his illusions today."

"All right."

Clerfayt stopped Giuseppe. The red sports car behind him also stopped, and the driver began to blow his horn. He had plenty of room to pass; but he insisted on his race.

"That's the way it is," Clerfayt said, sighing, and started again. "He's a human being; he seeks his own destruction."

The red car badgered them as far as Faido. The driver repeatedly tried to catch up. "He'll end up killing himself," Clerfayt said finally. "The last time, he almost failed to make the curve. We'd better let him pass."

He braked, but immediately stepped on the gas again. "That ham! Instead of passing, he almost crashed into our rear. He's just as dangerous behind us as ahead of us."

Clerfayt pulled the car to the right edge of the road. The smell of wood wafted toward them from a lumberyard. He stopped Giuseppe in front of some stacked lumber. This time, the red car did not pause. It roared by. The man inside waved contemptuously and laughed.

It became very still. Only the rushing of a brook and the soft patter of the rain could be heard. This was happiness, Lillian felt. This minute of stillness, full of dark, damp, fertile expectation. She would never forget it— the night, the gentle pattering, and the wet road glinting in the headlights.

A quarter of an hour later, they ran into fog. Clerfayt switched to the dim headlights. He drove very slowly. After a while, they were able to make out the edge of the road again. For a few hundred yards, the mist was swept away by the rain; then they again entered a cloud which was rising from the depths below.

Clerfayt braked the car very sharply. They had just emerged from the fog again. In front of them, wrapped around a milestone, hung the red sports car, one wheel over the edge of the abyss. Beside it stood the driver, seemingly unhurt.

"I call that luck," Clerfayt said.

"Luck?" the man replied furiously. "And what about the car? Look at it! I don't have collision insurance. And what about my arm?"

"Your arm is sprained, at worst. After all, you're able to move it. Man, be glad you're still standing on the road."

Clerfayt got out and inspected the wreck. "Sometimes milestones are good for something."

"It's your fault!" the man bellowed. "You got me into driving so fast. I'm making you responsible. If you had let me pass and not started to race with me—"

Lillian laughed.

"What does the lady think is so funny?" the man demanded angrily.

"That's none of your business. But since today is Wednesday, I'll explain it to you. The lady comes from another planet and doesn't know our customs down here. She's laughing because she sees you bewailing your car instead of giving thanks that you're still alive. The lady

104

cannot understand that I, on the other hand, admire you for it, so I'll send a tow car up here for you from the next village."

"Stop! You can't get away that easily! If you hadn't dared me to race, I would have driven slowly and not—"

"Too many conditions contrary to fact," Clerfayt said. "You'd better blame it all on the lost war."

The man looked at Clerfayt's license plate. "French! I'll have a devil of a time collecting my money." He fumbled with a pencil and a piece of paper in his left hand. "Give me your number. Write it down for me. Don't you see that I can't write with my arm like this?"

"Learn to. I've had to learn harder things in your country."

Clerfayt got in again. The man followed him. "Are you trying to duck out of this by running away?"

"Exactly. However, I'll send you a tow car."

"What? You mean to leave me standing here on the road in this rain?"

"Yes. This car of mine is a two-seater. Take a deep breath, look at the mountains, give thanks to God that you're still alive, and remember that better people than you have had to die."

They found a garage in Biasca. The owner was at his supper. He left his family and took a bottle of Barbera wine with him. "He'll need some alcohol," he said. "Maybe I will, too."

The car glided on down the mountain, curve upon curve, serpentine after serpentine. "This is a monotonous stretch," Clerfayt said. "It goes on to Locarno. Then comes the lake. Are you tired?"

Lillian shook her head. Tired! she thought. Monotonous! Can't this healthy specimen of life see that I am quivering all over? Doesn't he understand what's going on in me? Can't he feel that my frozen picture of the world has suddenly thawed and is moving and talking, that the rain is talking, the wet rocks are talking and the valley with its shadows and lights, and the road? Doesn't he have any idea that I shall never again be so at one with them as I am now—as if I were lying in the cradle and in the arms of an unknown god, frightened and still as trustful as a young bird, and yet already knowing that all this will exist for me only this one time, that I am losing it even as I possess it and it possesses me, this road and these villages, these dark trucks in front of the roadside inns, this singing behind lighted windows, the guitars, the gray-and-silver sky, and these names—Osogna, Cresciano, Claro, Castione, and Bellinzona—scarcely read and already subsiding behind me like shadows, as if they had never been? Doesn't he see that I am a sieve losing what it receives, not a basket that collects what is put into it? Doesn't he notice that I can scarcely speak because my heart is swelling so, and that among the few names it feels, his is one too, but that all of them really mean only one thing again and again: life?

"How did you like your first encounter down here?" Clerfayt asked. "A fellow who wails over his property and takes his life for granted. You will get to know many more such people."

"It's a change. Up above, everyone thinks his life frightfully important. So did I."

"We'll arrive in ten minutes," Clerfayt said. "Here is Locarno already."

Streets were leaping into being before them, lights, houses, blueness, and a broad square with arcades.

A streetcar rattled up and at the last moment blocked their way. Clerfayt laughed when he saw that Lillian was staring at it as if it were a cathedral. For four years, she had not seen one. There were no streetcars in the mountains.

Now the lake lay before them, broad, silvery, and restless. The rain had stopped. The clouds were moving fast and low across the moon. Ascona, with its piazza by the shore, lay still.

"Where are we going to stay?" Lillian asked.

"By the lake. In the Hotel Tamaro."

"How is it you know this place?"

"I lived here for a year after the war," Clerfayt replied. "Tomorrow morning, you'll understand why."

He stopped in front of the small hotel and unloaded the bags. "The owner of this place has a magnificent library," he said. "He's something of a scholar. And another man farther up on the mountain has a hotel that has Cézannes, Utrillos, and Lautrecs on the walls. That's the sort of thing you run into here. But how would it be if we drove a bit farther to eat?"

"Where to?"

"To Brissago on the Italian border. Ten minutes from here. To a restaurant called Giardino."

Lillian looked around. "Why, there's wisteria in flower!"

The lavender clusters of blossoms hung along the white walls of the houses. Over a garden wall, mimosa shook down its gold and feathery green. "Spring," Clerfayt said. "God bless Giuseppe. He displaces the seasons."

The car drove slowly along the lake. "Mimosa," Clerfayt said, pointing to the flowering trees by the lake. "Whole lanes of them. And there is a hill of iris and daffodils. This village is called Porto Ronco. And that one up there on the mountain is Ronco. It was built by the Romans."

He parked the car beside a long stone staircase. They climbed up to a little restaurant. He ordered a bottle of Soave, *prosciutto, scampi* with rice, and cheese from the Valle Maggia.

There were not many people in the restaurant. The windows were open, the air soft. A pot of white camelias stood on the table.

"You say you've lived here?" Lillian asked. "By this lake?"

"For almost a year. After my escape and after the war. I wanted to stay a few days, but I stayed much longer. I needed it. It was a cure of loafing, sunshine, lizards on the walls, staring at the sky and the lake, and so much forgetting that after a while my eyes were no longer fixed upon a single point; they began to see that nature had taken no notice at all of twenty years of human insanity. *Salute!*"

Lillian drank the light Italian wine. "Am I mistaken, or is the food here amazingly good?" she asked.

"It is amazingly good. The owner could be a chef in any great hotel."

"Why isn't he?"

"He used to be. But he would rather live in his native village."

Lillian looked up. "He wanted to come back—not go out into the world?"

"He was outside—and came back."

She set her glass down on the table. "I'm happy, Clerfayt," she said. "Though I must say that I have no idea what the word means."

"I don't know either."

"Haven't you ever been happy?"

"Often."

She looked at him. "In a different way each time," he added.

"When most of all?"

"I don't know. It was different each time."

"When most of all?"

"Alone," Clerfayt said.

Lillian laughed. "Where are we going now? Are there more fabulous restaurateurs and hotel owners here?"

"Many. At night, at full moon, a glass restaurant rises up out of the lake. It belongs to a son of Neptune. Old Roman wines are served there. But now we're going to a bar that has a wine that is already sold out in Paris."

They drove back to Ascona. Clerfayt left the car in front of the hotel. They walked over the piazza and down some steps to a bar in a cellar.

"I don't need any more to drink," Lillian said. "I'm already drunk on the mimosa. The air is full of it. What are those islands in the lake?"

"In Roman times, they say, there used to be a temple to Venus on that one. Now, someone has a restaurant there. But on nights of full moon the old gods still visit the place. Then in the mornings the owner finds that many bottles have been emptied, with their corks untouched. Now and then, Pan sleeps off his spree on the island and awakes at noon. Then he plays on his pipes a bit, and all radio broadcasts are full of static."

"The wine is wonderful. What is it?"

"Old champagne, perfectly stored. Luckily, the gods don't know anything about it, or they would have drunk it up long ago. There was no such thing as champagne until the Middle Ages."

They walked back. A crucified Christ hung on the wall of a house. Opposite was the door to a restaurant. The Saviour gazed mutely into the illuminated room, from which noise and laughter sounded. It seemed to Lillian that some comment should be made—but there was no comment to be made. It all belonged together.

She stood at the window of her room. Outside were lake, night, and wind. The spring busied itself in the clouds and in the plane trees on the piazza. Clerfayt came in. He put his arm around her. She turned and looked at him. He kissed her. "Aren't you afraid?" she asked.

"Of what?"

"Of my being sick."

"I am afraid that I'll have a front tire blow out on me at a hundred and twenty-five miles an hour," he said.

Abruptly, Lillian took a deep breath. We're alike, she thought. Both of us have no future. His reaches only to the next race, and mine to the next hemorrhage. She smiled.

"There is a story about that," Clerfayt said. "In Paris in the times of the guillotine a man was being led to execution. It was cold, and the way was long. En route, the guards stopped for some wine, which they drank from the bottle. After they'd drunk, they offered the bottle to their prisoner. He took it, looked at it for a moment, and then said, 'I suppose none of us has an infectious disease,' and drank. Half an hour later, his head rolled into the basket. My grandmother told me that story when I was ten years old. She was in the habit of drinking a bottle of Calvados a day. People predicted she would die an early death. She's still alive, and the prophets have been dead a long time. I've brought along a bottle of the old champagne. It's still feels the life that was once in it, so it's said. I'll leave it here for you."

He put the bottle on the window sill, but immediately picked it up again. "Wine should not stand in the moonlight. The moon kills its fragrance. That's one of the things my grandmother used to say, too."

He went to the door.

"Clerfayt," Lillian said.

He turned around.

"I didn't leave in order to be alone," she said.

VIII

The suburbs of Paris stretched out gray, ugly, and rain-streaked; but the farther they penetrated into the city, the more the enchantment began. Corners, angles, and streets rose up like paintings by Utrillo and Pissarro; the gray paled until it was almost silvery; the river appeared, with its bridges and scows and budding trees, with the colorful rows of *bouquinistes* and the square blocks of the old buildings on the right bank of the Seine.

"From that spot," Clerfayt said, "Marie Antoinette was taken away to be beheaded. An extraordinary restaurant is right opposite. In this city, you can combine hunger with history everywhere. Where would you like to stay?"

"There," Lillian said, pointing across the river at the light façade of a small hotel.

"Do you know the place?"

"How would I know it?"

"From the last time you were here."

"When I was last here, I stayed mostly in hiding in a green-grocer's cellar."

"Wouldn't you prefer to stay somewhere in the sixteenth *arrondissement*? Or with your uncle?"

"My uncle is so stingy that he probably lives in a single

111

room. Let's drive across the bridge and ask whether they have any vacancies. Where do you stay?"

"At the Ritz."

"Of course," Lillian said.

Clerfayt nodded. "I'm not rich enough to live elsewhere," he said.

They drove across the bridge to the boulevard Saint-Michel and onto the quai des Grands-Augustins and stopped in front of the Hôtel Bisson. As they got out of the car, a hotel employee came out the front door carrying bags. "There's my room, "Lillian said. "Someone is just leaving."

"Do you really want to stay here? Just because you saw the hotel from across the river?"

Lillian nodded. "That's just the way I want to live. Without recommendations and prejudices."

The room was available. The hotel had no elevator, but luckily the room was on the second floor. The stairs were old and dished. The room was small and sparsely furnished, but the bed seemed good, and there was a bathroom. All the furniture was cheap modern stuff except for a small baroque table that stood there like a prince among slaves. The wallpaper was old, and the electric light inadequate—but in compensation there shone outside the window the river with Conciergerie, quays, and the towers of Notre-Dame.

"You can leave here any time you please," Clerfayt said. "That's something people are apt to forget."

"Where to? To you in the Ritz?"

"Not to me, but to the Ritz," Clerfayt replied. "During the war, I stayed there for half a year. I wore a beard and went by another name. On the cheaper side, facing the rue Cambon. On the other side, facing the place Vendôme, were the German big shots. It was something to remember."

The porter brought up the bags. Clerfayt went to the door. "Would you like to have dinner with me this evening?"

"When?"

"Around nine?"

"At nine, then."

She watched him as he went out. Throughout this day's drive, they had exchanged not a word about the evening in Ascona. French was a convenient language, she thought. You slid from *tu* to *vous* and vice versa; it made the gradations of intimacy a kind of game. She heard Giuseppe's starting roar and went to the window. Perhaps he'll be back, she thought, but perhaps not. She did not know, and it was not very important. The important thing was that she was in Paris, that it was evening, and that she was breathing. The traffic lights on the boulevard Saint-Michel turned green, and like a cavalry charge a horde of Citroëns, Renaults, and trucks dashed across the bridge behind Giuseppe. Lillian could not remember ever having seen so many automobiles. During the war, there had been very few on the streets. The noise was intense, but it reminded her rather of an organ on which iron hands were playing a mighty *Te Deum*.

She unpacked her things. She had not brought much with her; nor did she have much money. She telephoned her uncle. There was no answer. She telephoned again. A stranger's voice responded. Her uncle had given up his telephone years ago, it seemed.

For a brief moment, she was panic-stricken. Her monthly check had been coming to her through a bank, and it was a long time since she had heard from her uncle. He couldn't be dead, she thought. Strange, that always occurred to one first. Perhaps he had moved. She asked the hotel clerk for a city directory. There was only the old one, from the first year of the war, nor was there any new telephone book. Even now there was still a shortage of coal. The room grew chilly in the evening. Lillian put on her coat. For safety, she had taken along some heavy sweaters and woolen underthings, with the thought that if they were superfluous in Paris, she could give them away to someone. She was glad that she had them.

The twilight began creeping through the window, gray and dirty. Lillian took a bath to make herself warm, and got into bed. For the first time since she had left the sanatorium, she was alone. She was really alone now for the first time in years. The money she had would, at most, last a week. With darkness, a new form of panic began to grip her. Where could her uncle be? Perhaps he had gone traveling for a few weeks. Perhaps he had had an accident, and perhaps he was dead. Perhaps Clerfayt, too, was already swallowed up in this unknown city, had taken himself off into another hotel, another existence, and she would never hear from him again. She shivered. Romantic daring quickly faded in the face of a few facts, in the face of cold and loneliness. In the warm cage of the sanatorium, the radiators would be humming now.

There was a knock at her door. It was the hotel porter with two packages. She saw that the small one contained flowers. Flowers could only come from Clerfayt. In her gratitude and in the dimness of the room, she gave the man far too large a tip. Quickly, she opened the second box. A woolen blanket lay inside. "I imagine you will need this," Clerfayt had written. "There's still not enough coal in Paris."

She unfolded the blanket. Two small cartons fell out of it. Light bulbs. "French hotels always economize on light," Clerfayt had written. "Replace your bulbs with these—they will make the world twice as bright."

She followed his advice. At least it was now possible to read. The porter brought her a newspaper. She looked into it, but after a while she laid it aside. These things no longer concerned her. Her time was too short. She would never know who was elected president next year, nor what party was uppermost in the Chamber of Deputies. Nor did such distant matters interest her; her whole being was filled with the will to live. To live her own life.

She dressed. She had her uncle's last letter; he had written her from that address six months ago. She would go there and inquire further.

There was no need of hunting. Her uncle was still in his old flat; he had only given up his telephone.

"Your money?" he said. "As you like. I've been having

your monthly allowance sent to Switzerland; it was hard to get a permit to transfer the funds. Naturally, I can have it paid to you in France. To what address?"

"I don't want it in monthly installments. I want to have all of it right now, at once."

"What for?"

"To buy clothes."

The old man stared at her. "You're like your father. If he—"

"He's dead, Uncle Gaston."

Gaston looked down at his big, bleached hands. "You don't have much money left. What do you mean to do here? My word, if I had the luck to live in Switzerland!"

"I haven't lived in Switzerland. I've lived in a hospital."

"You don't know anything about managing money. You'd spend it in a few weeks. You'd lose it—"

"Possibly," Lillian said.

He stared at her in consternation. "And what do you do when you've lost it?"

"I wouldn't be a burden on you."

"You ought to marry. Are you all right now?"

"Would I be here if I weren't?"

"Then you ought to get married."

Lillian laughed. It was too obvious; he was anxious to shift the responsibility for her to someone else. "You ought to get married," Gaston repeated. "I could arrange for you to meet some suitable people."

Lillian laughed again; but she was curious to see how the old man would go about it. He must be almost eighty, she thought, looking at his ostrich-like head, but he acts as if he has to provide for another eighty years. "All right," she replied. "And now tell me one thing—what do you do when you are alone?"

He stared at her in astonishment. "All sorts of things— I don't know—I keep busy—what an odd question. Why?"

"Don't you ever feel the impulse to take everything you have and go out into the world and squander it?"

"Just like your father!" the old man replied contemptuously. "He never had any sense of responsibility, or foresight either. I've a good mind to have you placed under guardianship."

"You can't do it. You think I'll throw my money away —but I think you're throwing your life away. Let's leave it at that. And see that I can have the money tomorrow. I want to buy those clothes soon."

"Where?" the old man asked quickly.

"At Balenciaga's, I think. Don't forget that the money belongs to me."

"Your mother—"

"I want it tomorrow," Lillian said, giving Gaston a light kiss on the forehead.

"Listen, Lillian, don't rush into any extravagances. You're perfectly well dressed. Clothes from those fashion houses cost a fortune!"

"Probably," Lillian replied. She looked across the dark courtyard at the gray windows of the houses opposite, which gleamed dark as slate in the last remnants of daylight.

"Like your father!" The old man was sincerely horrified. "Just like him. You could have lived without a care if it hadn't been for his fantastic projects—"

"Uncle Gaston, I've been told that there are two ways to part with your money nowadays. One is to save it and have it go in the inflation. The other is to spend it. And now tell me how you have been."

Gaston made a nervous gesture. "You can see. Things are hard nowadays. These times! I'm a poor man."

Lillian looked around. She saw fine old furniture standing about. Sofas and chair swatched in dust sheets, a crystal chandelier tied up in gauze, and a few good paintings. "You always used to be stingy, Uncle Gaston," she said. "But why are you still?"

His dark bird's eyes scrutinized her. "Do you want to live here? I don't have much room—"

"You have plenty of room, but I don't want to live here. How old are you anyway? Weren't you twenty years older than my father?"

The old man was irritated. "If you know, why do you ask?"

"Don't you have any fear of death?"

Gaston was silent for a moment. "You have dreadful manners," he said at last, softly.

"That's true. I shouldn't have asked you. But I ask myself that so often that I forget the question frightens others."

"I'm still in good shape. If you're counting on a legacy from me, you might have long to wait."

Lillian laughed. "I'm not counting on that. And I'm staying in a hotel and won't be a burden to you here."

"What hotel?" Gaston asked quickly.

"The Bisson."

"God be thanked! I wouldn't have been surprised if you were at the Ritz."

"I wouldn't either," Lillian said.

Clerfayt called for her. They drove to the Restaurant Le Grand Vefour. "How was your first collision with the world?" he asked.

"I have the feeling that I've come among people who think they're going to live forever. At least they act that way. They defend their possessions and let their lives slip by."

Clerfayt laughed. "And yet while the war was on, they all vowed that they would never again make the same mistake if they came through it alive. Human beings are great at forgetting."

"Have you forgotten it, too?" Lillian asked.

"I've made a great effort to. I haven't quite succeeded."

"Is that why I love you?"

"You don't love me. If you loved me, you wouldn't use the word lightly—and wouldn't tell me."

"Do I love you because you don't think of the future?"

"Then you would have had to love every man in the sanatorium. Let's see—we're going to have sole with roasted almonds and drink a young Montrachet with it."

"Then why do I love you?"

"Because I happen to be here. And because you love life. I am an anonymous specimen of life to you. Extremely dangerous."

"For me?"

"For the one who is anonymous. He can be replaced at random."

"So can I," Lillian said. "So can I, Clerfayt."

"I'm no longer quite so sure of that. If I had any sense, I'd clear out as soon as possible."

"You've barely arrived."

"I'm leaving tomorrow."

"Where to?" Lillian asked, without believing him.

"Far away. I have to go to Rome."

"And I have to go to Balenciaga's to buy clothes. That's farther than Rome."

"I really am going. I must see about a contract."

"Good," Lillian said. "That will give me time to plunge into the adventure of the fashion houses. My uncle Gaston is already talking of placing me under guardianship—or marrying me off."

Clerfayt laughed. "He would like to put you into a second prison before you know what freedom is."

"What is freedom?"

"I don't know either. I only know that it is neither irresponsibility nor aimlessness. It's easier to say what it is not than what it is."

"When are you coming back?" Lillian asked.

"In a few days."

"Do you have someone in Rome?"

"Yes," Clerfayt said.

"I thought so."

"Why?"

"It would be strange if you had been living alone. I wasn't living alone either, when you came."

"And now?"

"Now," Lillian said, "I'm far too drunk on life itself to be able to think it over."

She went to Balenciaga the following afternoon. Aside from sports things suitable for the sanatorium, Lillian had hardly any wardrobe. Some of her dresses dated from wartime; others had been her mother's, which she had had made over by a seamstress.

She watched the women who sat around her. She studied their clothes and probed their faces for the kind of excitement that filled her. She did not find it. She saw spiteful, aging parrots, too heavily made up, who gazed at the younger ones out of lidless eyes, and young women of brittle elegance whose knowing looks took in everything but the incomprehensible fascination of simple existence. Among these sat a band of good-looking Americans, chattering enthusiastically in their naïve way. Only here and there, burning to perishability in the busy emptiness like a lighted candle between window decorations, was a face that had some magic—usually an aging face—one that confronted age without terror, and on which time lay, not like rust, but like the patina upon a noble vessel, intensifying its beauty.

The parade of the mannequins began. Lillian heard the muted noise of the city seeping in from outside, like deliberate drumming from a modern jungle of steel, concrete, and machines. The mannequins on their slender ankles seemed wafted in like artificial animals, long chameleons who changed their clothes like the colors of their skins and silently glided past the chairs.

She settled on five dresses. "Would you like to try them right away?" the saleswoman asked.

"May I?"

"Certainly. These three will fit you just as they are; the others are a little too wide."

"When can I have them?" Lillian asked.

"When do you need them?"

"At once."

The saleswoman laughed. "At once means in three or four weeks at the earliest, here."

"I need them at once. Can I have the models that fit me?"

The saleswoman shook her head. "No, we need them every day. But we'll do what we can. We're overwhelmed with work, Mademoiselle. If we were to carry out all the orders in turn, you would have to wait six weeks. Shall we try the black evening dress now?"

The models were brought to a booth lined with mirrors.

The seamstress came along to take the measurements. "You've chosen very well, Mademoiselle," the saleswoman said. "The dresses suit you as if they were designed for you. Monsieur Balenciaga will be delighted when he sees them on you. A pity he is not here now."

"Where is Monsieur Balenciaga?" Lillian asked merely from politeness as she slipped out of her dress.

"In the mountains." The saleswoman mentioned the site of Lillian's sanatorium. To Lillian, it sounded like some place name in the Himalayas. "He's making a health cure there," the seamstress said.

"Yes, that is the place for it."

Lillian straightened up and looked into the mirror. "You see, that is what we meant," the saleswoman said. "Most women buy what they like. You bought what suits you. Don't you agree?" she asked the seamstress.

The seamstress nodded. "Now for the coat!"

The evening dress was coal black and clinging, but the coat that made up the costume was wide and capelike, of a half-transparent material that stood out as if it were starched.

"Striking!" the saleswoman said. "You look like a fallen archangel."

Lillian looked at herself. Out of the big three-leafed mirror three women returned her look, two in profile and one full face, and when she moved a little to the side, she saw, reflected from the wall mirror behind her, a fourth, who had her back turned to her and seemed on the point of going away.

"Striking!" the saleswoman repeated. "Why can't Lucille wear it this way?"

"Who is Lucille?"

"Our best model. The one who showed the dress."

Why should she wear it this way? Lillian thought. She will wear a thousand other dresses, and will go on modeling dresses for many years, then marry and have children and grow old. But I will wear it only this summer. "Can't you make up this one dress in less than four weeks?" she said. "I need it and I have little time."

"What do you think, Mademoiselle Claude?" the seamstress asked.

The saleswoman nodded. "We will begin on it at once."

"When?" Lillian asked.

"It can be ready in two weeks."

"Two weeks—" It was like two years.

"If all goes well, ten days. We need several fittings."

"All right. If there's no help for it."

"There is no help for it."

She went for fittings every day. The quiet of the booth cast a strange spell over her. Sometimes she heard the voices of other women from outside, but in the gray-and-silver haven of her own booth, she was isolated from the bustle of the city. The seamstress moved around her like a priestess around an idol. She pinned, pleated, gathered material, cut, murmured inaudible comments from a mouth bristling with pins, knelt, eased here and drew in there in an ever-repeated ritual. Lillian stood still and beheld in the mirrors three women who resembled her and at the same time were far away from her, to whom something was being done before her eyes that only distantly had anything to do with her, and that nevertheless profoundly transformed her. Sometimes the curtain of her booth was lifted and another client looked in—with the swift, keen glance of the eternal warriors of the sex, ever watchful, and ever on their mettle. At such times, Lillian felt that she no longer had anything in common with all that. She was not out to capture a man; she was out to capture life.

In the course of these days, a relationship of strangely detached intimacy developed between herself and the various women in the mirror, who were different with every new dress. She spoke to them without speaking; the images smiled at her without smiling. They were grave, and, in a subdued way, close to one another, like sisters whom life has flung apart, so that they never thought to see each other again. Now, they met as if in dream, and it was a silent rendezvous, already filled with gentle sadness—soon they would have to part once more, and this time, surely, for good. Even the dresses, with their Spanish feeling, had a little of that mood—the stark black of the velvets; the hectic red of the silks; the wide coats which made the body almost insubstantial, and the heavy brocades of the short *torero* jackets, with their suggestion of sand and sun and sudden death.

Balenciaga returned. He sat in on a fitting and said not a word. Next day, the saleswoman brought something silvery into the booth; it looked like the skin of a fish that had never felt the sun. "Monsieur Balenciaga would like you to have this dress," the saleswoman said.

"I have to call a halt. I've already bought more than I should have; every day I've ordered something more."

"Try it on. You'll be pleased with it." The saleswoman smiled. "And I assure you that the price will be satisfactory. The House of Balenciaga would like to have you wearing its clothes."

Lillian put on the silvery nothing. It was almost pearly in color, but instead of making her pale, it raised the color of her face and shoulders to a golden bronze tone. She sighed. "I'll take it. It's harder to say no to such a dress than to the blandishments of Don Juan and Apollo."

Not always, she thought, but at the moment it was so. She was living in a weightless world of gray and silver. Mornings, she slept late; then she went to Balenciaga; afterward she wandered at random through the streets; and in the evenings she had dinner by herself in the hotel's restaurant. The restaurant happened to be one of the best in Paris; she had not known that. She had no desire for company and missed Clerfayt only slightly. The anonymous life that poured in upon her from all sides, from streets, cafés, and restaurants, was powerful enough and new enough to her so that she did not yet greatly miss a life of her own. She let herself drift; the crowd sustained her and did not shock her; she loved it because it was life, unknown, thoughtless, foolish life devoted to the thoughtless and foolish goals which bobbed on its surface like colored buoys on a choppy sea.

"You have bought wisely," the saleswoman said to her

at the last fitting. "There are dresses that will never be out of fashion. You can wear them for years."

Years, Lillian thought, shivering and smiling. "I will only need them for this summer," she said.

IX

It was like awakening from a mild intoxication. For almost two weeks, she had lost herself among dresses, hats, and shoes like a drinker in a wine cellar. The first dresses were delivered, and she sent the bills to Uncle Gaston, who, after all, had only sent her her monthly sum. He had made the excuse that these financial rearrangements were taking a great deal of time.

Next day, her uncle appeared, highly excited. He sniffed around the hotel, told her that she was completely irresponsible, and wonder of wonders, demanded that she move to his apartment.

"So that you can have me under your control?"

"So that you can live more economically. It's a crime to spend so much on things to wear. They would have to be made of gold to be worth these prices."

"They are made of gold. It's a pity you don't see it."

"To sell sound, interest-bearing securities for a few scraps of cloth—" Gaston groaned. "I'll have to have you placed under guardianship!"

"Just try to. Every judge in France would understand my actions. In the end, it would be you who would be sent to a mental hospital for observation. If you don't let me have my money, and soon, I'll buy twice as many things and send you the bills."

"Twice as many of these rags! You're—"

"No, Uncle Gaston, I'm not crazy. You are. You who stint yourself on everything, so that a dozen heirs whom you hardly know and heartily detest can go through the money later on. But let's not talk about it any more. Stay to dinner with me. The restaurant here has very good food. I'll put on one of my new dresses for you."

"Out of the question. To throw more money out on—"

"But you will be my guest. I have credit here. And while we eat, you can tell me more about how sensible people live. At the moment, I'm as hungry as a skier after six hours' practice. No, hungrier. Going for fittings gives you an appetite. Wait downstairs for me. I'll be ready in five minutes."

She came down an hour later. Gaston, pale with ill-humor and the boredom of waiting, sat in the lobby at a small table which held a leafy plant and a scattering of magazines. He had not ordered an *apéritif*. To her delight, he did not recognize her at once. He actually twirled his mustache when he saw her descending the dimly lit staircase, pulled himself straighter, and threw her the look of and old-fashioned roué. "It's I, Uncle Gaston," she said. "You wouldn't be having incestuous thoughts, I hope."

Gaston coughed. "Nonsense," he growled. "It's only that my eyes are bad. When was the last time I saw you?"

"Two weeks ago."

"I don't mean that time. Before."

"About five years ago—and then, I was half starved and all to pieces."

"And how are you now?"

"Now, I'm still half starved, but my mind is made up."

Gaston took a pair of pince-nez from his pocket. "For whom have you bought these dresses?"

"For myself."

"You don't have any—"

"The only marriageable men up in the mountains were ski instructors. They were not bad, as long as they wore their ski outfiits, but out of them, they seemed like farmers."

"You're all alone?"

"Yes, but not the way you are," Lillian said, preceding him into the restaurant.

"What would you like to eat?" Gaston said. "Of course it's my treat. I'm not hungry. And you? Light, nourishing foods, I suppose. An omelette, fruit salad, Vichy water . . ."

"For me," Lillian replied, "sea urchins to start with— a dozen of them. And a vodka."

Involuntarily, Gaston looked down the line of prices. "Sea urchins are bad for you."

"Only for misers. They stick in their throats, Uncle Gaston. Then a *filet poivré* . . ."

"Isn't that too sharp? Boiled chicken, I'd think. Or didn't you have oatmeal at the sanatorium?"

"Yes, Uncle Gaston. I've eaten enough oatmeal and enough boiled chicken up in the mountains, looking out on the glories of nature, to last me my lifetime. Enough! And with the steak, let's have a Château Lafite. Or don't you like that wine?"

"I can't afford it. I've become very poor, my dear Lillian."

"I know. That's what makes it so exciting to eat with you."

"What do you mean?"

"With every drop, I drink a drop of your heart's blood."

"Ugh!" Gaston said, jolted out of his poverty-stricken air. "What a thing to say. And in connection with such a wine! Let's talk about something else. Can I taste your sea urchins?"

Lillian passed the plate across to him. Gaston gobbled down three. He continued to eat sparingly, but kept up with her on the wine. If he were going to have to pay for it, he wanted to have something of it. "Child," he said, when the bottle was empty, "how time flies! I remember you when you—"

Lillian felt a brief, sharp pang. "I don't want to remember any of that, Uncle Gaston. Tell me one thing: Why was I named Lillian? I hate that name."

"It was your father's choice."

"Why?"

"Would you like a liqueur with the coffee? Cognac? Chartreuse? Armagnac? I could have guessed it!" Gaston had visibly thawed. "All right, two armagnacs. Yes, as I was saying, your father—"

"What?"

The ostrich winked. "As a young man, he was in New York for a little while without your mother. Later on, he wanted his daughter to be called Lillian. Your mother had no objection. I learned, privately of course, that while he was in New York he was supposed to have had a—well, a very romantic affair. With a girl named Lillian. Forgive me, but you asked—"

"I'm so glad!" Lillian said. "I always thought the name was something Mother must have picked out of a book. She used to be a great reader."

The ostrich head nodded. "Yes, she was. Enough for two—your father kept away from books. Well, Lilly? Are you really intending to stay on in this place?" He looked around. "Don't you think it's a mistake?"

"I was just going to ask you about that. After the wine, you've actually become almost human."

Gaston sipped at his armagnac. "I'll give a little party for you."

"You threatened me with that once before."

"Don't you want one?"

"Not if it's a tea or a cocktail party."

"A dinner. I still have a few bottles of wine—only a few, but they're the equal of this."

"Good."

"You've become a beautiful girl, Lilly. But hard! Hard! Your father was not like that."

Hard, Lillian thought. What does he mean by hard? And am I like that? Or is it only that I have no time for the fraud of so-called good manners, which strews a little glitter over black truths, and thinks that that has made them disappear.

From her window, she could see the spire of Sainte-Chapelle. It thrust its filigree sharpness into the sky above the gray walls of the Conciergerie. She recollected the Sainte-Chapelle of earlier days. On the first day of good sunshine, she went to see it.

It was almost noon, and the room, with its high stained-glass windows, was flooded with light, as if it were a transparent tower of radiance. It seemed to be nothing but windows, full of Madonna blues and glowing reds and yellows and greens. So powerful was the torrent of colors, she could feel the hues on her skin, as if she were taking a bath in colored light. Aside from Lillian, there were only a few American soldiers in the church, and these soon left. She sat on a bench, wrapped in light as if it were the filmiest and most regal of all dresses, and she would have liked to be able to undress and see the transparent brocade gliding over her skin. It was a cataract of light, a weightless ecstasy, a falling and suspension at the same time; she felt she was breathing light; it was as though the blues and reds and yellows were coursing through her lungs and blood, as though the dividing line through skin and consciousness had been abolished and the light were penetrating her as she had seen it in X-ray photographs, except that the X rays went as deep as the skeleton, whereas these seemed to irradiate the mysterious force that made the heart beat and the blood pulse. It was life itself, and while she sat there, tranquil, without stirring, letting the light rain down upon her and into her, she belonged to it and was one with it. She was not isolated and solitary. Rather, the light received her and sheltered her, and she had the mystic feeling that she could never die as long as it held her so, and that something in her would never die—that part which belonged to this magical light. It was a great consolation, and she pledged herself never to forget it. Her life, those days that still remained to her, she felt, must be like this, a beehive filled with the ethereal honey of radiance: light without shadow, life without regret, combustion without ashes—

She recalled the last time she had been in Sainte-

Chapelle. That had been during the time a hunt was on for her father. She and her mother had spent their days in churches, because those were the safest places to be. Lillian had come to know most of the churches of Paris from the vantage point of the darkest corner, where she and her mother hunched, pretending to be at prayer. But after a while, *they* had begun sending spies even into the churches, and the dim aisles of Notre-Dame no longer meant safety. Then friends had advised her mother to spend the days in Sainte-Chapelle, because the attendants there were reliable. At the time, Lillian had recoiled from the vivid light, feeling herself there like a criminal dragged from his dark den into the merciless glare of a police searchlight, or like a leper exposed to the probing brightness of an operating room. She had hated it and never forgotten it, and felt it as a painful imposition.

Now, all such feelings were gone. The shadows of the past had dissolved like mist in the first mild surge of the light. Imposition was no longer there; only happiness. There was no resisting this light, she thought. It melted and transfigured memory's horrible capacity for carrying the past into the present, not simply as a lesson, but in the form of petrified life; for cluttering the present with such encumbrances as a room is cluttered with useless old furniture. In this light, memory became what it ought to be: stronger and conscious existence, not dead, old existence. Lillian stretched her whole body in the rippling light. It seemed to her that she could hear it. One could hear so many things, she thought, if only one could be quiet enough. She breathed deeply. She breathed in the gold and blue and wine red. She felt even the sanatorium and its last shadows dissolving in these colors; the gray-and-black gelatine sheets of the X-ray photographs curled up and burned with a small, bright flame. That was what she had been waiting for. That was why she had come here. She was happy. The happiness of radiance, she thought: the most immaterial in the world.

The attendant had to tap her on the shoulder. "Closing time, Mademoiselle."

She stood up and looked into the man's tired, care-worn face. For a moment, she could not understand his being unaware of what she felt—but even miracles were probably accepted as ordinary when you had them happening all the time. "Have you been here long?" she asked.

"For two years."

"Did you know the person who used to be here during the war?"

"No."

"It must be lovely, spending the day here."

"It's a living," the man said. "Pretty scanty. What with the inflation."

She took a bill from her purse. The attendant's eyes lit up. This was his miracle, she thought, and one could not object to it; it meant bread and wine and life, and happiness also. She went out into the gray courtyard. Did miracles really become monotonous, she thought, after you became accustomed to them? Did they become commonplace, just as the life down here, which up in the mountains had been the most glorious of concepts, seemed to have become commonplace, the constant slow-burning light of routine instead of a radiant chapel?

She looked around. The sun lay with a uniform glare upon the roofs of the adjoining prison; yet it contained all the rays that were performing their festival of light inside the chapel. Policemen crossed the courtyard, and a Black Maria with faces behind barred windows rumbled past. The radiant miracle was surrounded by buildings belonging to the police and judiciary. It stood amidst an atmosphere of filing cases, of crime, murder, litigation, envy, malice, in the dreary shadow of all that humanity called "justice." The irony was intense—but Lillian could not be sure that it did not also have a deeper meaning, that this had to be so in order for the miracle to be a miracle. Suddenly she thought of Clerfayt. She smiled. She was ready. She had heard nothing from him since he left Paris. That had not hurt her; she had not expected to hear. She did not need him yet; but it was good to know that he existed.

In Rome, Clerfayt had sat around offices, cafés, and workshops. He spent his evenings with Lydia Morelli. At first, he thought of Lillian sometimes; then he forgot her for days on end. He was touched by her, and that was something that did not easily happen to him with women. She seemed to him like a lovely young pup that exaggerated everything it did. She would settle down, he thought. She still labored under the illusion that she had to catch up on everything she had missed. Pretty soon she would find out that she had missed nothing. She would get her bearings and become like the others—like Lydia Morelli, for instance, or an inferior copy of Lydia. She did not have Lydia's sardonic cleverness, or her female ruthlessness. All in all, she was the type for a slightly sentimental man with poetic notions who could devote a great deal of time to her, he decided—not for him. She should have stayed with Volkov. Apparently, the fellow had existed only for her, and so, of course, had lost her on that very score. That was the law of life. Clerfayt was accustomed to living differently. He did not want to be drawn too deeply into anything. Lydia Morelli was right for him. Lillian had been a charming, brief holiday experience. She was too provincial for Paris, too demanding and too inexperienced. He didn't have the time for that.

Having come to this decision, Clerfayt felt relieved. He would telephone Lillian in Paris and see her again, to explain the thing to her. Perhaps there was nothing even to explain. She must surely have explained the whole thing to herself long ago. But then, why did he want to see her again? He did not waste much thought on this. Why not? After all, there had been almost nothing between them. He signed his contract, and stayed another two days in Rome. Lydia Morelli set out for Paris on the same day he did. He drove Giuseppe; Lydia took the train. She hated automobile trips and airplanes.

X

Lillian had always been afraid of the night. Night was associated with suffocation, with shadowy hands reaching for her throat, with the frightful and unbearable loneliness of death. In the sanatorium, she had kept the light on in her room, in order to escape the illumination of the full moon, reflected from miles of virgin snow, or the dim, unnerving pallor of moonless nights when the snow looked gray, when it stretched outside the windows like the most colorless thing in the world. The nights in Paris were kinder. The river was outside, and Notre-Dame, and now and then a drunk making a commotion in the street or a car whose whirring tires hummed over the pavement. When the first things arrived from Balenciaga, Lillian did not hang them in the wardrobe. She hung them around her in the room. The velvet dress hung above the bed, with the silver one close beside it, so that she could touch them when she started up out of sleep, out of primordial terror dreams, the dreams of falling, plummeting alone, with a smothered cry, from endless darkness into endless darkness. At such times, she could stretch out her arm and grasp the dresses, and they were like silver-and-velvet ropes which she could use to draw herself back out of the shapeless grayness, back to walls, time, relationships, space, and life. She ran her hands over them, felt the cloth, and stood up and walked about her room, often naked, and felt that her dresses surrounded her like friends; they hung on their hangers from the walls, from the doors of the wardrobe, and her shoes stood in a row on the dresser, golden and chestnut and black, perching on their high heels as though they had been left behind by a troupe of extremely chic Botticelli angels who had briefly flown to Sainte-Chapelle for midnight mass, and would be returning at dawn. Only a woman could know, she thought, how much comfort there could be in a tiny hat. She wandered about at night among her acquisitions, held the brocade up to the moonlight, pulled a small cap over her hair, tried on a pair of shoes, and sometimes a dress. In the pale light, she stood studying herself in the mirror, looking into the muted phosphorescence, into her face, at her shoulders to see whether they were already gaunt, at her breasts to see whether they were already drooping, and at her legs to look for those concave curves of emaciation in the thighs. Not yet, she thought, not yet, and continued the silent, ghostly game, another pair of shoes, a little hat with barely substance enough to cling to the head, and the few pieces of jewelry she owned, which at night had a singular witchery. And the image in the mirror smiled and questioned and looked back at her as though it knew more than she herself.

When he saw her again, Clerfayt stared at her—so much had she changed. He had telephoned her after his second day back in Paris—had done so as a burdensome duty, and with the thought of, at most, an hour with the girl. He stayed the evening. It was not the clothes alone; he perceived that at once. He had seen enough women who dressed well, and Lydia Morelli knew more about clothes than an army sergeant about drill. The change was deeper. It seemed to him that a few weeks ago he had left a half-grown girl, a slightly awkward creature not quite adult, and had come back to find a young woman who had just passed the mysterious border of adolescence, so that she still had its charm, but with it had acquired the magical sureness of a beautiful woman. He had decided to make a clean break with Lillian; now he was glad he still had a belated chance to try holding her. Away from her, he had magnified the aspect of her that had struck him as rather provincial. What with her over-intensity and social uncertainty, he had decided that she was what he would call hysterical. None of this was in evidence now. A flame was burning here, quietly and strongly, and he knew how rare that was. Kitchen candles in silver chandeliers were innumerable, and youth was often wrongly taken for the flame and might indeed have some flicker of it, until that was dimmed by calculation and resignation. But here was something different. Why had he not seen this thing before? He had felt it, but had not known what it was. It seemed to him he had seen a young trout which had been placed in an aquarium; it had kept bumping against the glass walls, pulling out the plants and stirring up mud. Now, it was no longer hampered by its cramped surroundings. It had found the river where it belonged and was no longer awkward and frantic. It played with its own swiftness and with the colors of the rainbow that flashed and danced upon its silver skin.

"My uncle Gaston wants to give a party for me," Lillian said a few evenings later.

"Oh?"

"Yes. He wants to marry me off."

"Still?"

"More than ever. He's terribly worried. Not only that I'll be ruined, but that he'll be involved in it, if I go on buying clothes the way I have been doing."

They were sitting in the Grand Vefour again. Once more, as on their first evening there, they had sole with roast almonds, and again they drank a young Montrachet. "You seem to have lost your tongue in Rome," Lillian said.

Clerfayt looked up. "Have I?"

Lillian smiled. "Or is it the woman who came in a while ago?"

"What woman?"

"Must I point her out to you?"

Clerfayt had not noticed Lydia Morelli come in. Now he spotted her. What the devil had brought her in here, of all places? He did not know the man she was with, except that his name was Johnson and that he was reputed to be very rich. Lydia had certainly lost no time, for he had told her only this morning that he would not be able to meet her this evening either. Now, too, he realized how she had tracked him down: he had been here several times with her a year ago. I ought to be careful with my favorite restaurants, he thought irritably.

"Do you know her?"

"Fairly well—not especially."

He saw that Lydia was studying Lillian and already knew to the last fold what Lillian was wearing, where the dress came from and how much it cost to within a hundred francs. He imagined that she had even appraised Lillian's shoes, although she could not see them. In such matters, Lydia was clairvoyant. He could have prevented this thing from happening if he had given the matter thought; but now, since it had come about, he decided to exploit it. The simplest emotions always remained the most effective. One of them was rivalry. If he could make Lillian jealous, so much the better.

"She's very well dressed," Lillian said.

He nodded. "She's noted for that."

Lydia was forty. She looked like thirty by day and like twenty-five in the evening, when the light was flattering. The light was always flattering in the restaurants to which Lydia went.

Clerfayt expected Lillian to make a remark about her age. "She's beautiful," Lillian said instead. "Have you had an affair with her?"

"No," Clerfayt replied.

"That was foolish on your part," Lillian said.

He looked at her in surprise. "Why?"

"She's very beautiful. Where is she from? From Rome?"

"Yes," he said. "From Rome. Why? Are you jealous?"

Lillian quietly set down her glass of yellow Chartreuse. "Poor Clerfayt," she replied. "I am not jealous. I have no time for that."

Clerfayt stared at her. With any other woman, he would have thought this a lie, but he knew at once that in Lillian's case it was not. She meant it, and it was so. Abruptly, without transition, without knowing the reason, he was in a vile temper. "Suppose we talk about something else."

"Why? Because you came back to Paris with another woman?"

"That's nonsense! What makes you think anything so absurd?"

"Isn't it true?"

Clerfayt thought only for a moment. "Yes, it is true."

"You have very good taste."

He remained silent, waiting for the next question. He was prepared to tell the truth. He knew that he had walked into this thing of his own accord, and was angry with himself; but he knew also that nothing could help him now, logic least of all. Lillian had escaped him, and in the most dangerous fashion—without a struggle. To win her back, he had no choice now but to do something extremely risky in a contest the clever usually waged only with mirrors—to make an admission that might lose him everything.

"I did not want to fall in love with you, Lillian," he said.

She smiled. "That's no remedy. Schoolboys act that way."

"In love no one is ever grown up."

"Love—" Lillian said. "What a sweeping word! And what a multitude of things it hides!" She looked at Lydia Morelli. "It is much simpler. Shall we go?"

"Where to?"

"I'd like to go back to my hotel."

Clerfayt did not reply. He paid the check. It's over, he

thought. They went out through the center door, passing Lydia Morelli's table. She ignored Clerfayt. The man in charge of the cars of restaurant guests had parked Clerfayt's car on the sidewalk quite near the entrance. Lillian pointed toward Giuseppe. "That's what gave you away. Drive me to the hotel."

"Not quite yet. Let's walk about the Palais-Royal. Is the garden open?" he asked the man.

"Only the arcades, sir."

"I've seen the garden," Lillian said. "What do you want to get into? Bigamy?"

"Stop that now. Come along with me."

They walked through the palace arcades. It was a cool evening; the smells of soil and spring were strong. Gusts of wind blew down from above into the garden; the wind was much warmer than the night that had settled in among the trees. Clerfayt stood still. "Don't say anything. And don't make me explain anything. I can't."

"What is there to explain?"

"Is there really nothing?"

"Really not," Lillian said.

"I love you."

"Because I haven't made a scene?"

"No," Clerfayt said. "That would be a hell of a reason. I love you because you have made an unusual scene."

"But I am not making one at all," Lillian replied, drawing the narrow fur collar of her jacket more tightly around her neck. "I don't think I know how to."

She stood before him, and the restless wind blew in her hair. Suddenly she had become a complete stranger to him, a woman whom he had never known and whom he had already lost. "I love you," he said again, and took her into his arms and kissed her. He smelled the faint fragrance of her hair and the bitter perfume of her throat. She did not resist him. She hung in his arms, her eyes wide open and absent, as if she were listening to the wind.

He shook her. "Say something! Do something! Tell me to go away, if that's what you want. Slap me in the face! But don't be like a statue."

She tautened, and he released her. "Why should you go away?" she asked.

"Do you want me to stay then?"

"To 'want' is such a cast-iron word, tonight. What am I to do with it? It fractures so easily, too. Do you feel the wind? What does it want?"

He looked at her. After a while, he said, with profound amazement: "I think you mean everything you say."

She smiled. "Why not? I've already told you that everything is far simpler than you assume."

He remained silent for a moment, not knowing what he should do. "All right, I'll drive you to the hotel," he said at last.

She walked along quietly at his side. What is the matter with me? he thought. I'm all mixed up, and annoyed with me and Lydia Morelli, and the only one I ought to be annoyed with is myself.

They reached the car. At that moment, Lydia Morelli and her escort came out of the restaurant. Lydia might have liked to snub Clerfayt again, but her curiosity about Lillian was too strong. Moreover, she and her escort were obliged to wait in the narrow street; Clerfayt's car had to be maneuvered out of the jam of cars parked side by side before they could have their own. With perfect composure, she greeted Clerfayt and introduced her escort. She gave an amazing display of adroitness as she went about getting the facts on Lillian. Clerfayt thought he would have to intervene, but he discovered in a moment that Lillian knew how to fend for herself. While the two parking attendants, with much shouting, were pushing cars back and forth and holding up traffic, and he was talking automobiles with Lydia's escort, the two women engaged in an apparently innocuous conversation, all thrusts and parries and deadly amiability. Lydia Morelli would surely have been victorious had she been fencing on her own plane; she was older than Lillian, and had far more skill and spite. But it seemed as if she were directing her thrusts at absorbent cotton. Lillian treated her with such disarming naïveté and such insulting courtesy that all of Lydia's strategy was useless; she was unmasked as the aggressor—and thereby already half defeated. Even her escort could not help noticing that she was the more aroused of the two.

"Your car, sir," the parking attendant told Clerfayt.

Clerfayt drove down the street and around the next corner. "That was a first-class performance," he said to Lillian. "She does not know who you are, where you are from, or where you are living."

"She will know by tomorrow, if she cares to," Lillian replied equably.

"From whom? From me?"

"From my dressmaker. She placed my dress."

"Doesn't it annoy you?"

"I couldn't care less." Lillian took a deep breath of the night air. "Let's drive across the place de la Concorde once more. Today is Sunday; they'll have the fountains illuminated."

"I think you don't care about anything, do you?" he asked.

She turned toward him and smiled. "In a very intense way, that's true."

"I thought so. What's done this to you?"

I know that I am dying, she thought, feeling the light of the street lamps gliding over her face. I know that more definitely than you, that's all, and so I hear the things that are mere noise to you as messages and cries and carols of joy, and feel the things that are commonplace to you as mercies and great gifts. "Look, the fountains!" she said.

He drove very slowly around the square. Under the silver-gray sky of Paris, the crystalline streamers rose, caught themselves narcissistically up in themselves and threw themselves toward and through one another. The fountains murmured; the obelisk stood marked with thousands of years of endurance like a bright, vertical axis among the most transitory things on earth, fountains that sprang toward the sky and died while they balanced for a moment forgetting the disease of gravity, and then, transformed again in falling, singing the earth's oldest

139

lullaby: the rush of water, the monotonous song of the eternal recurrence of matter and the eternal passing of individuality.

"What a square!" Lillian said.

"Yes," Clerfayt replied. "They set up the guillotine here. Over there, Marie Antoinette was beheaded. Now the fountains play."

"Drive to the Rond-Point," Lillian said. "I want to see the other fountains there, too."

Clerfayt drove down the Champs-Elysées. At the Rond-Point, the song and the white spray of the water were girded by yellow tulips as disciplined as a squadron of Prussian soldiers practicing "at attention" with the upright bayonets of their blossoms.

"Don't you care about this either?" Clerfayt asked.

Lillian had to think for a moment. Slowly, she brought her vision back from the splashing fountains and the night. He is making himself unhappy, she thought. How easily it all went. "It extinguishes me," she said. "Don't you understand that?"

"No. I don't want to be extinguished; I want to feel myself all the more strongly."

"That's what I mean. But it helps not to resist."

He would have liked to stop and kiss her; but he was not certain what would happen then. Curiously, he felt somehow cheated, and what he wanted most to do was to drive his car into the bed of yellow tulips, and crush them. He wanted to lash out at everything around him. That done, he would seize Lillian and drive somewhere with her—But where? To a cave, a hiding place, a room —or back again and again to the impersonal question of her bright eyes, which never seemed to look directly at him?

"I love you," he said. "Forget about everything else. Forget about the woman."

"Why? Why shouldn't you have someone? Did you think I've been alone all the time?"

Giuseppe took a leap forward and stalled. Clerfayt started it again. "You mean in the sanatorium?" he said.

"I mean in Paris."

He looked at her. She smiled. "I can't be alone. And now drive me to the hotel. I'm tired."

"All right."

Clerfayt drove along by the Louvre, past the Conciergerie, and across the bridge to the boulevard Saint-Michel. He was furious and helpless. He would have liked to beat Lillian—but that was out of the question. She had only admitted to something to which he had already admitted, and he did not doubt her for a moment. All he wanted now was to win her back again. She had suddenly become more important than anything else, the ultimate in desirability to him. He did not know what he ought to do, but something had to be done; he could not simply leave her at the hotel entrance. This was his last chance; he must find a magic word to hold her, or else she would get out, kiss him smilingly, absently, and vanish into the entrance of the hotel which smelled of bouillabaisse and garlic, climb the worn, crooked staircase past the nook where the porter dozed, his midnight snack of Lyons sausage and *vin ordinaire* at his side. Up the steps she would go, and the last he would see of her would be her slender ankles showing brightly in the gloom of the narrow stairway, and once she was in her room, two wings, no doubt, would sprout from her golden bolero jacket and she would fly out the window, swiftly, not to Sainte-Chapelle, of which she had spoken to him, but on a high-fashion witch's broom from Balenciaga or Dior, off she would whisk to some witches' sabbath in which only devils in evening dress took part—devils who had broken every speed record, talked fluently in six languages, knew philosophy from Plato to Heidegger, and, on the side, were piano virtuosos, poets, and world boxing champions.

The porter yawned and woke up. "Can you bring us something from the kitchen?" Clerfayt asked him.

"Certainly, sir. What shall it be? Vichy? Champagne? Beer?"

"First of all, we'll want some caviar. You must have some in the icebox."

141

"I can't open that, sir. Madame has the key."

"Then run to the Restaurant Lapérouse on the corner and get us some there. The place is still open. We'll wait here. I'll take care of your desk while you're gone."

He took money from his pocket. "I'm not in the mood for caviar," Lillian said.

"What are you in the mood for?"

She hesitated. "Clerfayt," she said at last, "I don't generally bring men home with me at this time of night. That's what really is worrying you, isn't it?"

"That's so," the porter put in. "Madame always comes home alone. It isn't normal, Monsieur. Would you like champagne? We still have some Dom Perignon 1934."

"Bring it, you blessed spirit," Clerfayt cried. "And if not caviar, what is there to eat?"

"I want some of that sausage." Lillian pointed to the porter's provisions.

"Take what's here, Madame. There's plenty more of it in the kitchen."

"Bring us a good-sized piece then," Clerfayt said. "With dark bread and a piece of Brie."

"And a bottle of beer," Lillian said.

"No champagne, Madame?" The porter's face fell. He was thinking of his percentages.

"The Dom Perignon in any case," Clerfayt declared. "Even if it is only for me. I have something I want to celebrate."

"What?"

"The breakthrough of feeling." Clerfayt posted himself in the porter's box. "Go along. I'll keep an eye on things until you're back."

"Can you run the switchboard?" Lillian asked.

"Of course. I learned that in the war."

She leaned her elbow on the counter. "You learned a great deal in the war, didn't you?"

"Most of what I know. After all, it's almost always wartime."

Clerfayt jotted down an order for a carafe of water, and a traveler's request to be wakened at six. He handed a baldheaded man the key to Number Twelve and two young Englishwomen the keys to Twenty-four and Twenty-five. A somewhat tipsy man came in from the street and wanted to know whether Lillian was free and what she charged. "A thousand dollars," Clerfayt said.

"No woman is worth that, you idiot," the man replied, and staggered out again into the murmuring, river-rippling night along the quay.

The porter came up from the kitchens with the bottles and the sausage. He was perfectly willing to go to the Tour d'Argent or Lapérouse if anything else were needed. He even had a bicycle for longer trips, he said.

"No, I don't think we need anything more, after all," Clerfayt said. "Do you have another room vacant?"

The man looked quite aghast. "But Madame already has her room."

"Madame is married. To me," Clerfayt explained, further befuddling the porter, who now could not understand why the Dom Perignon had been ordered.

"We have Number Six," the man said uncertainly. "Next door to Madame."

"Fine. Take everything up there."

The porter carried the food up to the room. After looking at his tip, he once more mentioned his bicycle. He would run errands all night, if necessary. Clerfayt wrote out a small list of purchases—toothbrush, soap, and a few other items to be left in front of the door in the morning. All that would be taken care of, the man promised. He went away, and came back once more with some ice for the champagne. Then he departed for good.

"If I had left you alone tonight, I was afraid I'd never see you again," Clerfayt said.

Lillian sat down on the window sill. "That's something I think every night."

"What?"

"That I may never see things again."

He felt a stabbing pain. She looked terribly lonely, with her lovely profile framed against the night. Lonely, not deserted. "I love you," he said. "I don't know whether that helps you at all, but it's so."

She did not reply.

"You know that I am not saying that because of this evening," he said, not knowing that he was lying. "Forget the evening. It was chance, stupidity, and confusion. I would not want to hurt you for anything in the world."

She remained silent for a while longer. Then she said thoughtfully: "I think I cannot be hurt at all, in a certain sense. I really think that. Perhaps that makes up for the other thing."

Clerfayt did not know what to say to this. He understood vaguely what she meant, but did not want to think of it. He wanted not to believe it. He looked at her. "At night, your skin is like the inside of a sea shell," he said. "It gleams. It does not swallow the light; it gives it back. Do you really want to have the beer?"

"Yes. And give me some of the Lyons sausage. With bread. Does that upset you?"

"Nothing upsets me any more. I feel as if I had been waiting forever for this night. Below the porter's box down there, smelling of sleep and garlic, the world has come to an end. We have just made it to safety in time."

"Have we?"

"We have. Don't you hear how quiet it has become?"

"You have become quiet," she replied. "Because you've gained your objective."

"Have I? It seems to me that I've walked into a fashion show."

"Oh, my silent friends." Lillian looked at the dresses, which still hung about in the room. "They keep me company and tell me about fantastic dances and masked balls. But I won't need them this evening. Shall I gather them up and lock them in the wardrobe?"

"Let them hang. What have they told you?"

"So many things. About *fiestas* and cities and love. And a great deal about the ocean. I've never seen it."

"We might drive to it." Clerfayt poured her a glass of beer. "In a few days. I have to go to Sicily. To a race there. I'm not going to win it. Come with me!"

"Do you always want to win?"

"I find it a good idea, once in a while. Idealists can do a lot with money."

Lillian laughed. "I'll tell that to my uncle Gaston."

Clerfayt looked at the dress of tissue-thin silver brocade which hung at the head of the bed. "That is a dress for Palermo," he said.

"I wore it a few nights ago."

"Where?"

"Here."

"Alone?"

"Alone if you like. I was having a party with Sainte-Chapelle, a bottle of Pouilly, the Seine, and the moon."

"You won't be alone from now on."

"I was less alone than you think."

"I know," Clerfayt said. "I talk about my loving you as though it were some kind of favor I were doing you. That's not how I mean it. I express myself crudely, because I'm not used to talking about such things."

"You don't express yourself crudely."

"Every man talks crudely when he tries not to lie."

"Come," Lillian said. "Open the bottle of Dom Perignon. Beer isn't your drink, I can see. It makes you a little too fumbling, philosophical, and full of generalities. What are you sniffing at? What do I smell of?"

"Of garlic, moonlight, and lies I can't quite analyze."

"That's good. Let's find our way back to earth and hold on there. It's so easy to fly off into space when the moon is full. And dreams don't even obey the laws of gravity."

XI

A canary was singing. Clerfayt heard it in his sleep. He woke up and looked around. It took a moment before he realized where he was. Sunlight, white clouds, and shimmering water were playing on the ceiling of the room, which seemed to be turned upside down. The blanket was bound with green satin ribbon. The bathroom door and the window were open, and Clerfayt could see the bird cage with its canary hanging in the window of a room across the courtyard. A woman with massive bosom and yellow hair sat at a table just within the window. She was eating, and, as far as he could make out, it was not breakfast but lunch; a half-bottle of Burgundy stood on the table.

He looked at his watch. He was not mistaken; it was noon. Not for months had he slept so long, and he became aware that he was very hungry. Opening the door, he peered out. There lay the package of things he had ordered the night before. The porter had remembered everything. He ran water in the tub, bathed, and dressed.

The canary was still singing. Its stout mistress was now having apple cake and coffee. Clerfayt went over to the other window, which looked out on the quay. The traffic was roaring by at full volume. The booksellers' stalls stood open, and a bright-colored tug moved by on the river, a barking spitz on its deck. Clerfayt leaned out, and in the adjoining window saw Lillian's profile. She, too, was leaning out, with an attentive, collected air, unaware that he was observing her, slowly letting down a shallow basket on a string. Down on the sidewalk, an oyster vendor had just set up his boxes. He seemed familiar with the procedure. The basket reached him; he lined it with damp seaweed and looked up. *"Marennes? Belons? The belons are better today."*

"Six *belons*," Lillian replied.

"Twelve," Clerfayt said.

She turned and laughed. "Don't you want any breakfast?"

"The *belons* will do fine for breakfast. And a light Pouilly instead of orange juice."

"Twelve?" the oysterman asked.

"Eighteen," Lillian amended. She turned to Clerfayt again. "Come over. And will you bring the wine."

Clerfayt went down to the restaurant for wineglasses and a bottle of Pouilly. He also brought bread, butter, and a piece of ripe Pont l'Evêque. "Do you do this often?" he asked.

"Almost every day." Lillian pointed to a letter on the table. "Day after tomorrow is the dinner at Uncle Gaston's. Would you like an invitation?"

"Not especially."

"Good. It would sabotage the purpose of the dinner, which is to find me a rich husband. Or are you rich?"

"Never for more than a few weeks. Will you get married if a rich-enough man turns up?"

"Give me some of your wine," she replied. "And don't be silly."

"I'd believe anything of you."

"Since when?"

"I've been thinking about you."

"When have you had time to think about me?"

"While sleeping. You're unpredictable. You function by other laws than the ones I know."

"Good," Lillian said. "That can never do any harm. What are we doing this afternoon?"

"This afternoon, I'm taking you with me to the Ritz. I'll deposit you in a secluded corner of the lobby behind a few magazines for fifteen minutes while I go to my room and change. Then we'll have a big lunch, and later a dinner and tomorrow the same, in order to undercut Uncle Gaston's plans for day after tomorrow."

She looked out the window and did not reply. "If you like, we can go to Sainte-Chapelle too," Clerfayt said. "Or to Notre-Dame, or even to a museum, you dangerous combination of bluestocking and Greek hetaera of the late period whom the winds of chance blew to Byzantium. I'm even ready to go up the Eiffel Tower or take a tour on the Bâteau Mouche."

"I've already taken the Seine tour—and was made an excellent proposition by a wholesale butcher. He wanted to set me up with a three-room apartment."

"What about the Eiffel Tower then?"

"The Eiffel Tower? Thither I'll go with thee, beloved!"

"So I thought. Are you happy?"

"What's that?"

"Don't you know yet? But who really knows what it is? Dancing on the head of a pin, maybe."

Lillian was on her way back from Uncle Gaston's dinner. The Vicomte de Peystre was driving her to her hotel. She had spent a disconcertingly boring evening over excellent food. The company had consisted of several women and six men. The women had been like hedgehogs, so sharply had they bristled with inquisitive hostility. Of the men, four had been unmarried, all wealthy, two young, and the Vicomte de Peystre the oldest and wealthiest. "Why do you live on the left bank?" he asked. "For romantic reasons?"

"By chance. That is the best reason I know."

"You ought to live on the place Vendôme."

"It's amazing," Lillian said, "how many people know where I ought to live better than I do."

"I have an apartment on the place Vendôme which I

never use. A studio, completely modern in its appointments."

"Would you care to rent it to me?"

"Very gladly."

"How much is the rent?"

Peystre shifted in his seat. "Why talk about money? Look at the place some time. If you like it, you may have it."

"With no conditions attached?"

"None whatsoever. Of course, it would give me pleasure if you would dine with me now and then—but that, too, is not a condition."

"That's very generous of you," Lillian said.

"Would you like to visit it tomorrow? We could have lunch together tomorrow afternoon."

Lillian studied the narrow face with its white brush of mustache. "My uncle really wanted to get me married," she said.

The Vicomte laughed. "You have plenty of time for that. Your uncle has old-fashioned views."

"Is the apartment large enough for two?"

"I think so. Why?"

"In case I want to share it with a friend."

Peystre studied her for a moment. "That is a possibility, too," he said then. "Although, to be candid, the apartment would be rather too small for that. Why not live alone for a time? You have only been in Paris for a few weeks. For the present, you ought to come to know the city. It has so much to offer."

"You are right."

The car stopped, and Lillian got out. "Well then, when? Tomorrow?" the Vicomte asked.

"I must give the matter thought. Would you mind if I asked Uncle Gaston's advice?"

"I wouldn't do that, if I were you. It might give him quite the wrong impression. You wouldn't do it anyhow."

"Wouldn't I?"

"Not when you tell me beforehand that you will. You are very beautiful and very young, Mademoiselle. It would be a pleasure to set you in the environment that is proper for you. And take the word of a man who is no longer young: you may find this sort of life picturesque, but it represents lost time for you. What Uncle Gaston may think is quite irrelevant. What you require is luxury. Grand luxury. Forgive my speaking so, but I know about these things. Good night, Mademoiselle."

She mounted the stairs. Uncle Gaston's gallery of prospective husbands had amused and depressed her in a macabre fashion. At first, she had felt like a dying soldier to whom someone is telling stories about a plushy life. Then, she had imagined that she was on a strange planet where people lived forever and had corresponding problems. She had not understood what the other guests were talking about. Things she was indifferent to were of the highest importance to them—and what she was seeking was surrounded, for these others, by a curious taboo. Vicomte de Peystre's offer seemed to her the most sensible thing she had heard this evening.

"Was it a nice party?" Clerfayt asked from the corridor.

"Are you here already? I thought you would be out drinking somewhere."

"I didn't feel like it."

"Were you waiting for me?"

"Yes," Clerfayt said. "You are turning me into a respectable person. I don't any longer want to drink. Not unless you are drinking with me."

"Did you used to drink a lot?"

"Yes. Always between races. And often between accidents. Out of cowardice, I think. Or to run away from myself. That's over now. I spent this afternoon in Sainte-Chapelle. Tomorrow, I'm going to the Cluny Museum. Someone who saw us together mentioned that you look like the lady on the unicorn tapestries they have there. You're having a great deal of success. Would you like to go out again?"

"Not tonight!"

"You've spent the evening with sober people who believe that life is a kitchen, a parlor, and a bedroom, not a sailboat with far too many sails, which may turn over at any moment. You have to offset all that."

Lillian's eyes began to shine. "So you have been drinking, after all?"

"I don't need to, with you. Wouldn't you like to drive around a little?"

"Around where?"

"Down every street and to every night club you've ever heard of. You're gloriously dressed—a shame to waste it on Uncle Gaston's candidates. At the least, we must take this dress out—even if you yourself don't want to. Dresses carry responsibilities with them."

"All right. Let's go driving. Slowly. Through many, many streets. Not one of them covered with snow. With flower girls on the corners. Let's take a carload of violets with us."

Clerfayt fetched Giuseppe out of the tangle of parked cars on the quay and waited in front of the hotel door. The restaurant next door began to close.

"The pining lover," someone said at his side. "Aren't you too old for such a part?"

It was Lydia Morelli. She had come out of the restaurant ahead of her escort.

"Much too old," Clerfayt replied.

Lydia draped the end of her white fur stole over her shoulder. "A new role! Rather ridiculous, my dear. With such a young chit."

"What a tribute," Clerfayt answered. "When you talk like that, it means she must be fascinating."

"Fascinating! That little fake with her room in a fourth-class hotel and her three Balenciaga dresses!"

"Three? I thought she had thirty. They look so different every time she wears them." Clerfayt laughed. "Lydia, since when have you taken to doing detective jobs on young chits and little fakes? Haven't we outgrown that long ago?"

Lydia was about to throw some retort at him, but her escort came out. She took his arm as if it were a weapon, and walked past Clerfayt.

Lillian came down a few minutes later. "Someone has

just told me that you are a fascinating person," Clerfayt said. "It's about time to hide you."

"Was it dull, waiting for me?"

"No. When you haven't waited for anything for a long time, waiting makes you ten years younger. Twenty years younger. I thought I would never again be waiting for anything."

"I've always waited for something." Lillian's eyes followed a woman in cream-colored lace who was leaving the restaurant accompanied by a bald-headed man; she wore a string of diamonds, each the size of a nut. "How they flash!" she said.

Clerfayt did not answer. Jewelry was dangerous territory; if she had a taste for that sort of thing, there were men better equipped than he to satisfy her desires.

"Nothing for me," Lillian said, laughing as if she had guessed his thoughts.

"Is that a new dress?" he asked.

"Yes. It came today."

"How many do you have now?"

"Eight, counting this one. Why?"

Lydia Morelli seemed to be well informed. That she had said "three" meant that she knew the exact figure.

"Uncle Gaston is appalled," Lillian said. "I've sent him the bills. And now let us drive to the best night club you know. You're right, clothes make demands."

"Shall we go on to still another?" Clerfayt asked. It was four o'clock in the morning.

"Yes, one more," Lillian said. "Or are you tired?"

He knew that he must not ask whether she was tired. "Not yet," he said. "Do you like it?"

"It's wonderful."

"Good, then we'll go to another club. One with gypsies."

Montmartre and Montparnasse were still burning with tardy postwar fever. The garish colors of the cabarets and night clubs were softened by the fog that regularly filled such places. The entertainment was all the usual fare, pure cliché. Without Lillian, Clerfayt would have been horribly bored. But for Lillian it was new; she did not respond to it as it was or as it struck him, but as she wanted to see it and saw it. To her, the clip joints were places of pure entrancement, the fiddle players hoping for tips became, in her eyes, inspired musicians, and the gigolos, *nouveaux riches,* shady and empty-minded men and women, people who did not go home because they did not know what to do there, or who were on the lookout for an adventure or a good deal—all these she saw as celebrants of a sparkling bacchanal of life, because that was how she wanted it and that was why she had come.

That's it, Clerfayt thought, that is what makes her different from all the others sitting around here. The others want an adventure, a deal, a little tuneful noise to fill their emptiness; but she is on the track of life itself, of life alone, and she seeks it like an obsessed huntress pursuing the white stag and the fabled unicorn, hunts it so passionately that the passion is contagious. She has no inhibitions, does not look to either side, and while I myself feel alternately old and used up or young as a child in her presence, there suddenly rise up for me out of forgotten years faces, desires, shadows of dreams, and, above all, like a flash of lightning in the twilight, the long-lost sense of the uniqueness of life.

The gypsy fiddler hung about the table, bending over his instrument, his velvet eyes alert as he played. Lillian listened, carried away by the music. For her, this is all real, Clerfayt thought; for her, it is the Hungarian steppe, the lonely nocturnal lament, solitude, the first fire at which man sought protection, and even the oldest, most banal, most sentimental song is for her a song of mankind, of its sadness, and its seeking to hold what cannot be held. Lydia Morelli might well be right—it was provincial, if you wished to take it that way. But goddamn it, you had to adore her for that very thing.

"I think I've drunk too much," he said.

"What is too much?"

"When one no longer recognizes oneself."

"Then I always want to drink too much. I don't love myself."

She is afraid of nothing, Clerfayt thought. Just as this night club is the temple of life to her, so every banality has for her the force it possessed when it was said for the first time. It's unendurable. She has to die and she knows it; she's taken the knowledge into herself as another might take morphine, and it transforms everything for her; she fears nothing, nothing is blasphemy, nothing banality. And, damn it all, why am I sitting here and feeling this mild horror of it all, not also throwing myself into this uncritical whirl?

"I adore you," he said.

"Don't say that too often," she replied. "One has to be very independent to say a thing like that."

"Not with you."

"Say it all the time," she said. "I need it like water and wine."

Clerfayt laughed. "What you say is as true as what I say. But who cares whether a thing is true? Where are we going now?"

"To the hotel. I want to move out."

Clerfayt made up his mind to be surprised by nothing henceforth. "All right. Let's go and pack," he said.

"My things are already packed."

"Where do you want to move to?"

"To a different hotel. For two days, someone has been telephoning me at this time of night. A woman who tells me to go back where I came from—and a few other things besides."

Clerfayt looked at her. "Haven't you told the night clerk not to put the calls through?"

"I've told him that. But she manages to get through. Yesterday, she told him she was my mother. She speaks French with an accent."

Lydia Morelli, Clerfayt thought. "Why haven't you said anything to me about it?"

"What for? Is the Ritz full?"

"No."

"Good. Uncle Gaston will faint tomorrow when he hears where I'm staying."

Lillian had not packed. Clerfayt talked to the night clerk and was able to borrow a huge wardrobe trunk that a German major had left behind during the retreat. He stowed Lillian's dresses away in it. She sat on the bed, laughing. "I'm sorry to leave here," she said. "I've loved everything so much. But I love without regrets. Do you know what I mean?"

Clerfayt raised his head. "I'm afraid I do. You don't regret leaving anything."

She laughed again, her legs outstretched, a glass of wine in her hand. "It no longer matters. I've left the sanatorium; since then, I can leave any place I like."

No doubt she will leave me, too, in the same way, Clerfayt thought. Like changing a hotel. "Here is the German major's sword," he said. "He must have forgotten it in the excitement—impossible laxness for a German officer. I'll leave it right here in the trunk. Incidentally, you're charmingly drunk. Luckily, I reserved a room for you in the Ritz two days ago. Otherwise, it would be difficult to get you past the concierge in your present state."

Lillian reached for the major's sword and saluted, still sitting. "I'm very fond of you. Why don't I ever call you by your first name?"

"Nobody else does."

"That would be a reason for me to."

"Now, I think you're all packed," Clerfayt said. "Do you want to take the sword with you?"

"Leave it here."

Clerfayt pocketed the key and helped Lillian into her coat. "Am I too thin?" she asked.

"No. I think you've gained a few pounds."

"That's the only thing that counts," she murmured.

They had a cab follow them with the suitcases and trunk. "Does my room in the Ritz face on the place Vendôme?" Lillian asked.

"Yes. Not the rue Cambon."

"How is it you were there during the war?"

"I went there after I escaped from prison camp. It was an excellent hiding place. Nobody would have dreamed of looking for me there. My half-brother lived on the place Vendôme. We are Alsatians. My brother has a German father; my father was French."

"Couldn't your brother have done something for you? When you were in camp?"

Clerfayt laughed. "He would have loved to have me in Siberia. As far away as possible. Do you see the sky? Morning is coming. Hear the birds? In cities, you only hear them at this time. Nature lovers must go to night clubs, so they can hear thrushes on the way home."

They turned into the place Vendôme. The broad gray square was very still. Under the clouds, the morning gleamed a rich gold. "When you see how wonderfully people built in the past, you assume they must have been happier than we," Lillian said. "Do you think they were?"

"No," Clerfayt replied. He let the car coast to a stop before the hotel entrance. "I am happy at this moment," he said, "no matter whether we know what happiness is or not. I am happy at this moment, in this stillness, on this square, with you. And when you have had a good sleep, we'll drive south, and make our way to Sicily and the Targa Florio by easy stages."

ideal guardian for Lillian: Levalli was an esthete, bald, fat, and homosexual.

All day, Lillian lay on the beach or in the garden that surrounded the villa. The garden was neglected, romantic, full of marble statues. Lillian never felt any desire to see Clerfayt driving, but she loved the low growl of the motors which penetrated into the stillness of the orange groves. The sound was carried in by the wind, together with the heavy fragrance of orange blossoms. It merged with the murmur of the sea to form an exciting concert—as if modern jungle drums were mingling with the oldest sound in the world, the murmur of water, from which all life came. To Lillian, it seemed as if Clerfayt were speaking to her. The sound hung invisibly above her all day long; she abandoned herself to it as she abandoned herself to the hot sky and the white sheen of the sea. Clerfayt was always there—whether she slept under the stone pines in the shadow of some god's statue, or sat on a bench reading Petrarch or Augustine's *Confessions;* whether she curled up by the sea without a thought in the world, or sat on the terrace in the mysterious hour before twilight, when the Italian women were already saying *feliccissima notte* and back of every word there seemed to linger the question mark of an unknown god. Always, the distant rumble was there, the drum roll of sky and evening, and it always awoke a resonance in her blood, which throbbed gently and responded.

Then, in the evening, Clerfayt would come, accompanied by the growl, which rose to thunder when the car came close. "Like the gods of classical times," Levalli said to Lillian, "our modern *condottieri* appear amid thunder and lightning, as if they were sons of Jupiter."

"Don't you like it?"

"I do not like motors of any kind. They remind me too much of the noise of bombers during the war."

The sensitive, corpulent man placed a Chopin piano concerto on the record player. Lillian looked at him thoughtfully. Odd, she thought, how one-sidedly we are always bound by our own experience and our own danger. I wonder whether this esthete and connoisseur of the arts ever thinks of what the tuna may feel when it is swung up on the deck of one of his fishing boats to be slaughtered?

Shortly before the race, Levalli gave a party. He had invited nearly a hundred guests. The garden was lit with candles and hurricane lamps; the night was warm and sparkling with stars, the sea smooth, making a vast mirror for the huge moon which floated low and red on the horizon, like a balloon from another planet.

Lillian was enchanted. "You like it?" Levalli asked.

"It's everything I've desired."

"Everything?"

"Almost everything. For four years, I dreamed of this sort of thing, when I was a captive between walls of snow in the mountains. This is the very opposite of snow—and absolutely the opposite of mountains—"

"I'm glad," Levalli said. "I give parties rarely these days."

"Why? Because otherwise they would become a habit?"

"It's not that. It's that they make me—how should I put it?—melancholy. When we give parties, it's usually because we want to forget something—but we don't forget it. The others don't forget it either."

"There's nothing I want to forget."

"Really?" Levalli asked politely.

"Not any more," Lillian replied.

Levalli smiled. "An old Roman villa is supposed to have stood on this spot," he said, "and they had glorious festivals by torchlight and the glow of fire-spewing Etna. Do you think that the ancient Romans came any nearer the secret?"

"What secret?"

"Of why we live."

"Do we live?"

"Perhaps not, since we ask. Forgive my talking about it. Italians are melancholics; they look the opposite, but are not."

"Who isn't?" Lillian said. "Not even stable hands are cheerful all the time."

She heard Clerfayt's car approaching, and smiled. "It is said," Levalli remarked, "that the last Roman lady to own this villa used to have her lovers killed in the mornings. She was a romantic and could not endure the disenchantment after the illusion of the night."

"What a lot of trouble to go to," Lillian replied. "Couldn't she simply send them away before dawn? Or go away herself?"

Levalli offered his arm. "Going away is not always so simple—when one takes oneself along."

"It is always terribly simple when one knows that there are limits to the desire for possession—and that one cannot hold on to anything, not even oneself—"

They walked toward the music. "Is there nothing you want to possess?" Levalli asked.

"There's too much I want to possess," Lillian replied. "And so, nothing."

He kissed her hand. "Let's stroll over there to the cypresses. A little beyond them, we've set up a glass dance floor lighted from within. I've seen that done in garden restaurants on the Riviera, and thought it would be a nice idea for our party. And there come your dancing partners—from Naples, Palermo, and Rome."

"One can be either a spectator or a participant," Levalli said to Clerfayt. "I prefer being a spectator. Anyone who tries to do both does both imperfectly."

They were sitting on the terrace, watching the couples dancing on the irradiated glass floor against the background of the cypresses. Lillian was dancing with Prince Fiola.

"A flame," Levalli said to Clerfayt. "Look how she dances! Do you know the women in the Pompeian paintings? The exquisiteness of women in art is that the elements of accident have been sheared away and beauty alone has remained. Have you seen the paintings in the Minoan palace in Crete? The Egyptians of the time of Ikhnaton? The women with elliptical eyes and thin faces, the corrupt dancing girls and the sensual young queens? The flame burns in all of them. Look at this dance floor.

Over gentle fires of hell ignited by glass, electricity, and technology, the women appear to be gliding—that's why I had it set up. The flares of the artificial hell below, which appears to be burning them from beneath and illuminating the folds of their skirts, and the cold light of the moon mingling with the rays of the stars illuminating their temples and shoulders—isn't it an allegory to make one laugh or dream for a few minutes? They are beautiful, these women who capture us by persuading us that they will make us into gods, and then make us into fathers, citizens, breadwinners. Aren't they beautiful?"

"They are beautiful, Levalli."

"In every one of them there is a Circe. The irony is that they themselves have no notion of it. They are still lovely in their youth as they dance there, but behind them, almost invisible, there already dances the shadow of respectability, with the twenty pounds of weight they will gain, with the boredom of family, the preoccupation with petty ambitions, petty desires and goals, the tedium, the confinement, the eternal recurrence, the slow attrition. All this is present already except in that one girl who is dancing with Fiola over there, the one you have brought here. How have you done it?"

Clerfayt shrugged.

"Where did you find her?"

Clerfayt hesitated. "To remain in your style, Levalli—at the gates of Hades. This is the first time in years I've known you to be so lyrical."

"The opportunity doesn't offer very often. So. At the gates of Hades. I'll ask no further. It is enough to let the imagination play. Out of the gray twilight of hopelessness which Orpheus alone escaped. But even he had to pay the price: double solitude—paradoxical as that sounds—because he tried to lead a woman out of Hades. Are you prepared to pay, Clerfayt?"

Clerfayt smiled. "I'm superstitious. I don't answer such questions shortly before a race."

It is Oberon's night, Lillian thought, as she danced with Fiola and Torriani. Everything is enchanted, with lights,

161

with blue shadows, with life and unreality at the same time. No footsteps can be heard, only gliding and music. This is what I imagined when I sat in my room amid the snow, with the fever chart by the bed, and the radio tuned to music from Naples and Paris. It is as though dying were impossible on such a night of moon and sea and the soft breeze carrying the perfume of mimosa and orange blossoms. You meet and hold each other for a while, and lose each other, and find yourself in another man's arms again; the faces change but the hands are the same.

Are they the same? she thought. There sits my lover, with the melancholy man who for a brief time on earth is the owner of this dream of a garden, and I can see that they are talking about me. It is the melancholy man who is talking now, and no doubt he wants to know the answer to the same question he asked me. The secret! Isn't there an old fairy tale in which a dwarf rejoices because no one knows his secret, his name?

She smiled. "What are you thinking of?" asked Fiola, observing the smile.

"Of a fairy tale in which a person's secret was that no one knew his name."

Fiola flashed his teeth. They seemed twice as white in his dark brown face as the teeth did in the faces of the others.

"Isn't that your secret, too?" he asked.

She shook her head. "What does a name matter?"

Fiola looked at the row of mothers who sat under the palms beside the dance floor. "Everything to some people," he said.

Dancing by, she saw that Clerfayt was looking thoughtfully at her. He holds me, she thought, and I love him because he is there and does not question. When will he begin to question? I hope never. Perhaps never. We will have no time for that. "You are smiling as if you were very happy," Fiola said. "Is that your secret?"

What foolish questions he asks too, Lillian thought. He should have learned that a man ought never to ask a woman whether she is happy.

"What is your secret?" Fiola asked. "A great future?"

She shook her head again. "None," she said cheerfully. "No future at all. You have no idea how easy that can make so many things."

"Look at Fiola," said old Contessa Vitelleschi, seated in the mothers' corner. "He seems to think there are no young women here besides that foreigner."

"That's natural enough," Teresa Marchetti replied. "If he danced so often with one of our girls, he would be virtually engaged and her brothers would take it as an affront if he did not marry her."

The contessa peered at Lillian through her lorgnette. "Where does that female come from?"

"Not from Italy."

"I can see that. Probably some mongrel—"

"Like me," Teresa Marchetti said sharply. "American, Indian, Spanish—but useful enough to bring some of Papa's dollars to Ugo Marchetti, to clear the rats out of his tumble-down *palazzo*, install bathrooms, and keep his mistresses in style."

Contessa Vitelleschi pretended not to have heard. "It is easy for you to talk. You have a son and a bank account. I have four daughters and debts. Fiola ought to marry. It's a fine state of affairs when the few well-to-do bachelors we have left marry English models, as they've taken to doing lately. The country is being stripped bare."

"There ought to be a law against it," Teresa Marchetti said sarcastically. "Also a law against impoverished younger sons marrying rich American girls who do not know that after the fiery courtship they are going to be banished to the feudal dungeon of Italian marriage."

Again the contessa did not listen. She was keeping her eye on two of her daughters. Fiola had stopped at one of the tables set out under the trees. Lillian took her leave of him and had Torriani escort her to Clerfayt. "Why don't you dance with me?" she asked Clerfayt.

"I am dancing with you," he replied. "Without getting up."

Torriani laughed. "He doesn't like to dance. He's vain."

"That's true," Clerfayt said to Lillian. "I dance miserably. You ought to know that from the time in the Palace bar."

She shook her head. "I forgot that ages ago."

She returned to the dance floor with Torriani. Levalli sat down beside Clerfayt again. "A flame," he said. "Or a dagger." He sat for a while in silence, then burst out: "Don't you think these lights under the floor are tasteless? The moon is bright enough. Luigi!" he called. "Turn out the lights under the dance floor. And bring some of the old grappa. She makes me sad," he said abruptly to Clerfayt, and in the darkness his face looked stricken, with deep-sunken hollows. "Beauty in a woman makes me sad. Why?"

"Because one knows it will pass and wishes it could remain."

"Is it as simple as that?"

"I don't know. That reason satisfies me."

"Does it make you sad, too?"

"No," Clerfayt said. "Quite different things make me sad."

"I understand." Levalli sipped his grappa. "I know them, too. But I run away from them. I want to be a fat Pierrot, and nothing else. Try some of this grappa."

They drank in silence. Lillian danced past them again. I have no future, she thought. That is almost like having no gravity. She looked at Clerfayt. That makes us alike, she thought. His future extends from one race to the next. She formed a soundless sentence with her lips. Clerfayt was sitting in darkness now. She could scarcely discern his face. But that, too, seemed unnecessary. You did not have to look life in the face. You needed only to feel it.

XIII

"What is my position?" Clerfayt shouted through the noise, when he stopped at the pit.

"Seventh," Torriani shouted. "How is the road?"

"Stinking. In this heat it just eats the rubber. Have you seen Lillian?"

"Yes. She's in the stand."

"Thank God she isn't sitting here in the pit with a stop watch!"

Torriani held a jug of lemonade to Clerfayt's lips. The manager came over. "Ready?" he shouted. "Get going!"

"We're not magicians," the chief mechanic shouted back. "The devil himself can't change wheels in thirty seconds."

"Come on! Snap into it!"

The gasoline spurted into the tank. "Clerfayt," the manager said, "Duval is ahead of you. Harry him. Harry him till he's boiling mad. Then keep him behind you. We don't need more than that. We're holding the first two places."

"Go ahead! Ready!" the chief mechanic shouted.

The car roared off. Careful, Clerfayt thought, don't strain the motor! The stands were flashes of color and whiteness and light; then there was only the road, the blazing blue sky, and the dot on the horizon that must be dust and Duval with his car.

The stretch climbed for four hundred yards. The mountain range of the Madonie, citrus orchards, the flickering silver of olive groves, curves, serpentines, hairpin turns, flying road gravel, the hot breath of the motor, burning feet, an insect that slammed like a bullet into his glasses, cactus hedges, rising and descending curves, cliffs, rubble, mile after mile; then, gray and brown, the old fortress city of Caltavuturo, dust, more dust, and suddenly a spiderlike insect: a car.

Clerfayt was faster on the curves. Bit by bit, he gained ground. Ten minutes later, he recognized the car; it had to be Duval. Clerfayt hung on behind him, but Duval would not yield the road. He blocked Clerfayt's every attempt to pass. It was impossible that he had not seen him. Twice the cars had taken a very sharp curve so close together that the drivers could look into each other's faces, Duval past and Clerfayt just entering the curve. Duval was obstructing Clerfayt on purpose.

The cars raced along close together. Clerfayt waited tensely until the road began climbing in sweeping curves, where he could see ahead. He knew that a broad curve was coming along soon. Duval took it wide on the outside, to prevent Clerfayt from passing him on the right and to cut across the middle of the curve. Clerfayt had counted on that; he cut the curve in front of Duval, shooting past him on the inside. The car skidded, but he caught it; surprised, Duval slowed for just a second, and Clerfayt was past. The dust was behind him now; he could see Etna with a puff of light smoke above it poised majestically against the simmering sky, and they rocketed on, Clerfayt in the van, up toward Polizzi, the highest point of the course.

It was this brief interval, the moment of passing after having ridden for miles through thick dust, and then the blue sky, the pure air, which struck into his dust-crusted face like wine, the heat of the churning motor, the sunlight, the volcano in the distance, the world which was present once more, simple, grand, tranquil, unconcerned with races and with men; it was this, and the Promethean moment when the car reached the top, that carried Clerfayt away, out of himself, beyond himself. He thought of nothing, but he was simultaneously everything; he was the car that he held in his hands, the volcano whose cone funneled down to hell, and the sky of blue, hot metal toward which he was hurtling. Seconds later, the road plunged down once more from the height of Polizzi, dropped in curve upon curve, and the car with it. Shifting, shifting—on this course, the one who shifted best would win. Down it went into the valley of the Fiume Grande, and immediately thereafter up again into a lunar landscape, then down again, like a giant swing, until near Collesano the palms began anew, and the agaves, the flowers, the greenness, and the sea. At Campofelice came the only straight stretch of the race—five miles of it along the beach.

Clerfayt did not think of Lillian again until he stopped to change tires. He saw the stands vaguely, like a window box full of bright-colored flowers; the roaring of the motor had ceased, and in the silence that was hardly such but seemed so to him, he had the feeling that a while before he had been blown high by an eruption, out of the crater of the mountain, and was now hovering like Icarus, floating slowly down to earth on wide asbestos wings into the waiting arms of an infinite emotion that was broader than love and had become personified, somewhere in the stands, by a woman, a name, and a mouth.

"Go!" the manager shouted.

The car raced off again; but Clerfayt was no longer driving alone. Like the shadow of a high-flying flamingo, that emotion flew along with him, sometimes behind him like a tail wind and sometimes ahead of him like a transparent banner, but at all times close to him.

In the next round, the car began to dance. Clerfayt caught it, but the rear wheels skidded on him again; he fought it with the steering wheel, then a curve appeared ahead of him, dotted with people like a country baker's cake with flies. The car was still out of control, skidding and thumping. Clerfayt shifted on the short stretch that still remained before the curve. He stepped on the gas, but the car jerked his arms around. He felt a tearing at his shoulder; the curve swelled gigantically into the glistening sky; the number of people tripled, and they, too, swelled, they, too, became giants, till it seemed impossible to avoid them. Blackness rushed down from the sky. He bit into something, and someone seemed to be pulling his arm out of its socket. But he held on tightly, while hot lava shot into his shoulder. In the tumbling landscape, there was only one remaining patch of blue, sharp and blinding; he held on to it with his eyes, while the car bucked beneath him; and then he saw the opening, the only one not crawling with gigantic two-legged flies; he wrenched the wheel around again, stepped hard on the accelerator and—miracle—the car obeyed him, shot through the gap, up the slope, was caught between shrubbery and stones; the tattered casing of the rear tire cracked like a whip, and the car stood still.

He saw the people rushing toward him. They had splashed apart like water struck by a stone; now they came back shouting, faces distorted, arms outstretched, shaking their fists, with their mouths open black holes. He did not know whether they wanted to kill him or congratulate him, and he did not care. There was only one thing that mattered: they must not touch the car, must not help him, or he would be disqualified. "Go away! Go away! Don't touch it!" he shouted, standing up and again feeling the pain, feeling warmth, seeing blood dropping from his nose on his blue overalls. He could raise only one arm; but he used it to threaten, to fend them off. "Don't touch! Don't help!" Then he staggered out of the car and stood in front of the radiator. "Don't help! Not allowed!"

They stood still. They saw that he could walk. The blood was not dangerous; he had only cut open his face. He ran around and looked at the tire. The casing was flapping loosely. He cursed. It was the new tire. Quickly, he cut off the loose strip of casing; then he felt the tire. It still had enough air to cushion the bumps in the road if he did not take the curves too fast. His shoulder was not broken; the arm was only sprained. He must try to drive on with his right arm alone. He had to reach the pit; Torriani was there to relieve him, and mechanics were there, and a doctor.

"Off the road!" he shouted. "Cars are coming!"

He had no need to say more. The bellowing song of the next car approached from behind the slopes, mounted; the people crawled up the hill, the howling filled the world, tires screeched, and the car shot like a low projectile, a grenade of dust, around the curve.

Clerfayt was already back in the seat of his car. The howl of the other vehicle had been better than any injection. "Back!" he shouted. "I'm coming!"

The car slid backward. The motor caught as he jerked the wheel around and steered it forward. He clutched, shifted, gripped the steering wheel again, reached the road, holding the wheel tightly, driving slowly, and with only one thought in his mind: the car must reach the pit; it isn't far to the straight stretch, and from there on I can hold it; there aren't many more curves.

The next car howled up behind him. Clerfayt held the road as long as he could. He clenched his teeth, knowing that he was blocking the other man, knowing that it was forbidden, that it was unfair; but he could not help himself. He held the center of the road until the car behind him overtook him on the right as they entered a curve. The driver, face white with dust behind his glasses, raised his hand in salute as he passed. He had seen Clerfayt's face and the tire. For a moment, Clerfayt felt a surge of comradeship; then he heard the next car behind him and the comradeship was transformed into rage, into a rage that was the worst kind of all: without reason, and impotent.

That's what comes of it, thought he. I should have paid attention instead of dreaming. Driving cars is a romantic affair only for amateurs. There should only be the car and the driver; everything else is a danger or brings danger—to hell with flamingos, to hell with emotions; I could have held the car, I should have cut the curves easier, I should have spared the tires: now it's too late, I'm losing too much time; here's another damned car passing me, and there comes the next; the straight stretch is my enemy; they're swarming over me like hornets and I have to let them pass; to hell with Lillian, what business has she being here, and to hell with me, what have I to do with her?

Lillian sat in the stand. She felt the mass hypnosis of the tightly pressed crowd, and tried to fight it off; but it was impossible to escape it. The noise of the many motors was as stupefying as a thousandfold anesthetic which traveled directly from ears to brain, paralyzing and strait-jacketing it, and delivering it over to the mass frenzy.

After a while, she became accustomed to it, and suddenly the reaction followed. The noise seemed to separate itself from what was going on down below. The din hung independently over the landscape, while underneath it the little colored cars swished by. It was like a child's game: little people in white and colored overalls trundled wheels and automobile jacks around; managers held up flags and shields; and, in between, the unreal voice of the announcer came over the loud-speaker, reciting times in minutes and seconds, which only gradually acquired a meaning. A horse race was like this, and a bullfight also—because the danger was voluntary, it became like play, something you did not really take seriously unless you were right in it.

Lillian felt something within her protest against this shallow intoxication. She herself had been close to death for too long for this playing with death not to strike her as frivolous. It seemed to her similar to the conduct of street urchins who dash across the street just in front of approaching automobiles. That children did this, and were killed, she knew; it was not admirable for men to behave in the same way. Life was something too great, and death also had something too great about it; they were not to be played with. Having courage was a different thing from having no fear; courage was consciousness of danger, fearlessness mere ignorance.

"Clerfayt!" someone beside her said. "Where is he?" She was instantly alert. "What has happened to him?" "He should have passed long ago."

People in the stands were growing restive. Lillian saw Torriani looking up at her, waving, then pointing to the road and again looking up at her and signaling her to be calm, that nothing had happened. That frightened her more than anything else. He's crashed, she thought, and sat very still. Fate had struck while she sat unsuspecting, had struck somewhere on one of the many curves of this cursed course. The seconds became leaden, the minutes hours. The carrousel on the white ribbon existed now only like a bad dream; her chest became a black cavity, hollowed out with waiting. Then came the loudspeaker's mechanical voice: "Clerfayt's car, Number Twelve, has overshot a curve. We have no further news as yet."

Slowly, Lillian raised her head. Everything was the same as it had been before—the sky, the blue brightness, the window box of gay garments, the white lava of the Sicilian spring—but somewhere now there was a point without color, a mist in which Clerfayt was struggling or had already ceased to struggle. The frightful incredibility of dying reached out for her again with wet hands, and the breathlessness that was followed by a silence never to be understood: the silence of non-existence. Slowly, she looked down along her own body, and then around. Was she alone infected by the invisible leprosy of this knowledge? Did she alone feel it so intensely, as if all the cells within her were disintegrating, as if every cell were without breath and every one suffocating in its own single death? She looked at the faces of the people around her. She saw nothing in them but avidity for sensation, that frightful avidity that enjoyed death as stimulation. The avidity was not open, but concealed, clothed in false concern, false fright, and in the satisfaction of themselves not being affected: avidity that for a moment thrilled the sluggish sense of life like a shot of digitalis stimulating a phlegmatic heart.

171

"Clerfayt is all right," the announcer stated. "He has not been seriously injured and has brought the car back onto the course himself. He is driving; he is back in the race."

Lillian heard the murmur that passed through the stands. She saw the change of expressions. There was relief now in those faces, and disappointment, and admiration. Someone had escaped, had displayed courage; he had not weakened; he was continuing to drive. Everyone in the stands now felt that same courage in himself, as if he were the man who were driving on after a crack-up; and for a few moments, even the most despicable gigolo felt like a man, the most henpecked of husbands became an intrepid, death-defying hero. Sex, accompaniment of every danger to others, not to oneself, shot adrenalin into the spectators' blood from a thousand glands. This was what they had bought their tickets for!

Lillian felt rage like a flickering curtain before her eyes. She suddenly hated these people around her, hated every one of them, hated the men who pulled themselves up straighter and the women who played up to them with veiled looks. She hated the wave of sympathy that now spread out, the cheap generosity of the crowd, who, having had their sacrifice snatched from them, now decided to take him to their heart; and then she hated Clerfayt and knew that this was only a reaction to her fear, and she hated him nevertheless because he, too, played along in this childish game with death.

For the first time since she had left the sanatorium, she thought of Volkov. Then she saw Clerfayt approaching down below. She saw his bloody face, and she saw him slowly climbing out of the car.

The mechanics were checking the car. They changed the tires. Torriani stood beside Clerfayt. "It's that damned tire," Clerfayt said. "I could only hold the wheel with one hand. The car is all right. You must take it."

"Of course!" the manager called out. "Get going, Torriani!"

Torriani leaped into the seat. "Ready!" the first mechanic shouted. The car shot away.

"What's wrong with your arm?" the manager asked Clerfayt. "Broken?"

"No. Sprained or dislocated. In the shoulder. The devil only knows how it happened."

The doctor came. Clerfayt had a moment of mad pain. He sat down on a box. "Am I out?" he asked. "I hope Torriani can make it."

"You can't go on driving," the doctor said.

"Leucoplast," the manager replied. "Wide strips of it around the shoulder. Patch him up, just in case."

The doctor shook his head. "It won't do much good. He'll feel it right away if he starts driving again."

The manager laughed. "Last year, he burned the soles of both his feet. Went on driving anyway. And I mean burned, not just singed."

Clerfayt sat drooping on his box. He felt limp and empty. The doctor bound his shoulder tightly with bandages. I should have watched out, Clerfayt thought. Being faster than yourself doesn't mean you're God—not quite. It isn't true that only man can use his brain to invent aids that make him faster than his natural speed. Isn't a louse faster than itself when it sits in an eagle's feathers?

"What happened?" the manager asked.

"The damn tire. I overshot the curve. Took a small tree along. Banged into the steering wheel. Stinking luck!"

"It would have been stinking luck if the brakes, the motor, and the steering were wrecked. The buggy is still running. Who knows who else will drop out before the end? The race isn't over yet by a long shot. This is Torriani's first Targa. I hope he can make it."

Clerfayt stared at the pieces of metal that the mechanics had pinched off. I'm too old, he thought. What am I doing here? But what else can I do?

"There he is!" the manager bellowed, binoculars at his eyes. "Holy Mary, there he is. What a boy! But he'll never make it. We're too far behind."

"Who's still in the race on our team?"

"Weber. In fifth place."

Torriani hurtled past. He waved and vanished. The manager executed a snake dance. "Duval has dropped out. And Torriani has made up four minutes. Four minutes! Holy Mother of God, protect him!"

He looked as if he were about to fall to his knees and pray. Torriani continued to catch up. "In that beat-up coffee grinder!" the manager bawled. "I could kiss the boy, the darling! He's driven an average of almost sixty. Record for the round! Holy Anthony, protect him!"

Torriani made up time in every round. Clerfayt did not want to begrudge him the pleasure, but he could feel his own bitterness growing. A sixteen-year advantage in age was showing up. He knew that that was not always true. Caracciola with a broken hip and suffering infernal pain had won races over much younger drivers and champions; Nuvolari and Lang after the war had driven as if they were ten years younger. But sooner or later, everyone had to leave the stage, and he knew that his time was coming close.

"Valente has frozen pistons. Monti is lagging. We're holding third and fourth places!" the manager screeched. "Clerfayt, can you relieve Torriani if anything happens?"

Clerfayt saw the doubt in the manager's eyes. They still ask me, he thought. Soon they will no longer ask. "Let him go on as long as he can," he replied. "He's young; he can stand the gaff."

"He's too nervous."

"He's driving beautifully."

The manager nodded. "Anyhow, it would be suicide for you, with your shoulder, on those curves," he said without conviction.

"It wouldn't be suicide. But I'd have to drive slower."

"Holy Mother of God!" the manager resumed his prayers. "Make Torelli's brakes freeze. Not so he'll crash, but enough to stop him. Protect Weber and Torriani! Give Bordoni a hole in his gas tank!" The manager became devout, after his fashion, during every race; the moment it was over, he would begin swearing again with relief.

One round before the end, Torriani's car rolled up to

the pit. Torriani was slumped over the steering wheel. "What's the matter?" the manager bellowed. "Can't you go on? What's the matter? Lift him out. Clerfayt! Holy Mother of God, Mother of Sorrows—he has heat stroke. It isn't that hot yet! In the spring. Can't you go on? The car . . ."

The mechanics were already at work. "Clerfayt!" the manager implored him. "Just bring the car back. Weber is two rounds ahead; it won't matter, even if we lose a few minutes. You'll still be fourth. Get in! God in Heaven, what a race!"

Clerfayt was already seated in the car. Torriani had collapsed. "Just bring the car back!" the manager begged him. "And fourth prize. Third for Weber, of course. And a little hole in Bordoni's tank. And besides, in your kindness, Holy Virgin, a new flat tires for the rest of the field. Sweet blood of Jesus—"

One round, Clerfayt thought. It passes. It's a bearable pain. It's less than hanging on the cross in a concentration camp. I've seen a boy whose sound teeth were drilled right down to the roots by the *Sicherheitsdienst* in Berlin, to make him squeal on his friends. He did not squeal on them. Weber is ahead. It doesn't matter what I do. It does matter. How it whirls! This jalopy isn't a plane. Down with the damned gas pedal. Fear is halfway to an accident.

The mechanical voice of the announcer droned: "Clerfayt is in the race again. Torriani has dropped out."

Lillian saw the car shoot past. She saw the bandaged shoulder. That fool, she thought, that child who has never grown up! Thoughtlessness isn't courage. He'll crash again. What do they know about death, all these healthy fools? Up in the mountains, they know, they who have had to fight for every breath like a reward.

A hand beside her thrust a calling card into her fingers. She tossed it away and stood up. She wanted to leave. A hundred eyes were fixed upon her. It was as though a hundred blank lenses, reflecting the sunlight, were following her. For a second they followed her attentively. Blank eyes, she thought. Eyes that see and do not see.

Had it not always been like that? Everywhere? Where not? In the sanatorium, she thought again. There it had been different. The eyes there had been knowing.

She descended the steps of the stands. What am I doing here among these alien people? she thought, and stopped as if she had been struck. Yes, what am I doing here? she thought. I wanted to come back here, but can one go back? I wanted to go back with all the strength of my heart; but do I belong here now? Have I become like the others? She looked around. No, she thought, she did not belong. You could not come back into the warmth of not-knowing. You could not undo what was done. The dark secret, which she knew and which the others seemed to ignore, could not be forgotten. It remained with her, no matter where she fled. She felt as if the gay and gilded set of a play had suddenly fallen down, and she could see the bare scaffolding behind. It was not disenchantment, only a moment of intense clarity of vision. She could not turn back. She knew it now. There was no help to be had from outside. But there was one compensation; the last fountain that remained to her would leap all the higher. Her strength would no longer have to be distributed among a dozen springs, but would be confined to a single one, to herself, and with it alone she had to try to reach the clouds and God. She would never reach them—but was not the attempt already fulfillment, and the falling back of the dancing waters upon themselves already a symbol? Upon yourself, she thought. How far you fled and how high you had to aim, to attain that!

She moved on. It was as if a nameless burden had all at once been taken from her. Something like a dull, out-worn responsibility dropped from her shoulders upon the wooden stairs of the stand, and she stepped out of it as if it were an old dress. Even though the theater set had col-lapsed, the scaffolding remained, and anyone who was not afraid of its bareness was independent and could play with it and before it as he pleased, and as his fear or courage permitted. He could stage his own solitude in a thousand variations, even in the variation of love. The play never ceased. It was only transformed. You became your own sole actor and audience simultaneously.

The applause of the crowd began to chatter like a machine-gun salvo. The drivers were coming in. Small, parti-colored, they shot through the finish line. Lillian stood still on the steps until she saw Clerfayt's car. Then she slowly descended, the alien applause roaring around her, into the coolness of a new, precious knowledge which might as easily bear the name of Freedom as of Solitude, and into the warmth of a love already murmuring the word Abandonment, and both came upon her like a summer night with leaping fountains.

Clerfayt had wiped away the blood, but his lips were still oozing. "I can't kiss you," he said. "Were you frightened?"

"No. But you ought not to drive any more."

"Of course not," Clerfayt replied patiently. He was familiar with this reaction. "Was I so bad?" he asked, cautiously twisting up his face.

"He was great," said Torriani, who was sitting on a box, his face the color of cheese, drinking cognac.

Lillian threw a hostile look at him. "It's over," Clerfayt said. "Don't think about it any more, Lillian. It wasn't dangerous. It only looked that way."

"You ought not to drive," she repeated.

"All right, Lillian. Tomorrow we'll tear up the contract. Are you satisfied?"

Torriani laughed. "And day after tomorrow, we'll paste it together again."

The manager came by, and the mechanics pushed the car into the pit. It stank of burned oil and gasoline. "Are you coming tonight, Clerfayt?" the manager asked.

Clerfayt nodded. "We're in the way here, Lillian," he said. "Let's get away from this filthy stable." He saw her expression. It still held the same curious gravity. "What's the matter?" he asked. "Do you still want me not to drive any more?"

"Yes."

"Why?"

She hesitated. "I don't know how to put it—but somehow it's terribly immoral."

"Ye gods!" Torriani said.

"Be quiet, Alfredo," Clerfayt replied.

"It sounds silly, I know," Lillian said. "I don't mean it that way. It's something else. A few minutes ago, I knew perfectly well what I meant—now I don't quite."

Torriani took a long swallow. "After a race, drivers are as sensitive as crabs when they've shed their shells. Don't give Clerfayt any complexes."

Clerfayt laughed. "You mean we shouldn't tempt God, Lillian?"

She nodded. "Only if there's no other choice. Not out of frivolity."

"Ye gods!" Torriani repeated disgustedly. "Frivolity!" He got up and went over to Gabrielli.

"I'm talking nonsense," Lillian said in despair. "Don't listen to me."

"You're not talking nonsense," Clerfayt replied. "Only it's surprising to hear this from you."

"Why?"

"Do I ever ask you to go back to the sanatorium?" he said quietly.

She looked at him. She had imagined until now that he knew nothing, or that he had assumed there was not much wrong with her. "I don't need to go back to the sanatorium," she said quickly.

"I know that. But I don't ask you to either."

She saw the irony. "I suppose I shouldn't talk that way, is that it?"

"Of course you should," he said. "Always."

She laughed. "I love you very much, Clerfayt. Are all women as silly as I've been after a race?"

"I don't remember. Is that a Balenciaga dress?"

"I don't remember that either."

He felt his cheekbones and his shoulder. "Tonight, I'll have a face like a streaky pudding. Shall we drive out to Levalli's while I can still steer?"

"Don't you have to go to see your manager?"

"No. That's only a victory celebration in the hotel."

"Don't you like to celebrate victories?"

He laughed. "Every win is one less."

Lillian looked at him.

"One less to win," he said. His face was already beginning to swell. "Will you make wet compresses for my face this evening and read aloud to me a chapter from the *Critique of Pure Reason?*"

"Yes," Lillian said. "And some day I'd like to go to Venice."

"Why?"

"There are no mountains there, and no automobiles."

XIV

They stayed in Sicily another two weeks. Clerfayt's shoulder mended. They lived in Levalli's neglected garden, and by the sea. The villa was a cabin overhanging the sea and time, which whispered and rushed away beneath it without beginning and without end.

Clerfayt had a few weeks free until the next race. "Shall we stay here?" he asked. "Or go back?"

"Where to?"

"To Paris. Or anywhere. When you're at home nowhere, you can go anywhere. It is getting hot here now."

"Is the spring over already?"

"Down here it is. But we can take Giuseppe and follow it. In Rome it is just beginning."

"And when it is past there?"

Clerfayt laughed. "We'll follow it again, if you like. Then it will be beginning in Lombardy and by the lakes. After that we can follow it into Switzerland, up the Rhine, until we see it by the sea in all the colors of the Dutch tulip fields. It's as though time were standing still."

"Have you ever done that?"

"Yes, a hundred years ago. Before the war."

"With a woman?"

"Yes, but it was different."

"It is always different. Even with the same woman. I'm not jealous."

"I wish you were."

"I would think it terrible if you had experienced nothing and were to tell me that I was the first woman in your life."

"You are."

"I'm not; but if for my sake you forget the names of the others for a while, that is enough."

"Shall we go?"

Lillian shook her head. "Not yet. I don't want to pretend to myself that time is standing still. I want to feel it and not deceive myself. It stood still all those endless winters in the sanatorium; but I did not stand still. I was dragged back and forth along it as if it were a wall of ice."

"Are you standing still now?"

She kissed him. "I am turning in a circle. For a while. Like a dancer."

Then she became impatient and wanted to leave. From one day to the next it seemed to her that she had been in Sicily for months. They had been months, she thought, months for her. Her calendar differed from that of the people around her. Between day and day there stretched each time the night, like a gorge weeks in length; the night and her ordeal. She never let Clerfayt spend the whole night with her. She saw to it that he was never beside her in the mornings when she awoke. He thought it was a whim of hers; but she did not want him to hear her coughing.

She flew to Rome, intending to fly on from there to Paris. Clerfayt was to drive the car back, with Torriani, and they were going to meet in Paris.

For a day, she wandered around among the ruins of Rome. Next day she sat at the outdoor tables of the café on the Via Veneto. She was supposed to take the evening plane, but she hesitated. A groundless melancholia had taken possession of her, a feeling of great sweetness, with no other component of sadness except, perhaps, the one last cause which stands, silver and gray, on the horizon of every life that is not lived on the level of simple book-keeping. She spent the night in the hotel, and did not go to the airline office until next morning. In the show window she saw a poster of Venice. What she had said to Clerfayt suddenly came to her. Without further thought, she went in and had her ticket changed for one to Venice. It seemed to her that she must go there before she went to Paris. She had to get something clear in her mind; she did not know precisely what it was, but she had to do it before she saw Clerfayt again.

"When is the plane leaving?" she asked.

"In two hours."

She returned to the hotel and packed. She assumed that Clerfayt must already be in Paris, but she was reluctant to telephone or write him that she was not coming. She could do that from Venice, she thought, and knew that she would not do it. She wanted to be alone, she felt—alone and unattainable, uninfluenceable, before she returned. Returned? she thought. Where to? Had she not thought that once before, at the race? Where to? Had she not flown away, and was she not flying now like one of those legendary birds that are born without feet and must fly until they die? But wasn't that what she'd wanted? And wasn't the question now whether she oughtn't to leave Clerfayt also?

The plane dropped down into the pink late afternoon of the lagoon. Lillian was given a corner room in the Hotel Danieli. As they rode up in the elevator, the man who ran it informed her that this hotel had been the scene of the stormy romance between the aging George Sand and the young Alfred de Musset.

"And what happened? With whom did he deceive her?"

"With no one, Mademoiselle. The young man was in despair. Madame Sand deceived him." The man smiled. "With an Italian doctor. Monsieur de Musset was a poet."

Lillian saw the spark of irony and amusement in the man's eyes. Probably she deceived herself, she thought, and loved the one man while she was with the other.

The elevator operator opened the door. "She left him," he recounted. "She went away without telling Monsieur de Musset that she was going."

Like me, Lillian thought. Do I want to deceive myself also?

She entered her room, and abruptly stood still. The whole room was filled with the hovering, rose-colored evening light that exists only in Venice. She went to the window and looked out. The canal was blue and still, but it rhythmically lifted and lowered the rows of gondolas whenever a *vaporetto* churned up to San Zaccaria and stopped. The first lights were flaring, intensely white and all but lost in the wealth of pinks and blues, except for the orange warning lights along the shallows. These hung tenderly like a glowing chain around the neck of San Giorgio Maggiore. There seemed to be no heaviness in this city, Lillian thought; it was as far away as anything could possibly be from all mountains. Further, it was not possible to flee. Nothing ground and crushed you here; everything caressed. And everything was strange and magical. No one knows me here, she thought. And no one knows that I am here. She felt this anonymity as a queer, tempestuous joy, the joy of having escaped a joy, for a short time or forever.

That feeling intensified when she walked through the piazza. Something of the adventure of all beginnings was in it. She had no destination; she let herself drift and landed in the lower restaurant of Quadri, because she thought it lovely that a small eating establishment whose walls were decorated with eighteenth-century scenes and gold brackets should simply open out on the street. She ordered *scampi,* drinking a light white wine with it. Beside her, masked figures danced on the walls. She felt like them, as if she had escaped, had her face hidden behind an invisible domino, in the same mild intoxication of irresponsible freedom that every mask granted. A thousand beginnings lay before her in the roseate dusk, like the thousand narrow lanes of this city which was so fond of masks. Where did those beginnings lead? To unknown, unnamed new discoveries, or only to seductive, well-known pleasures from which you emerged with a hangover and an acute regret at having wasted on them the most precious thing there was: time? Yet it has to be wasted, Lillian thought, it has to be wasted thoughtlessly, in spite of everything, or else you are like the man in the fairy tale who wanted so much for his gold piece that he could not decide what it should be, and died before he made up his mind.

"What is going on this evening?" she asked the waiter.

"This evening? Perhaps you would like the theater, Signora."

"Can seats still be had?"

"Very likely. There are almost always some seats to be had."

"How do I reach it?"

The waiter began to describe the route. "Can't I take a gondola?" she asked.

"Certainly. In the old days, people always did. It isn't done so much any more. The theater has two entrances. It isn't far to walk."

Lillian took a gondola at the Palazzo Ducale. The waiter had been right; except for hers, only one other gondola was heading for the theater. It was occupied by an elderly American couple, who were taking flash-bulb photographs. They took a picture of Lillian's gondola, too. "A woman ought not to be alone in Venice," the gondolier said as he helped her step out. "A young woman still less. A beautiful woman never."

Lillian looked at him. He was old and did not give the impression of offering himself as the needed medicine. "Can one ever feel alone here?" she said, gazing at the red twilight above the roofs.

"Here more than anywhere else, Signora. Unless you were born here, of course."

Lillian arrived just in time, as the curtain was rising. The play was an eighteenth-century comedy. She looked around the theater in the muted illumination from the stage and the wings. It was the most beautiful theater in the world and must, before the introduction of electric light, have been magical with a host of candles lighting the painted balconies. It still was.

She looked at the stage. She did not understand much Italian, and soon gave up trying to listen. The strange feeling of loneliness and melancholy which she had had in Rome overpowered her again. Was the gondolier right? Or did the feeling come from the symbolic situation: that you could arrive at a place, listen to a play of which you understood nothing, and have to leave it just as you were beginning to catch some inkling of its meaning? Nothing serious was taking place on the stage—that much she could see. It was a comedy, seduction, deception, a somewhat cruel joke about a fool, and Lillian did not know what it was that so stirred within her, that developed into a curious sob, so that she had to put her handkerchief to her lips. She did not realize until the feeling came again and she saw the dark spots on her handkerchief.

She remained sitting for a moment, trying to suppress it; but the blood welled up again. She had to go out, but she was not sure she could manage it alone. In French, she asked the man beside her to take her out. He shook his head irritably without looking at her. He was following the action of the play, and did not understand what she wanted. She turned to the woman on her left. Desperately, she searched for the Italian word for "help." She could not think of it. *"Misericordia,"* she murmured at last. *"Misericordia, per favore!"*

The woman looked up in astonishment. "Are you sick?" she asked in English.

Lillian nodded, handkerchief to her lips, and indicated by a gesture that she wanted to leave.

"Too many cocktails," the blonde, elderly woman said. "Mario, darling, help the lady to get some fresh air. What a mess!"

Mario stood up. He supported Lillian. "Just to the door," she whispered.

He took her arm and helped her out. Heads turned briefly. On the stage, the self-assured lover was just that very moment enjoying a triumph. Mario opened the door to the foyer, and in the bright light stared at Lillian. Before him stood an extremely pale young woman in a white dress, blood dripping through her fingers on to her clothes. "But, Signora, this is too much of an understatement. You are really sick," he said in astonishment. "Shall I take you to a hospital?"

Lillian shook her head. "Hotel Danieli. Please—a car," she choked out. "Taxi—"

"Signora, there are no taxis in Venice. Only a gondola, or a motorboat. You must go to a hospital."

"No, no. A boat. To the hotel. There must be a doctor there. Please—just take me to a boat—you have to go back. . . ."

"Oh," Mario said, "Mary can wait. She doesn't understand a word of Italian anyhow. And the play is very dull."

The pale Pompeian red of the foyer after the dark red of the curtains. The white of the stucco reliefs. Doors. Steps and wind; then a square, noises of plates and forks, a restaurant on the street, laughter and the bustle of diners. Past that to a dark, ill-smelling, narrow canal, out of which a gondolier and a boat appeared, like a ferry for crossing the Styx. "Gondola, Signora, gondola?"

"Yes. Quick, quick! The Signora is sick."

The gondolier stared. "Shot?"

"Don't ask questions. Draw up. Quick."

The narrow canal. A small bridge. Walls of houses. The slap of water. The long-drawn-out cry of the gondolier at intersections. Moldering steps, rusted doors, tiny gardens with geraniums, rooms with radios and bare yellow light bulbs, washing hung out to dry, a rat balancing like a trapeze artist on the side of a house, the sharp voices of women, smells of onions and garlic and oil, and the heavy, dead smell of the water.

"We'll be there in a moment," Mario said.

A second canal, broader. Then the stronger waves and the breadth of the Canal Grande. "Shall we stop a motorboat?"

She lay on the rear seats, athwart them, just as she had

fallen there. "No," she whispered. "Go on. Better not change . . ."

The hotels, illuminated; the terraces, *vaporetti,* chugging, smoking, filled with passengers, motorboats with men in white uniforms—how terribly alone you were in the midst of the sweet tumult of life when you were fighting for it and when everything was transformed into a nightmare in which you struggled for breath. The rows of gondolas at their stands swayed on the reflecting water like black coffins, like black, huge water vultures striving to hack at her with their metallic beaks—past all this, and then the *piazzetta,* a mist of light, spaciousness and stars, an area of brightness with the sky for ceiling, and under the Bridge of Sighs an unbearably sweet tenor singing "Santa Lucia" for a boatload of tourists. Suppose this were dying now, Lillian thought—lying this way, her head back, the rush of the water close to her ears, the scrap of song ahead, and an unknown man beside her asking again and again in English: "How are you feeling? Hold on another two minutes. We're almost there." But no, she knew that this was not dying.

Mario helped her out of the boat. "Pay for me," she whispered to the doorman at the canal entrance of the Hotel Danieli. "And get a doctor. Right away."

Mario suported her across the lobby. There were not many people in it. A group of Americans at one table stared at her. Dimly, she saw a face she knew, but she could not recall who it was.

The elevator operator was still on duty. With an effort, Lillian smiled at him. "All kinds of things happen in this hotel," she whispered. "Didn't you say so?"

"Don't try to talk, Signora," Mario said. He was a courtly guardian angel with a velvety voice. "The doctor is coming. Doctor Pisani. He's very good. Don't talk. Bring ice cubes," he said to the elevator operator.

She lay in her room for a week. The windows stayed open —it was already that warm. She had not informed Clerfayt. She did not want him to see that she was sick. Nor did she want to see him at her bedside. This was her affair, hers alone. She slept and half slept through the days, heard the hoarse cries of the gondoliers until late at night, and the slapping sounds made by the tied-up gondolas on the Riva degli Schiavoni. The doctor came now and then, and Mario came also. It was only a small hemorrhage, nothing very dangerous; the doctor understood her, and Mario brought her flowers and told her about his difficult life with elderly ladies. If only he could find a rich young one who would understand him. He did not mean Lillian. In a single day, he had seen through her and grasped her point of view. He was completely open with her and spoke with her as if she were a fellow-worker in the same vineyards as he. "You live on death the way I do on women who see their time running out," he said, laughing. "Or to put it another way: You also see your time running out, but you have your gigolo who always stands by you. His name is Death. The difference is that he remains faithful to you. On the other hand, you play him false whenever you can."

Lillian listened with amusement. "Death is the gigolo for all of us. Only most people don't know it," she said. "What are you planning to do later on, Mario? Marry one of your aging ladies?"

Mario shook his head gravely. "I'm saving. When I have enough, a few years from now, I'm going to open a smart bar with a little eating place. Something like Harry's Bar. I have a fiancée in Padua who is a very good cook. Her *fettucini!*" Mario kissed the tips of his fingers. "Will you come with your friend?"

"I'll come," Lillian said, touched by his delicacy. He wanted to make her feel better by pretending to believe she would go on living, at least the few years until he had his place. Yet hadn't she herself secretly believed in a little personal miracle? Hadn't she believed that the very thing she had been warned against might turn out to be good for her? I have been a romantic sentimentalist, she thought. Like a child, I've expected that some mother-figure divinity would rescue me from every desperate situation with one good-natured slap on the backside. She saw Mario's head against the window, in the rose-quartz light of afternoon, and thought of a remark she had heard an English racing driver make in Sicily: that Latin peoples had no sense of humor. They needed none; they had long passed beyond that particular mode of facing up to life. Humor was a flower of cultivated barbarism; the eighteenth century had had little of it, but on the other hand had had a great deal of the *courtoisie* which chose to ignore what could not be assimilated. Those condemned to death in the French Revolution went to the block with exquisite manners. Not laughing; they went as if they were on their way to court.

Mario brought her a rosary that had been blessed by the Pope, and a painted Venetian box for letters.

"I cannot give you anything in return, Mario," she said.

"I don't want anything in return. It is good to be able to give sometimes, instead of always having to live on gifts."

"Do you really have to?"

"My profession is too profitable for me to give it up. But it isn't easy. It's real work. What is so nice about you is that you don't want anything from me."

The face that Lillian had seen in the hotel lobby the evening of her hemorrhage turned out to be that of the Vicomte de Peystre. He had recognized her, and on the next day had begun sending her flowers. At first these came without a name; after a week he sent his card.

"Why are you in the hotel?" he asked, when at last she telephoned him.

"I love hotels. Would you like to send me to a hospital?"

"Of course not. Hospitals are for operations. I hate them just as much as you do. But a house with a garden, by one of the quiet canals—"

"Do you have one here, too? Like your apartment in Paris?"

"It would not be difficult to find one."

"Do you have one?"

"Yes," de Peystre said.

Lillian laughed. "You have homes everywhere and I don't want one anywhere. Which of us will give them up more easily? Rather, take me out to eat somewhere."

"Are you allowed out?"

"Not really. That makes a bit of an adventure of it, doesn't it?"

It made it an adventure, she thought, as she went down to the lobby. If you escaped death frequently, you were reborn just as frequently, and each time with a deeper gratitude—so long as you dropped the idea of having a claim upon life.

Surprised, she stood still. That is it, she thought. That is the secret. Did I have to come to Venice, to this magical hotel with its afternoons of vermilion and cobalt blue, to find it out?

"You are smiling," de Peystre said. "Why? Because you are tricking your doctor?"

"Not my doctor. Where are we going?"

"To the Taverna. We take the boat here."

The side entrance of the hotel. The swaying gondola. A moment of recollection and of nausea, which swiftly passed as she stepped in. The gondola was no longer a floating coffin, nor was it a black vulture hacking at her with metallic beak. It was a gondola, dark symbol of an appetite for splendor so overweening that it had been necessary to pass a law that all gondolas must be black, because otherwise their owners would have ruined themselves on extravagant decoration.

"I know Venice only from my window," Lillian said. "And from a few hours the first evening."

"Then you know it better than I. I have been coming here for thirty years."

The canal. The hotels. The terraces with their tables, white tablecloths and glasses. The slapping water. The narrow canal, like a branch of the Styx. How is it I know all this? Lillian thought, for a moment depressed. Oughtn't there to be a window with bird cage and canary coming along now?

"Where is the Taverna?" she asked.

"Near the theater."

"Does it have a terrace?"

"Yes. Have you been there?"

"Very briefly. Not to eat. I passed by."

"It's an excellent restaurant."

She heard the rattle of dishes and the voices before they turned the corner.

"You're smiling," de Peystre said. "Why?"

"That is the second time you've asked me that. Because I'm hungry. And because I know I am going to be fed."

The proprietor personally waited on their table. He brought sea food, fresh, broiled, and poached, and an open white wine.

"What brings you here all by yourself?" de Peystre asked.

"A whim. But I am going back."

"To Paris?"

"To Paris."

"To Clerfayt?"

"So you already know that? To Clerfayt."

"Can't that wait a while?" de Peystre said cautiously.

Lillian laughed. "You are persistent. Are you making an offer?"

"Not if you don't want me to. And if you do want it, without conditions. But why don't you take a little time to, let us say, to look around?"

A man with toys came over to the table. He wound up two plush Scotch terriers and set them walking over the table top. "I don't need to look around any more," Lillian said. "I have no time for repetitions."

De Peystre picked up the plush dogs and handed them back to the peddler. "Are you so sure that things will always be repetitions?"

Lillian nodded serenely. "For me, yes. Changes in detail are unimportant. Variations do not interest me."

"Only the essence?"

"Only what I make of it. And that would be the same even if the man were different. That is what you mean, isn't it? I have very simple reactions, it seems to me."

The toy peddler set down a whole poultry yard on the

table. The proprietor came over, pushed the man away, and served peaches flaming in rum and *espresso*. "Do you never have the feeling that you might be missing something?" de Peystre asked.

Lillian looked at him for a moment. Then she asked: "What, for example?"

"An adventure. A surprise. Something new. Something you do not know."

"I had that feeling when I came here. I felt that I was missing New York, Yokohama, Tahiti, Apollo, Dionysus, Don Juan, and Buddha. Now I no longer feel that."

"Since when?"

"Since a few days ago."

"Why not?"

"Because I have learned that one can only miss oneself."

"Where did you learn that?"

"At the window in my hotel."

"Now I will ask you for the third time why you are smiling," de Peystre said.

"Because I'm breathing. Because I'm here, because it's evening and because we're talking nonsense."

"Is it nonsense?"

"It's always nonsense. Do they have cognac here?"

"There's grappa, aged and very good," de Peystre said. "I envy you."

Lillian laughed.

"You've changed," de Peystre said. "You're different from the way you were in Paris. Do you know what the difference is?"

She shrugged. "I don't know. Perhaps it's because I've given up an illusion—the illusion that we have a claim upon life—and with that the illusion that life has been unjust and hasn't granted our claims."

"Highly amoral."

"Highly," Lillian repeated, finishing her grappa. "I hope I can stick to it. At least for a while."

"It seems that I have come too late," de Peystre said. "A few hours or a few days too late. When are you leaving? Tomorrow?"

"Yes."

"It sounded as if you were. Alas."

" 'Alas,' " Lillian said, "is by no means as sad a word as people think."

"Is that another of your new insights?"

"One that I learned today."

De Peystre drew her chair back. "I shall live in hope of your insights of tomorrow."

" 'Hope,' on the other hand," Lillian said, "is a much sadder word than people think."

XV

Clerfayt had looked for her in Paris; then he had assumed that she had returned to the sanatorium. He telephoned, and discovered his error. He had gone back to hunting for her in Paris, and found her nowhere. At last he had concluded that she had wanted to leave him. Even Uncle Gaston had crossly informed him that he did not know where his niece was, and did not care. Clerfayt had tried to forget her and to go on living as he had done before; but it was like trying to dance in glue.

A week after his return, he ran into Lydia Morelli. "Has your swallow left you?" she asked.

"She really must have got under your skin. You never used to ask about other women."

"Has she left you?"

"Left!" Clerfayt replied, smiling. "What a silly word."

"One of the oldest in the world." Lydia studied him.

"Are we playing a conjugal scene from the eighteen-nineties?"

"So you're really in love?"

"And you're jealous."

"I am jealous; but you are unhappy. That's a difference."

"Really?"

"Yes. I know whom I'm jealous of; you don't. May I have a drink?"

Clerfayt went to dinner with her. During the evening, his feelings about Lillian condensed into the old chagrin of the man who has been left before he himself was able to leave. Lydia had pricked his sensitive point with a sharp needle.

"You ought to get married," she said later.

"To whom?"

"I don't know. But it's time that you did."

"You?"

She smiled. "I wouldn't want to do that to you. Anyhow, you haven't nearly enough money for me. Marry someone with money. There are plenty of women with money. How long do you count on going on racing? That's a job for young men."

Clerfayt nodded. "I know that, Lydia."

"Don't look so glum. We're all growing older. The thing is to provide for the future before it's to late."

"Is that really so essential?"

"Don't be a fool. What else?"

I know someone who does not want to provide for the future, he thought. "Have you considered whom I ought to marry, Lydia? You're so solicitous all of a sudden."

She looked keenly at him. "We might discuss the matter. You've changed."

Clerfayt shook his head and stood up. "So long, Lydia."

She came close to him. "You'll be back, won't you?"

"How long have we known each other?"

"For four years. With many holes in between."

"Like a brocade that has been eaten by moths?"

"Like two people who have never wanted to assume a responsibility—who have everything and don't want to give anything away."

"Neither the one nor the other is true."

"We've fitted each other well, Clerfayt."

"Like all people who don't fit in anywhere?"

"I don't know about that. Shall I tell you a secret?"

"That there are no secrets, and that everything is one?"

195

"No, that's for men. This secret is about women. It's that nothing is altogether as bad and nothing is altogether as good as we think. And nothing is final. Come tonight."

He did not go. He was down at the mouth and felt vile. It was not the way it usually was in such cases. He not only missed Lillian, he missed something in himself. Without noticing, he had absorbed something of her way of life. A life without a tomorrow, he thought. But you couldn't live that way; there was a tomorrow, at least for him, and in spite of his occupation; there had to be one.

She has isolated me, he thought with anger. She has made me twenty years younger, but also more foolish. In the past, I would have looked up Lydia Morelli and spent a few enjoyable days with her, and that would have been that; now I would feel like a high-school boy if I did and I'd have a hangover as though I'd been drinking bad wine. I ought to marry Lillian, he thought. Lydia is right, though not the way she thinks. Suddenly he felt liberated, and was amazed at feeling so. He had never before thought he would ever marry. Now it seemed to him perfectly natural. He could no longer imagine his life without Lillian. That was neither tragic nor romantic nor sentimental; it was simply that life without her seemed nothing but a monotonous succession of years, like rooms all alike in which the lights had gone out.

He gave up looking for her. It was pointless; if she returned, she would either come to him or she would not. He had no idea that she was already back in the Hôtel Bisson. But she stayed there alone for several days more. She did not want Clerfayt to see her until she felt well enough to appear healthy. She kept to her room and slept a great deal. While Clerfayt watched over her trunks in the Hotel Ritz, she lived out of the two suitcases she had taken to Sicily.

She felt as if she had come back into port after a great storm, but as if the port had meanwhile changed. The set had been shifted; or, rather, the set had remained the same, but the lighting was different. It was clear and definite now, merciless but without sadness. The storm was over. So was the rose-colored deception. There was no escaping. And no complaint either. The noise was dying down. Soon she would be able to hear her heart. Not only its call—its answer also.

The first person she looked up was Uncle Gaston. He was surprised, but after a few minutes exhibited something resembling a prudent degree of pleasure. "Where are you staying now?" he asked.

"I'm back at the Bisson. It's not expensive, Uncle Gaston."

"You think money multiplies overnight. If you go on the way you've been going, you'll have nothing left before long. Do you know how long your funds will last if you go on spending at the rate you've been doing?"

"No. I don't want to know either."

I must hurry up and die, she thought with a touch of irony.

"You've always lived beyond your means. In the old days, people used to live on the interest of their principal."

Lillian laughed. "I've heard that in the city of Basel on the Swiss border a person is considered a spendthrift if he doesn't live on the interest of the interest."

"Ah, Switzerland," Gaston said, as if he were speaking of the Venus Kallipygos. "What a currency! A fortunate nation!" He looked at Lillian. "I could fix up one room in my apartment for you. That would save you hotel bills."

Lillian looked around. He would spin his little intrigues and try to marry her off, she thought. And keep watch on her. He was afraid that she might cost him some of his own money. Not for a moment did it occur to her to tell him the truth. "I won't be an expense to you, Uncle Gaston," she declared. "Never!"

"Young Boileau has often asked after you."

"Who is he?"

"The son of the watch-company Boileaus. A very fine family. The mother—"

"Oh, he's the one with the harelip?"

"Harelip! What coarse expressions you use. A little blemish that often occurs in old families. Besides, it's been operated on. You hardly notice it. Men aren't fashion models, after all."

Lillian regarded the self-righteous little man. "How old are you, Uncle Gaston?"

"Are you harping on that again? You know perfectly well."

"And how old do you think you will live to be?"

"That's a totally tactless question. You do not ask that of elderly people. It's in God's hands."

"Many things are in God's hands. He will have a lot of questions to answer someday, don't you think? I have a few to ask him, too."

"What?" Gaston's eyes flew wide. "What's that you're saying?

"Nothing." Lillian had to check a brief surge of anger. Here this indestructible molting old rooster stood before her, victorious, champion on a racecourse one foot long; old as he was, he would certainly live at least several years longer than she; he knew everything, had an opinion on everything, and was on intimate terms with his God.

"Uncle Gaston," she said with an effort, "if you could live your life over again, would you live it differently?"

"Of course!"

"How?" Lillian asked, a faint hope rising.

"I certainly wouldn't get caught again in the devaluation of the franc. Back in 1914, I would have bought American stocks—and then in 1938, at the latest—"

"All right, Uncle Gaston," Lillian interrupted. "I understand." Her anger had evaporated.

"You understand nothing. Otherwise you wouldn't be so reckless with the little money you have left. Of course, your father—"

"I know, Uncle Gaston. A spendthrift. But there is an even bigger spendthrift than he was."

"Who?"

"Life. It spends you and me and everybody else."

"Stuff and nonsense. That's parlor Bolshevism! Time you cleared your head of that stuff. Life is too serious for that."

"It certainly is. Bills have to be paid. Give me money. And don't act as if it's your own. It belongs to me."

"Money! Money! That's all you know about life."

"No, Uncle Gaston, that's all you know."

"Be thankful if it's so. Otherwise you'd have been without a cent long ago." Reluctantly, Gaston wrote out a check. "And what about later?" he asked bitterly, waving the slip of paper in the air to dry the ink. "What are you going to do later?"

Lillian gazed at him in fascination. I think he's actually saving on blotting paper, she thought. "There is no later," she said.

"That's what they all say. And then, when they have nothing left, they come begging, and out of our little savings we have to—"

Her anger returned, clear and violent. Lillian snatched the check from her uncle's hand. "Stop your wailing! And go and buy yourself American stock, you patriot!"

She walked along the wet streets. It had been raining while she was at her uncle's, but now the sun was shining again, and reflecting from the asphalt and the puddles at the curb. Even in puddles the sky is reflected, she thought, and found herself laughing. In that case, perhaps God was reflected even in Uncle Gaston. But where in him? God was harder to find in her uncle than the blue and glitter of the sky in the filthy water that flowed into the sewer openings. God was hard to find in most people she knew. They sat in their offices, behind their desks, as though they were all going to be double Methuselahs; that was their dreary secret. They lived as if death did not exist. But they did it like shopkeepers, not like heroes. They had repressed the tragic knowledge of the end and played ostrich and cultivated the petty-bourgeois illusion of Eternal Life. They went on trying to cheat each other on the brink of the grave and to pile up the things that soonest made them slaves of themselves: money and power.

She took a hundred-franc note, studied it, and tossed it into the Seine. It was a childishly symbolic gesture of protest, but she did not care. In any case, she did not throw away Uncle Gaston's check. She walked on and reached the boulevard Saint-Michel. Traffic roared around her; people ran, jostled, hurried; the sun flashed upon hundreds of automobile roofs; motors roared; everywhere were destinations which had to be reached as quickly as possible, and each of these petty destinations concealed the last one so thoroughly that it seemed as if it did not exist.

She laughed and crossed the street between two quivering rows of hot monsters, momentarily spellbound by a red light, as Moses had once crossed the Red Sea with the people of Israel. In the sanatorium it had been different, she thought; there, the final destination always glowered like a black sun in the sky. You lived under it, and in spite of it, but you did not repress it; that gave you deeper understanding and deeper courage. To know that you were to be slaughtered and could not escape, and to face it with this ultimate understanding and courage, was to be no longer entirely a sacrificial animal. The victim had surmounted the butcher to that small extent.

She reached her hotel. Her present room was again on the first floor, so that she would have only the one flight of stairs to climb. The shellfish seller was standing at the door of the restaurant. "Wonderful shrimp, today," he said. "Oysters are almost past. They won't be good again until September. Will you still be here then?"

"Certainly," she replied.

"Would you care for some shrimp for lunch? The gray ones taste better. The pink ones only look nice. Gray ones?"

"Gray ones. I'll let the basket down. And ask Lucien, the headwaiter, for a half-bottle of *vin rosé,* very cold."

She slowly climbed the stairs. Then she let down her basket and drew it up again. The wine was uncorked, and so cold that the bottle was misted over. She sat down on the window seat, feet drawn up, leaning against the frame, the wine at her side. The waiter had packed a glass and napkin into the basket. She drank, and began shelling the shrimp. Life was good like this, she thought, and did not want to pursue the thought any further. Dimly, she felt a consciousness of some compensation, but she did not want to know anything about it now. Not at this moment anyhow. That her mother had died of cancer, after drastic operations, had something to do with it. There were always things worse than what you yourself had. She blinked into the sun. She felt its light upon her. That was how Clerfayt saw her when, altogether without hope, he came by the Bisson on patrol one more time.

He wrenched open the door. "Lillian! Where have you been?" he cried.

She had seen him crossing the street. "In Venice, Clerfayt."

"But why?"

"I told you in Sicily that some day I wanted to go to Venice. I thought about it again in Rome."

He closed the door behind him. "Why didn't you telegraph me? I would have come. How long were you there?"

"Are you interrogating me?"

"Not yet. I've looked everywhere for you. Who was with you?"

"You say this is not an interrogation?"

"I've missed you! My God, I thought all sorts of things. Can't you understand that?"

"Yes," Lillian said. "Would you like some of these shrimp? They taste of seaweed and the ocean."

Clerfayt took the paper plate and the shrimp and threw them out the window.

Lillian watched them flying. "You hit a green Citroën sedan. If you'd waited a second longer, they would have landed on the head of a fat lady in an open Renault. Please give me that basket with the string. I'm still hungry."

For a second, Clerfayt looked as if he were going to throw the basket after the shrimp. Then he handed it to her. "Tell him to send up another bottle of *rosé*," he said. "And come away from the window so that I can take you into my arms."

Lillian slid down from the window seat. "Have you brought Giuseppe with you?"

"No. He's standing on the place Vendôme sneering at a dozen Bentleys and Rolls-Royces parked around him."

"Get him and let's drive into the Bois."

"Sure, we can drive to the Bois," Clerfayt said, kissing her. "But we'll go out together and get Giuseppe together; otherwise you'll be gone when I come back. I'm taking no more risks."

"Did you miss me?"

"Now and then, when I wasn't hating you or stewing for fear that you were the victim of some sex murder. Who were you with in Venice?"

"I was alone."

He looked at her. "I suppose it's possible. With you, one never knows. Why didn't you let me know?"

"We don't do that, do we? Don't you go to Rome sometimes and not turn up again for weeks? And even come back with a mistress?"

Clerfayt laughed. "I knew that would be coming sooner or later. Is that why you stayed away?"

"Of course not."

"Too bad."

Lillian leaned out the window to draw up her basket of shrimp. Clerfayt waited patiently. There was a knock at the door. He answered, took the wine from the waiter and drank a glass while listening to Lillian call out the window that she wanted a larger portion of shrimp. Then he looked around the room. He saw her shoes standing about, a slip lying on a chair, and her dresses hanging inside the wardrobe, whose door was ajar. She was back again, he thought, and a profound, unfamiliar, and stirring peace filled him.

Lillian turned around, basket in hand. "How good they smell! Will we go to the ocean again some time?"

"Yes. To Monte Carlo. There's a race there in the summer."

"Can't we go before?"

"As soon as you like. Today? Tomorrow?"

She smiled. "You know me. No, not today or tomorrow." She took the glass he held out to her. "I didn't intend to stay so long in Venice," she said. "Only a few days."

"Why did you stay on then?"

"I didn't feel well."

"What was the matter?"

She hesitated. "I had a cold."

She saw that he did not believe her. That pleased her. His incredulity made the hemorrhage seem more improbable to her, too; perhaps it had, after all, really been less important than she thought. Suddenly she felt like a fat woman who had lost twenty pounds without noticing it.

She leaned against him. Clerfayt held her tightly. "And when are you going away again?" he asked.

"I don't go away, Clerfayt. It's just that sometimes I'm not present."

A barge on the river tooted. On the deck, a young woman was hanging colored wash on lines. At the door to the galley, a girl was playing with a dog. The captain stood at the wheel in shirt sleeves, whistling.

"See that?" Lillian asked. "I always feel envious when I see that kind of thing. Domestic peace. What God meant us for."

"If you had it, you'd steal away from the boat the next place it anchored."

"That doesn't prevent me from being envious. Shall we go to get Giuseppe now?"

Carefully, Clerfayt lifted her in his arms. "I don't want to get Giuseppe or drive to the Bois now. We can do that later."

XVI

"In other words, you want to lock me up," Lillian said, laughing.

Clerfayt did not laugh. "I don't want to lock you up. I want to marry you."

"Why?"

Lillian bent from the edge of the bed and held the bottle of *rosé* toward the light. The window shimmered through the wine as if blood had been poured over the panes. Clerfayt took the bottle from her hand. "To make sure you don't again vanish without a trace some day."

"I left my trunks in the Ritz. Do you think that marriage is a better guarantee of return?"

"Not return. Staying. Let's approach this from a different angle. You don't have much money. You don't want to take any from me—"

"You haven't any yourself, Clerfayt."

"I have my percentage share of two races. Besides that, there's what I had left and what I'm going to make. We have plenty for this year."

"Good, then let's wait until next year."

"Why wait?"

"So that you'll see it's nonsense. How would you pay

for my wardrobe next year? You said yourself that your contract runs out at the end of this year."

"They've offered me an agency for our cars."

Lillian lifted her leg and studied its lines. They're getting too thin, she thought. "You mean to say you want to sell cars?" she asked. "I can't imagine that."

"Neither can I, but I've done lots of things that I couldn't imagine myself doing. For example, wanting to marry you."

"Why do you always want to do everything at once? Like becoming a respectable automobile dealer and marrying?"

"You act as if both were a national disaster."

Lillian slid out of bed and reached for a wrapper. "Where would you sell cars?"

Clerfayt hesitated. "The Toulouse franchise will be open."

"Good Lord!" Lillian said. "When?"

"In a few months. In the fall. Or end of the year at the latest."

She began combing her hair. "I'm getting too old to win races," Clerfayt said, still lying on the bed and talking to her back. "I'm not Nuvolari or Caracciola. I suppose I might try to become a manager somewhere, but then I'd have to keep moving all the time from one track to the next, like our fat Cesare—he will not even see his wife in the winter, now that they're starting to hold races in Africa and South America. No, I've had enough of it. I want to change my life."

Why do they always want to change their lives? Lillian thought. Why do they want to change the very thing about them that has made an impression on a woman? Doesn't it ever occur to them that by doing that they'll probably lose the woman? Even Mario on the last day was ready to give up his career as gigolo and start an honorable life with me. And Clerfayt, who thinks he loves me, and whom I loved because he seemed to be just as much without a future as myself, wants to change course now, and actually thinks I'm bound to be glad about it.

"I've often thought about whether people like us ought

to marry," she said. "None of the reasons convinced me. The best was still one a tubercular chess player mentioned: that it's good to have someone with you at the moment of death agony. But I don't know whether at that time you're not so hopelessly alone anyhow, even if hordes of people who care about you are standing around your bed, that you may not even be aware of it. Camilla Albei, who used to be at the sanatorium, was always very concerned about having a lover to be there at the end. To be on the safe side, she went to great lengths to keep up relations with three men at the same time. She dragged out her last affair with a disgusting, arrogant man beyond all reason, simply to have him available that way. Then she was run over by a car on the village street and died half an hour later. Not even the disgusting man came to her side—he was sitting in Luft's pastry shop eating *Mohrenköpfe* with whipped cream. The village policeman, whom she'd never seen before, held Camilla's hand, and she was so grateful that she tried to kiss it. She didn't have the strength to, though."

"Lillian," Clerfayt said quietly. "Why are you always dodging me?"

She put down the comb. "Don't you understand why? What has happened, Clerfayt? We've met by chance— why won't you let it remain that way?"

"I want to hold on to you. As long as I can. That's simple, isn't it?"

"No. It isn't the way to hold on to anyone."

"All right. Then let's put it differently. I don't want to go on living as I have been doing."

"You want to settle down?"

Clerfayt looked at the rumpled bed. "You infallibly find the most horrible word for things. Let me put it this way. I love you and want to live with you. Laugh at that, for all I care."

"I never laugh at that." She looked up. Her eyes were filled with tears. "Oh, Clerfayt, what silliness all this is!"

"Isn't it?" He stood up and took her hands. "We were so sure it could never happen to us."

"Let it be as it is. Let it be. Don't destroy it."

"What is there to destroy?"

Everything, she thought. You cannot build domestic happiness in Toulouse on butterfly wings, even if you set them in cement. How egoism blinded people! If this concerned some other man, Clerfayt would understand exactly how I felt; in his own case, he's blind. "I am sick, after all, Clerfayt," she said at last, hesitantly.

"That's one more reason not to be alone."

She did not answer. Boris, she thought. Boris would understand me. Clerfayt is now talking like him; but he is not Boris.

"Shall we get Giuseppe now?" she asked.

"I can get him. Will you wait here?"

"Yes."

"When do you want to go to the Riviera? Soon?"

"Soon."

Clerfayt stood still behind her. "I own a wretched little place on the Riviera."

In the mirror, she saw his face and his hands on her shoulders. "You really are developing unexpected qualities."

"We could fix it up and make it nicer," Clerfayt said.

"Can't you sell it?"

"Take a look at it first."

"All right," she said, suddenly impatient. "When you get to the hotel, send my trunks over."

"I'll bring them with me."

He left. She remained at her dressing table, looking into the fading dusk. Anglers were sitting on their heels along the river's edge. A few *clochards* were preparing their supper by the wall of the quay. What strange paths what is called love can take, she thought. Had not Levalli said that behind every young bacchante there lurked the housewife, and behind the reckless conqueror the sober bourgeois with his instinct for possession? Not for me, she thought; but what had happened to Clerfayt? Had she not loved him because he reached out for life as if every moment were going to be his last? Toulouse! She began to laugh. She had never wanted to speak of her illness because she had thought that the sick must always

207

be somewhat repulsive to the healthy. Now it seemed to her that the reverse could also be true: the healthy could sometimes seem almost vulgar to the sick, like a *nouveau riche* to an impoverished aristocrat. It seemed to her that Clerfayt had abandoned her in a strange fashion today and had shifted over to the big, bustling majority, to the side that was unattainable to her. He was no longer one of the lost; he suddenly had a future. To her surprise, she became aware that she was crying, gently and noiselessly; but she was not unhappy. It was only that she wished she could have held on to everything a little longer.

Clerfayt came with the trunks. "How did you manage so long without your things?"

"I ordered new ones. That's always possible to do with clothes."

It was not true; she had only decided at this moment to pay another visit to Balenciaga tomorrow. There was a double reason to do so, she thought; she had to celebrate having escaped with her life in Venice, and she had to be extravagant as a protest against Clerfayt's offer to marry her and live in Toulouse.

"Can't I give you a few dresses?" Clerfayt asked. "I'm fairly rich at the moment."

"For my wedding trousseau?"

"On the contrary. Because you went to Venice."

"Good, give me one. Where are we going tonight? Is it possible to sit in the Bois yet?"

"If we take coats. Otherwise it's still too cool. But we can drive through. The woods are bright green and enchanted with springtime and blue exhaust fumes. The side roads are practically solid with parked cars every night. Love is hanging its banners out of the windows everywhere."

Lillian snatched up a dress of black filmy material with a ruche of Mexican red, and waved it out the window. "To love," she said. "Divine and earthly, small and great! When are you leaving again?"

"How do you know that I have to leave again? Are you following the racing calendar?"

"No. But with us, there's no telling who is leaving whom."

"That is going to change."

"Not before the end of the year!"

"It's possible to get married earlier, too."

"Let's first celebrate our meeting again and farewell. Where do you have to go?"

"To Rome. And then to the thousand-mile race through Italy. Next week. You can't come along. It's just driving and driving, nothing more than that, until you can't tell yourself apart from the road and the motor."

"Will you win?"

"The Mille Miglia is a race for Italians. Caracciola won it once, for Mercedes, but otherwise the Italians fight it out among themselves. Torriani and I are only driving as third team. In case something happens. May I stay here while you dress?"

Lillian nodded. "What kind of dress shall it be?" she asked.

"One of those I held in captivity."

She opened the trunk. "This one?"

"Yes. I know it very well."

"You've never seen it."

"Not on you; but I know it all the same. It hung in my room for a few nights."

Lillian turned around, a mirror in her hand. "Really?"

"I admit it," Clerfayt said. "I hung your clothes out like a witch doctor in order to lure you back. I've learned that from you. It was black magic, and a comfort. A woman may leave a man, but she'll never leave her clothes."

Lillian inspected her eyes in the mirror. "So my shadows were with you."

"Not your shadows—your shed and left-behind snakeskins."

"I would have thought it would be another woman."

"I tried that. But you've spoiled me for anyone else.

Compared to you, they seem like bad colored prints as against a genuine Degas."

Lillian laughed. "Like one of those ungainly ballet *rats* he was always painting?"

"No. Like a drawing Levalli has in his house—a dancer in movement that simply carries you away. Her face is only suggested, so that everyone can project into it his own dream."

Lillian laid her pencils aside. "There always has to be something left out for that, doesn't there? If everything is painted down to the last details, there isn't any room left for the imagination. Is that what you mean?"

"Yes," Clerfayt said. "We are caught only in our own dreams, never in those of others."

"Caught or lost."

"Both. Just as sometimes, before waking, we dream that we are falling and falling into an endless black space. Do you ever have that dream?"

"I've had it," Lillian said. "I used to have it almost every afternoon, back in the sanatorium, when we were taking what the Crocodile would call our siesta—I used to feel like a stone falling into a bottomless pit. Is there any wine left?"

Clerfayt brought her a glass. She put her arm around his neck. "It's odd," she murmured, "but as long as we don't forget that we're falling and falling, nothing is lost. Life seems to love paradoxes—when we think we're perfectly safe, we're always ridiculous and on the verge of a tumble; but when we know we're lost, life showers gifts on us. Then we don't have to do a thing—it runs after us like a poodle."

Clerfayt sat down on the floor at her side. "How do you know all that?"

"I'm just talking. And all the things I say are only half-truths—like everything else."

"Love, too?"

"What has love to do with truth?"

"Nothing. It's the opposite of it."

"No," Lillian said, getting up. "The opposite of love is

death—and love is the bitter enchantment that makes us forget death for a short time. That is why everyone who knows anything about death also knows something about love." She slid the dress on over her head. "That, too, is a half-truth. Who actually knows anything about death?"

"Nobody—except that it is the opposite of life, not of love, and that, too, is dubious."

Lillian laughed. Clerfayt was back in his old vein. "Do you know what I would like?" she asked. "To live ten lives all at once."

He stood up and caressed the narrow shoulder straps of her dress. "What for? It would always only be one life, Lillian—just as a chess player who plays against ten different partners is in reality always playing only one game—his own."

"I've found that out, too."

"In Venice?"

"Yes, but not the way you think."

They were standing at the window. A muted sunset hung over the Conciergerie. "I'd like to get my life all mixed up," Lillian said. "For instance, I'd like to live a day or an hour of my fiftieth year—then one of my thirtieth—then one of my eightieth—all in a single day, just as I happen to feel like it—not one after the other strung along the chain of time."

Clerfayt laughed. "You change fast enough for me as you are. Where shall we eat?"

They went downstairs. He doesn't understand what I mean, Lillian thought. He thinks when I say that, that it's capriciousness; he doesn't realize that I'd only like to coax the hereafter to let me have a few days that I'll never live to see. On the other hand, I'll never be a cranky old woman of eighty, or a man's aging disappointment, whom he would rather never see again, an old flame who comes as a kind of shock when he runs into her in later years. I'll remain young in my lover's memory and so have an advantage over all the women after me who'll live longer and grow older than I.

"What are you laughing at?" Clerfayt asked on the stairs. "At me?"

"At myself," Lillian said. "But don't ask me why. You'll find out at the proper time."

He brought her back to the hotel two hours later. "Enough for today," he said smilingly. "You need sleep."

She looked at him in astonishment. "Sleep?"

"Rest. You told me you'd been sick."

She searched his face for the hidden joke. "Do you really mean that?" she asked finally. "I suppose you're going to tell me next that I look tired."

The night porter appeared, wearing a knowing grin. "Salami tonight? Caviar? The *patronne* has left the caviar out."

"A sleeping pill," Lillian declared. "Good night, Clerfayt."

He held her fast. "Do understand me, Lillian. I don't want you to strain yourself and perhaps have a relapse."

"You weren't so anxious at the sanatorium."

"In those days I thought I'd be driving away and never seeing you again."

"And now?"

"Now I am sacrificing a few hours this evening because I want to keep you as long as I can."

"How practical!" Lillian said spitefully. "Good night, Clerfayt."

He looked at her sharply. "Bring up a bottle of Vouvray," he said to the porter.

"Very well, sir."

"Come." Clerfayt took Lillian's arm. "I'll take you up."

She shook her head and pulled free. "Do you know the last person I had such an argument with? Boris. But he was better at it. You're right, Clerfayt. It's an excellent idea for you to go to bed early; you have to be well rested for your race."

He glared at her. The porter came with the bottle and two glasses. "We don't need the wine," Clerfayt said coldly.

"Oh yes, I need it."

Lillian took the bottle and one glass. "Good night,

Clerfayt. Let's not dream of falling tonight—into endless space. Dream of Toulouse instead!"

She flourished the glass and started up the stairs. He stood until she was out of sight. "Cognac, sir?" the night porter asked. "A double?"

"For yourself," Clerfayt said, thrusting a few bills into his hand.

He walked along the quai des Grands-Augustins as far as the Restaurant La Périgordine. Through the lighted windows, he saw late diners enjoying the specialty of the house, truffles roasted on embers. Two people, obviously long and serenely married, were paying their check; a pair of young lovers were ardently telling each other lies. Clerfayt crossed the street and walked slowly back along the closed stalls of the booksellers. Boris, he thought furiously. That topped it off! The wind brought the smell of the Seine. A few scows loomed black in the plangent darkness. From one of them came the wail of an accordion.

Lillian's windows were lighted, but the curtains were drawn. Clerfayt saw her shadow moving back and forth across them. She did not look out, although the windows were open. Clerfayt knew that he had behaved like an idiot, but he could not help it. He had meant exactly what he said. And Lillian had looked very tired; in the restaurant, her face had suddenly looked so worn. As if it were a crime to be solicitous, he thought. What would she do now? Pack? It occurred to him that she must know he was still there since she had not heard Giuseppe roaring away. Quickly, he crossed the street and sprang into the car. He started it, stepped unnecessarily hard on the gas, and shot off toward the place de la Concorde.

Lillian carefully placed the bottle of wine on the floor beside the bed. She heard Giuseppe drive away. Then she found a raincoat in her trunk and put it on. It scarcely went with the dinner dress, but she did not feel like changing; the coat covered her dress fairly well. She did not want to go to bed. She had had enough of that in the sanatorium.

She went down the stairs. The night porter sprang to attention. "Cab, Madame?"

"No, thanks, no cab."

She went out on the street, and got as far as the boulevard Saint-Michel with scarcely an encounter. But then came a hail of propositions, white, brown, black and yellow. It was as though she had stepped into a swamp and the gnats were falling upon her. In a few minutes, she received a brief but intensive course of instruction in whispered eroticism of the simplest kind—compared to which a pair of street curs were a couple of romantic lovers.

Somewhat stunned, she sat down at a sidewalk café table. The professional whores scrutinized her sharply; they had their beat and were prepared to defend it tooth and claw against any competition. Her table immediately became a center of attention; women of her type did not sit alone in these cafés at this time of night. Even American girls were usually in pairs.

Here Lillian was the target for new propositions—she was offered indecent photographs, cheap jewelry and terrier pups. Someone volunteered to protect her, someone else to take her for a drive. Was she interested in meeting young Negroes? Would she like to know a few Lesbian ladies? She did not become flustered, but gave the waiter a tip in advance. He looked at the amount, and bestirred himself to drive the worst of the rush away. This gave her a chance to drink her Pernod in peace and look around.

A pale man with a beard at an adjoining table began to draw her. A rug peddler tried to sell her a grass-green prayer rug, but was chased away by the waiter. Finally, a young man approached and introduced himself as a garret poet. Realizing that her only defense was to have someone with her, she invited the poet to have a glass of wine. He wondered if he might take a sandwich instead. She ordered a roast beef sandwich for him.

The poet's name was Gérard. After eating his sandwich, he read her two poems and recited two others from memory. They were elegies on death, dying, transitoriness, and the meaninglessness of life. Lillian grew cheerful. The poet was thin, but a hearty eater. She asked him whether he could take care of another roast beef sandwich. He most certainly could, he declared, and he thought that she understood poetry; didn't she feel with him that life was dreary? Why did one want to bother with it? He ate two more sandwiches and came forth with even more pessimistic verse. He began discussing the problem of suicide. Tomorrow, of course, not today, not after such a big meal. Lillian felt gayer and gayer, the poet was skinny, but he looked healthy enough to live another fifty years.

Clerfayt sat around the Ritz bar for a while. Then he decided to telephone Lillian. The porter answered. "Madame is not in the hotel," he said, when Clerfayt identified himself.

"Where is she?"

"She went out half an hour ago."

Clerfayt calculated. In so short a time, she could not have packed. Nevertheless, he took the precaution of asking: "Did she take suitcases with her?"

"No, sir. She was wearing a raincoat."

"Good. Thank you."

A raincoat, he thought. It would be just like her to go to the station without baggage and leave—to go back to her Boris Volkov, who is so much better than I.

He ran to the car. I should have stayed with her, he thought. What the hell is the matter with me? How clumsy you get as soon as you're really in love! How the veneer of superiority drops away. How alone you are, and how all the skills of experience evaporate! You go about in a fog making nothing but mistakes.

He had the night porter describe what direction she had taken. "Not toward the Seine, sir," the man said reassuringly. "To the right. Perhaps she just wanted to walk a little and will be back soon."

Clerfayt drove slowly along the boulevard Saint-Michel. Lillian heard Giuseppe, and a moment later saw him. "What about death?" she asked Gérard, who was doing justice to a plate of cheese. "Suppose death is even drearier than life?"

"Who can say," Gérard retorted, chewing despondently, "whether life is not a punishment we must endure for a crime we committed in another world? Perhaps this is hell and not what the Church foretells for us after death."

"It also foretells heaven."

"Then perhaps we are all fallen angels condemned to a number of years of penance on earth."

"We can shorten the sentence if we want to."

"Suicide!" Gérard nodded enthusiastically. "And we shrink from it. Yet it is liberation! If life were fire, we'd know what to do. Jump out of it! The irony—"

Giuseppe came by again, this time from the direction of the place Edmond-Rostand. Irony, Lillian thought, is all we have, and sometimes it has a certain allure; that's the case now as I sit listening to this lecture. She saw Clerfayt searching the crowd on the street so intensely that he did not notice her a few yards out of range.

"If you could have your wish, what would be the supreme demand you would make on life?" she asked Gérard.

"The unfulfillable," the poet replied promptly.

She looked gratefully at him. "Then you don't have to wish for anything more," she said. "You have your wish already."

"And also for a listener like you!" Gérard declared with gloomy gallantry, shooing away the artist who had completed Lillian's portrait and was skulking around the table with the sketch. "Forever. You understand me!"

"I'll take that picture," Clerfayt said to the crestfallen artist.

He had come up behind them on foot, and was looking Gérard over with little cordiality. "Beat it," Gérard told him. "Don't you see we're talking? We've had enough disturbances. *Garçon,* two more Pernods. And send this gentleman away."

"Three Pernods," Clerfayt replied, sitting down. The artist stood beside him, eloquently mute. "It's lovely here," Clerfayt said to Lillian. "Why haven't we come here more often?"

"And who are you, unbidden stranger?" Gérard asked, assuming that Clerfayt was some kind of pimp who was trying one of the usual tricks to make Lillian's acquaintance.

"Director of the insane asylum of Saint-Germain-des-Prés, my boy. This lady is one of our patients. She has a pass for this evening. Has anything happened? Have I come too late? Waiter, take this knife away. The fork, too."

As a poet, Gérard liked to believe in the astonishing. "Really?" he whispered. "I've always wanted to—"

"You don't have to whisper," Clerfayt interrupted. "She knows she is a lunatic and loves being one. It gives her complete irresponsibility. Immunity from any law. She could commit murder and nothing would happen to her."

Lillian laughed. "It's just the other way around," she said to Gérard. "This is my former husband. He seems to have run away from the asylum. It's characteristic that he should call me mad."

The poet was no fool. Moreover, he was a Frenchman. He saw the situation, and rose with a winning smile. "Some go too late and some go too early," he declared. "Go at the right time—thus spake Zarathustra. Tomorrow, Madame, a poem will be waiting for you here in the charge of the waiter."

"It's nice that you came," Lillian said. "If I had gone to bed, I would have missed all this. The green light and the sweet rebellion of the blood. The mud and the swallows above it."

"Sometimes you're too quick for me, Lillian," Clerfayt replied. "Forgive me. You do in hours what other women need years for—like the plant that grows up in minutes under the hands of a yogi, and blossoms—"

And dies, Lillian thought. "I have to, Clerfayt," she said. "I have so much to make up for. That's why I'm so superficial, too. There's time enough to be wise later on."

He took her hand and kissed it. "I'm an idiot. And getting worse every day. But I don't mind. I like it. If only you are with me. I love you very much."

A furious, rapid quarrel sprang up in front of the café. In seconds, a policeman was there, several Algerians were gesticulating, a girl was railing, newsboys were running and shouting.

"Come," Lillian said. "There is still that wine in my room."

allowing this to plunge her into melancholy, self-recrimination and regrets, it had made it simpler to tell herself that now she would need even less money for her keep and could therefore afford one more dress. She had chosen it with particular care. She had had in mind something dramatic, but what she finally ordered proved to be simpler than any of her others. On the other hand, the one Clerfayt was paying for was dramatic; it was a protest against Toulouse and what she imagined Toulouse to be.

She smiled at herself in the mirror of a shop window. In many things one could not be superficial enough, she thought. And clothes could give one greater moral support than all appeals to justice, more than any amount of sympathy and understanding, more than all confessors, all wisdom, all perfidious friends, and even a lover. This was not frivolity; it was simply knowledge of the comfort and power that could lie in small things.

It was good to know that, Lillian thought, and for her, it was almost all that was left. She no longer had time for grand justifications, not even for rebellions. She had made the one rebellion that meant anything to her, and sometimes she was already beginning to wonder about that; now, all other recourses were closed to her and the only thing left was to settle her account with fate.

She knew that everything she was using to deceive and to console herself could also be viewed as a collection of rather cheap tricks; but she had already moved so far beyond the honorable major tricks which men practiced in trying to make their existence bearable that the differences in magnitude no longer existed for her. Moreover, it seemed to her that it took just as much, if not more, discipline, courage in facing facts, and self-conquest to believe in the petty tricks and to enjoy them, as it did to put your faith in the kind of tricks that had high-sounding names. She bought her clothes and derived as much comfort from that as another might from philosophy—just as she mixed up her love for Clerfayt with her love for life, and tossed them both into the air and caught them again, and knew that sooner or later both would smash. You could fly in a balloon until it came down to earth, but you could not hang houses from it. And when it came down to earth, it was just a big, flapping rag—not a balloon any more.

She met the Vicomte de Peystre when she turned into the Champs-Elysées near Fouquet's. He started. "How happy you look," he said. "Are you in love?"

"Yes. With a dress."

"How sensible," de Peystre said. "That is love without anxiety and without difficulties."

"In other words, not love."

"A portion of the only love that has any meaning: love of self."

Lillian laughed. "You call that a love without anxiety and difficulties? Are you made of cast iron or sponge rubber?"

"Neither. I am a belated scion of the eighteenth century and share the fate of all scions, to be misunderstood. Would you care to have something with me here on the terrace? A cocktail?"

"Coffee."

They took a table in the late-afternoon sunlight. "Sometimes it's almost the same thing," de Peystre said, "to sit in the sun or to talk about love or life—or about nothing. Are you still staying at the little hotel by the Seine?"

"I think I am. Sometimes I am no longer quite sure. When the windows are open in the morning, it often seems to me that I am sleeping in the midst of the noise on the place de l'Opéra. And at night it's sometimes as if I were drifting down the Seine—on a still boat or in the water, on my back, with my eyes wide open, without myself and entirely within myself."

"You have strange thoughts."

"On the contrary, I have almost none. Dreams sometimes, but not many of those either."

"Don't you need any?"

"No," Lillian said. "I really don't need any."

"Then we are alike. I don't need any either."

The waiter brought a sherry for de Peystre and a pot of coffee for Lillian. De Peystre frowned at the coffee. "That really should come after one has eaten," he declared. "Wouldn't you rather have an *apéritif?*"

"No. How late is it?"

"Almost five o'clock," de Peystre replied, astonished. "Do you drink by the clock?"

"Only today." Lillian beckoned to the headwaiter. "Have you heard anything yet, Monsieur Lambert?"

"Of course. From Radio Rome. They've been reporting for hours. All of Italy is either glued to the radio or in the streets," the headwaiter said excitedly. "The heavy cars ought to be starting out in the next few minutes. Monsieur Clerfayt is driving with Monsieur Torriani. They're not relieving one another, but driving together. Torriani is going along as mechanic. It's a sports-car race. Would you care to hear it on the radio? I brought my portable here today."

"That would be nice!"

'Is Clerfayt in Rome?" de Peystre asked.

"No, in Brescia."

"I know nothing about races. What kind is this one?"

"The Brescia thousand-mile race."

The headwaiter came to the table with his radio. He was a racing fan and had been garnering every scrap of news about the race for hours. "They are being started at intervals of a few minutes," he explained. "The fastest cars last. It's a race against the stop watch. I'll turn on the Milan station. Five o'clock—time for the news broadcast."

He turned the knobs. The radio began to squawk. Then the Milan station came in, the announcer rapidly disposing of political events as if he could not wait to reach the sports news. "We now bring you a report from Brescia," he went on in an altered, passionate voice. "A number of the contestants have already started on their way. The market place is so choked with people that they can scarcely move—"

The set squawked and spat. Then, piercing through the babel of voices, came the howl of a motor, which immediately grew fainter. "There's one roaring away," Monsieur Lambert whispered excitedly. "Probably an Alfa."

It had become quiet on the terrace. The curious came over toward the radio, or leaned forward from their various tables. "Who's leading?"

"It's too soon to say," the headwaiter replied with authority. "The fast cars are just starting."

"How many cars are there in the race?" de Peystre asked.

"Almost five hundred."

"Good Lord!" someone exclaimed. "And how long is the course?"

"A thousand miles, sir. At a good average, they'll take fifteen to sixteen hours. Or maybe less. But it's raining in Italy. They're having a heavy storm in Brescia."

The broadcast came to an end. The headwaiter carried his radio set back into the restaurant. Lillian leaned back. For a moment, a picture seemed to hang almost visibly in the still golden afternoon light of the terrace, between the subdued clink of ice in the glasses and the rattle of plates which, heaped one upon the other, kept score of the drinks each patron had ordered. The picture was colorless, transparent as are some jellyfish in water, so that she could still see behind it the chairs and tables: the scene of a gray market place, abstract noise which had lost its individual tone, and the ghosts of cars, one behind the other, with two tiny sparks of life in them whose sole aim was to risk itself. "It's raining in Brescia," she said. "Just where is Brescia, anyway?"

"Between Milan and Verona," de Peystre replied. "Would you care to have dinner with me tonight?"

The garlands hung down in shreds, battered by the rain. The flags slapped wetly against the flagpoles. The storm raged as though a second cavalcade with invisible automobiles were roaring through the clouds. The artificial and the natural thunder alternated; the ascending roar of a car was answered by the lightning and thunder from above. "Five minutes to go," Torriani said.

Clerfayt crouched behind the wheel. He was not very tense. He knew that he had no chance to win; but in a race there were always surprises, and in a long race freaks of fortune.

He thought of Lillian and the Targa Florio. That time, he had forgotten her, then hated her, because the remembrance of her had come to him suddenly during the race and had distracted him. Then the race had been more important than she. Now it was different. He was no longer sure of her, and for that reason thought of her all the time. The devil knows whether she is still in Paris, he thought. He had talked with her over the telephone only that morning; but in this racket the morning seemed infinitely far away. "Did you telegraph Lillian?" he asked.

"Yes," Torriani replied. "Two minutes to go."

Clerfayt nodded. The car rolled slowly from the market place toward the Viale Venezia and stopped. There was no longer anyone standing in front of it. The man with the stop watch would be, from now on and for more than half a day and half a night, the most important thing in the world for them. He ought to be, Clerfayt thought, but he isn't any longer. I think about Lillian too much. I ought to let Torriani drive, but now it's too late. "Twenty seconds," Torriani said.

"Thank God. Let's go, damn it all!"

The starter waved, and the car roared away. Shouts flew after it. "Clerfayt has started," the announcer cried, "with Torriani as mechanic."

Lillian returned to the hotel. She felt that she had fever, but decided to ignore it. She had it often, sometimes only two degrees, sometimes more, and she knew what it meant. She looked into the mirror. At least I don't look so done in at night, she thought, and smiled to herself at the trick she was employing again: to change the fever from an enemy to a nocturnal friend which lent a glow to her eyes and the animation of high temperature to her face.

When she stepped back from the mirror, she saw the

two telegrams on the table. Clerfayt, she thought, with a heartbeat of panic. But what could have possibly happened so quickly? She waited a while, staring at the small, folded and pasted papers. Cautiously, then, she picked up the first and opened it. It was from Clerfayt: "We're starting in fifteen minutes. Deluge. Don't fly away, flamingo."

She laid it aside. After a while, she opened the second. She was even more afraid than before that it might be from the management of the race, reporting an accident, but it was also from Clerfayt. Why is he doing this? she thought. Doesn't he know that a telegram at such a time is frightening?

She opened her wardrobe to choose a dress for the evening. There was a knock at the door. It was the porter. "Here is the radio, Mademoiselle. You can reach Rome and Milan easily with it."

He plugged it in. "And here is another telegram."

How many more will he send? she thought. He might just as well post a detective in the next room. She picked out a dress. It was the one she had worn in Venice. It had been cleaned and all the stains were gone. She had decided that it was her lucky dress, and wore it like a mascot. Now she held it firmly in her hand while she opened the last telegram. It was not from Clerfayt, but contained wishes of good luck for him. How was it that it had come to her? She looked at the signature once more in the deep dusk. Hollmann. She stared at it. She deciphered the point of origin. The telegram had been sent from the Bella Vista Sanatorium.

She laid the slip of paper on the table with great care. Today is the day for ghosts, she thought, sitting down on her bed. Clerfayt, sitting there in the radio set, waiting to fill the room with his roaring motor—and now this telegram which makes silent faces stare in through the window.

It was the first word she had had from the sanatorium. She had never written, had no impulse to. She had wanted to leave it completely behind her forever.

She had been so certain she would never return that the parting had been like death.

For a long while, she sat still. Then she turned the knobs of the radio; it was time for the news broadcasts. Rome rushed in with a surge of noise, with names, known and unknown villages and cities, Mantua, Ravenna, Bologna, Aquila, with hours and minutes, with the over-wrought voice of the announcer who spoke of minutes gained as if they were the Holy Grail, who described defective water pumps, frozen pistons, and broken gaso-line lines as if they were cosmic disasters, who hurled the race with time into the dimness of the room, the dashing for seconds, not for seconds of life, but in order to arrive, after hurtling along a wet road with ten thousand curves and a screaming mob, at a particular spot a few hundred yards sooner, only to leave it again im-mediately; a wild dash as if the atom bomb were behind one.

Why don't I understand it? Lillian thought. Why do I feel nothing of the thrill of millions of people who are lining the highways of Italy to watch this? Shouldn't I feel it more strongly? Isn't it something like my own life? A race to gather in as much as I possibly can? A pursuit of a phantom that speeds along in front of me like the artificial rabbit in front of the pack in a greyhound race?

"Florence," the voice on the radio announced trium-phantly, and began listing times, names, and brands of car, average speeds and maximum speeds. And then, bursting with pride: "If the leading cars keep up this pace, they'll be back in Brescia again in a new record time."

She started. In Brescia, she thought. Back in the little provincial town of garages, cafés, and shops, back where they had started. They play with death, they roar through the night, they endure the terrible weariness of early morning, with stiff, masklike faces encrusted with filth; they race on, on, as though all the glory of the world were at stake—and all this only to return again to the little provincial town from which they had come! From Brescia to Brescia!

She switched off the radio and went to the window. From Brescia to Brescia! Was there any more vivid symbol of meaninglessness? Had life given them such miraculous gifts as healthy lungs and hearts, incomprehensible chemical factories like liver and kidneys, a soft white mass inside the skull which was more fantastic than all the stellar systems—had life given them all that so that they could risk it and, if they had luck, go from Brescia to Brescia? What horrible folly!

She looked out at the endless chain of cars gliding along the quay. Was not every one of them driving from Brescia to Brescia? From Toulouse to Toulouse? From self-complacency to self-complacency? And from self-deception to self-deception? Me, too? she thought. Yes, probably me, too. In spite of everything. But where is my Brescia? She looked at Hollmann's telegram. Where it came from there was no Brescia. Neither a Brescia nor a Toulouse. At that place there was only the quiet, inexorable struggle for breath on the eternal border. There was no self-complacency and no self-deception there.

She turned away from the window and for a while walked about the room. She felt her dresses, and it suddenly seemed to her that ashes were trickling through them and in them. She picked up her brushes and combs and laid them down again, without knowing that she had held them in her hand. Like a dim shadow, there entered through the window a premonition that she had made a terrible mistake, a mistake that had been unavoidable and that was now irrevocable.

She began dressing for the evening. The telegram still lay on the table. In the light of the lamps, it seemed to be brighter than any other object in the room. She glanced at it from time to time. She heard the plashing of the river, and smelled the water and the foliage of the trees. What are they doing up there now? she thought, and began for the first time to remember. What were they doing, while Clerfayt raced behind the glare of his headlights over the dark roads outside Florence? She hesitated a while longer; then she picked up the telephone and gave the number of the sanatorium.

"Siena," Torriani shouted. "Gas up and change tires."

"When?"

"In five minutes. This damned rain!"

Clerfayt made a face. "We're not the only ones who have it. The others, too. Watch out for the pit."

The houses were coming closer together. The headlights wrenched them out of the pattering darkness. Everywhere people stood in raincoats and beneath umbrellas. White walls appeared, people who spurted away like splashes of water, umbrellas that swayed like mushrooms in the storm, the car skidding— "The pit!" Torriani screamed.

The brakes caught; the car shook itself and stood still. "Gas, water, tires, get going!" Clerfayt shouted into the echoing resonance of the motor. His ears were ringing as if they were empty old halls in a thunderstorm.

Someone gave him a glass of lemonade and a new pair of glasses. "What's our position?" Torriani asked.

"Fine! Eighteenth!"

"Lousy," Clerfayt said. "Where are the others?"

"Monti in fourth, Sacchetti in sixth, Frigerio in seventh place. Conti has dropped out."

"Who's first?"

"Marchetti, with a ten-minute lead. Then Lotti, three minutes behind him."

"And what about us?"

"Nineteen minutes behind. Don't worry—the first team in Rome never wins the race. Everybody knows that."

The manager appeared at their side. "The Lord has fixed it that way," he declared. "Mother of God, sweet blood of Christ, you know it, too!" he prayed. "Punish Marchetti because he was first. A little gas-pump breakdown no more. And one for Lotti, too. Holy Archangels, protect . . ."

"How did you get here?" Clerfayt asked. "Why aren't you still in Brescia?"

"Ready!" the mechanics shouted.

"Let's go!"

"I'm taking planes—" the manager began, but his words were snatched out of his mouth by the roar of the motor. The car raced away, scattering people to both sides, and the ribbon of the road to which they were glued again began its endless windings. What would Lillian be doing now? Clerfayt thought. He didn't know why he had expected a telegram at the pit. But telegrams could be delayed; perhaps it would be at the next pit. Then the night was there again, the lights, people whose shouts he could not hear because of the motor's roar, so that they seemed like characters in a silent movie, and finally there was only the road, this snake which seemed to run around the earth, and the mystical beast that screamed under the hood of the car.

XVIII

The connection came very quickly. Lillian had not expected it for hours, because she knew the French telephone system, and also because she had the feeling that the sanatorium was terribly far away, as if it were on another planet.

"Bella Vista Sanatorium."

Lillian was not sure whether she recognized the voice. It might still be Miss Heger. "Mr. Hollmann, please," she said, and became aware of how her heart was pounding.

"One moment, please."

She listened to the almost inaudible hum of the wires. Apparently, they were having to look for Hollmann. She glanced at the clock; it was after dinner at the sanatorium. Why am I so agitated? she thought. As if I were summoning a dead man.

"Hollmann. Who is speaking, please?"

She started in alarm—the voice was so clear. "Lillian," she whispered.

"Who?"

"Lillian Dunkerque."

There was a moment's silence. Then Hollmann said incredulously: "Lillian! Where are you?"

"In Paris. Your telegram for Clerfayt came to me. It was forwarded by his hotel. I opened it by mistake."

"You're not in Brescia?"

"No," she said, feeling a slight stab of pain. "I'm not in Brescia."

"Didn't Clerfayt want you to come?"

"No, he didn't want me to."

"I'm hanging over the radio," Hollmann said. "I suppose you are, too, of course."

"Yes, Hollmann."

"He's driving magnificently. The race is still wide open. I know him; he's waiting his chance, letting the others drive their machines into the ground. He won't put on the pressure till midnight, maybe even later—no, around midnight, I think. It's a race against the clock—you know that. The wearing part of it is that he never knows himself what his position is; he only finds out when he stops for gas, and what he hears then may be already outdated. It's a race with uncertainty—you understand me, Lillian?"

"Yes, Hollmann. A race with uncertainty. How are you?"

"Fine. The speeds are fantastic. Averages of seventy-five miles an hour and more. And many of the big motors are only now reaching the long straight stretches. Average speeds, Lillian, not maximum speeds!"

"Yes, Hollmann. You're feeling well?"

"Very well. Much better, Lillian. What station are you listening to? Switch on Rome; Rome is closer to the race than Milan, now."

"I have Rome. I'm glad to hear you're better."

"How about you, Lillian?"

"Very well. And—"

"It's probably the right thing that you aren't in Brescia —it's raining like mad there. Though I wouldn't have been able to stand it; I would have been right out there at the start. How are you feeling, Lillian?"

She knew what he meant. "Fine," she said. "How is everything up there?"

"Same as ever. Little has changed in these few months."

Few months, she thought. Had it not been years? "And

how is—" She hesitated, but suddenly she knew that she had only telephoned to ask this question. "How is Boris?"

"Who?"

"Boris."

"Boris Volkov? We don't see much of him. He no longer comes to the sanatorium. I think he's all right."

"Have you seen him at all?"

"Yes, of course. Though it's two or three weeks ago. He was walking his dog, the police dog; you know it, of course. We didn't talk. How is it down below? As you imagined?"

"Pretty much," Lillian said. "I suppose it always depends on what you make of it. Is there still snow on the mountain?"

Hollmann laughed. "Not any more. There are all those crocuses and things. Lillian—" He paused. "I'm going to be out of here in a few weeks. It isn't a swindle. The Dalai Lama has told me."

Lillian did not believe it. She had been told the same thing years ago. "That's wonderful," she said. "Then we'll see each other here. Shall I tell Clerfayt?"

"Better not, yet; I'm superstitious about those things. There—the latest news is coming in. You'll have to listen, too! So long, Lillian."

"So long, Hollmann."

She had wanted to add something about Boris, but she did not do so. For a while, she looked at the black receiver; then she carefully placed it on the hook and gave way to her thoughts without taking account of them, until she became aware that she was crying. Like the rain in Brescia, she thought, and got up. How foolish I am! One has to pay for everything. Did I think I had already done so?

"The word 'happiness' has acquired an excessive importance in our times," the Vicomte de Peystre said. "There have been centuries in which it was unknown. It was not a part of life. Read Chinese literature of the best epochs, or Indian or Greek classics. Instead of emotion, in which the word 'happiness' has its root, people sought an unperturbed, elevated sense of life. Where that is lost, the crises begin, the muddles of emotion, romanticism, and the search for happiness comes in as a foolish substitute."

Lillian laughed. "Isn't the other also a substitute?"

"One worthier of human dignity," de Peystre replied.

"Is the one impossible without the other?"

He looked at her thoughtfully. "Almost always. In your case not, I think. That fascinates me. You have both. It presupposes a state of such pure despair that names for it, and for the despair also, are already matters of indifference. It is far beyond anarchy—on the polar plateau of solitude without the slightest grief. In you, I think, grief and rebellion have long ago mutually annihilated one another. Consequently, little things have the same value as big things. Details begin to take on radiance."

"The eighteenth century is rising," Lillian said with semi-mockery. "Didn't you say you were its last scion?"

"Its last admirer."

"It seems to me people talked a lot about happiness in that century."

"Only in its bad periods. And even then, although people talked and raved about it, they were practical in the grand sense."

"Until the guillotine came."

"Until the guillotine came and the right to happiness was invented," de Peystre agreed. "The guillotine always comes."

Lillian finished her glass. "Isn't all this a long prelude to the proposition you want to make to me: to become your mistress?"

De Peystre remained impassive. "Call it that if you like. It is a proposal to give you the framework you require. Or, rather, the framework which to my mind would suit you."

"Like the setting for a stone."

"Like the setting for a very precious stone."

"A stone of pure despair?"

"Of blue-white loneliness. And blue-white courage, Mademoiselle. My compliments! And forgive my persistence. Diamonds with such fire are rare." De Peystre set down his glass. "Would you like to hear the latest reports on the race in Italy now?"

"Here? In Maxim's?"

"Why not? Albert, the master of this establishment, could gratify far more complicated wishes. If he cared to. And for you he would care to. I am sure he would; Albert has excellent eyesight."

The orchestra began, in keeping with tradition, to play melodies from *The Merry Window*. The waiter cleared the table. Albert cat-footed past them and gave instructions for a bottle of cognac to be brought to their table. It was neither dusty nor ornamented with the emblem of Napoleon; its only distinction was a small, handwritten label. "I told you he has excellent eyesight," de Peystre remarked. "This is for you to try. Naturally, we must first warm it with our hands, inhale the bouquet and discuss it a little. The usual ceremonies. We are being watched."

Lillian took her glass and without warming it in her hand or inhaling the fragrance, drank the liquor down. De Peystre laughed. Albert in his corner dispatched the flicker of a confirming smile from an impassive face. The smile was followed a few minutes later by a waiter with a small bottle of *framboise*. He set smaller glasses on the table and poured carefully. "Aged raspberry liqueur," de Peystre said reverently.

What would he do, Lillian thought, if I were to throw the raspberry liqueur into his overcultivated face? Probably he would understand that, too, and make a courtly phrase about it. She did not despise him; on the contrary, she found him as pleasant as a mild sedative, and had listened to him with interest. For her, he embodied the other side of existence. He had sublimated the anxiety of life into a cult of esthetic cynicism and tried to convert dangerous mountain paths into park walks. It changed nothing. When had she heard something like this before? Of course, with Levalli in Sicily. You needed money and little heart to live that way. You did not drive from Brescia to Brescia. You stayed in Brescia and told yourself that you were in Versailles early in the eighteenth century.

"I must go," she said.

"How often you say that," de Peystre declared. "It makes you irresistible. Is it your favorite phrase?"

She looked at him. "If you only knew how I would like to stay," she said slowly after a pause. "Even alone, if I must—but only to stay. To stay. Everything else is a lie, and the courage of fear."

She had him drop her off at her hotel. The night porter, in a state of high excitement, came forward to meet her. "Monsieur Clerfayt is in twelfth place! He's overtaken six competitors. The announcer says he is a marvelous night driver."

"He is, I know."

"A glass of champagne to celebrate?"

"One should never celebrate too soon. Racing drivers are superstitious."

Lillian sat in the small, dark lobby for a while. "If he goes on like this, he'll be in Brescia again early tomorrow morning," the night porter said.

"That, too," Lillian replied, and stood up. "I'm going to have a last cup of coffee on the boulevard Saint-Michel."

She was already treated there as a regular patron. The waiter watched over her. Gérard waited for her, and a group of students had formed a kind of guard of honor for her.

Gérard had the excellent trait of always being hungry. That gave her time to think while he gobbled. She loved looking out on the street where life drifted by with hot and comfortless eyes. It was difficult to believe that every single person possessed an immortal soul, when you saw this endless stream. Where would they all be going later? Did their souls disintegrate like their bodies? Or did they continue to drift about, haunting the boulevard, on these evenings of desire, pleasure, and despair, decomposing ghosts full of silent anxiety and the plea to be allowed to stay what they were and not to become soul fertilizer for others who at this moment were being thoughtlessly begotten behind the thousands of windows?

Gérard stopped eating at last. He had finished with an excellent Pont l'Evêque cheese. "How the crude animal process of ingesting nourishment in the form of roasted pieces of animal flesh and half-fermented milk products stimulates the poetic qualities of the soul!" he declared. "It is eternally astonishing and consoling!"

Lillian laughed. "From Brescia to Brescia," she said.

"I do not understand this clear and simple sentence; but it seems to be relatively unassailable." Gérard drank down his coffee. "It is even profound. From Brescia to Brescia! I shall use that as the title for my next volume of poems. You are taciturn tonight."

"Not taciturn. Only without words."

"From Brescia to Brescia?"

"Something like that."

Gérard nodded. He sniffed his cognac. "It is a phrase that grows better by the minute. It leads to a plethora of platitudes which are all as deep as mine shafts."

"I know another one," Lillian said. "Everything is the same."

Gérard set down his glass. "With or without imagination?"

"With all imagination."

He nodded, relieved. "For a moment, I was afraid that you were depressed and about to trot out some deadly laundry-room maxim."

"On the contrary—an extremely heart-warming insight."

"The details are the same as the whole; this wine bottle is just as enchanting as a Raphael; the pimply girl student at that table has something in her of Medea and Aspasia. Life without perspective: everything is equally important and unimportant; everything is foreground, everything God. Is that what you mean?" Gérard asked.

Lillian smiled. "Approximately. How fast you are!"

"Too fast." Gérard made a bitter grimace. "Too fast to experience it." He took a large swallow of cognac. "If you have really felt that," he went on lecturing, "there remain only three things for you—"

"As many as that!"

"To enter a Buddhist monastery, go crazy, or die—most suitably by suicide. Self-extinction is, as you know, one of the three ways in which we are superior to animals."

Lillian did not ask what the other two were. "There is a fourth possibility," she said. "But there is nothing particularly superior about it. Our trouble is that we think we have a claim upon life. We have none. When we know that, a good deal of bitter honey suddenly becomes sweet."

Gérard silently saluted her, with both hands held high. "He who expects nothing is never disappointed," he declared. "The ultimate in minor truths."

"For tonight," Lillian replied, laughing. "The loveliest truths die overnight. How many corpses have to be swept up every morning! And what strange things one sometimes talks about after sundown. I must go now."

"You always say that, but you always come back."

She looked at him in gratitude. "I do, don't I? It's odd that only poets know that."

"They, too, don't really know it. They only hope so."

She walked along the quai des Grands-Augustins as far as the quai Voltaire, and then back through the narrow streets behind the quays. She was not afraid of walking alone at night; she had no fear of people.

On the rue de Seine she saw someone lying on the ground. She thought it was a drunken woman, and walked past. But something in the attitude of the woman, who lay sprawled half on the sidewalk, half in the street, compelled her to return. She wished at least to pull her up to the sidewalk so that she would be safe from cars.

The woman was dead. Her eyes were open and staring at Lillian in the feeble light of the street lamp. As she raised the shoulders, the head dropped back with a dull thud against the pavement. Lillian uttered a smothered cry; for a moment, she had thought she had injured the woman. She looked into the face; it was infinitely empty. In perplexity, she looked around; she did not know what to do. A few windows were lighted, and from behind a wide one which was curtained, she heard music. Between the houses, the sky looked very high, and was starless. Someone called out from somewhere. Then Lillian saw a man approaching. She hesitated a moment; then walked rapidly toward him. "Gérard," she said, astonished and profoundly relieved. "How did you know—?"

"I followed you. That is the privilege of poets on spring evenings."

Lillian shook her head. "Come, a dead woman is lying there."

"She is probably drunk. Unconscious."

"No, she's dead. I know what the dead look like." She felt Gérard's resistance. "What's the matter?"

"I don't want to have anything to do with it," the poet of death said.

"We can't leave her lying like this."

"Why not? She's dead. What happens next is the concern of the police alone. I don't want to be mixed up in it. You oughtn't to either. They'll think we did it to her. Come!"

He tugged at Lillian's arm. She stood still and gazed into the face that no longer knew anything, and that knew everything that she herself did not know. The dead woman looked frightfully deserted. She had one leg drawn up under her checked skirt. Lillian saw her stockings, her brown shoes, the half-clenched hands, the short, dark hair, and a thin chain around her neck.

"Come!" Gérard whispered. "If we stay, there'll be nothing but trouble. It's no joke being involved with the police. We can telephone from somewhere. That's good enough."

She let herself be drawn away. She knew that Gérard was both right and wrong. He walked so fast that she could scarcely keep up with him. When they reached the better-lighted quay, she saw that he was very pale. "It's one thing to talk about it and something else again to face it, isn't it?" she said with bitter mockery. "Where can we telephone? At my hotel?"

"The night porter will overhear us."

"I can send him away on an errand."

"All right, then."

The porter came forward beaming. "He's in tenth place now, but he'll—"

He saw Gérard, and lapsed into reproachful silence. "A friend of Clerfayt's," Lillian said. "You're right, we must celebrate now. Would you bring us a bottle of champagne? Where is the telephone?"

The porter pointed to his desk, and went out. "Now," Lillian said.

Gérard was already looking in the telephone book. "It's an old book."

"The police don't change their numbers."

In tenth place, Lillian thought. He is still driving and driving, from Brescia to Brescia.

She heard Gérard speaking. The porter came back with glasses and the bottle. The cork popped like a shot; the porter had shaken the bottle too joyfully. Gérard started and stopped speaking. "No, no shot," he then said into the telephone, and hung up.

"I think you need a drink," Lillian said. "At the moment, it was all I could think of: to order the champagne; the porter has been waiting all evening for it. I suppose it isn't a sacrilege."

Gérard shook his head, and drank greedily. He looked over at the telephone. Lillian saw that he was afraid the police would be tracing the call. "They thought someone had fired a shot," he said. "It was the cork. Why is tragedy often so frightfully comic?"

Lillian handed the bottle to him to refill their glasses. "I must go," he said.

"This time it's you who must go. Good night, Gérard."

He looked at the bottle. "If you don't want any more, can I take it along?"

"No, Gérard. You can stay and help drink it, or make your safe retreat. It's a choice."

He took himself off, disappearing through the door with rapid strides. Now the night comes, alone, she thought, and gave the bottle to the porter. "You drink it. Is the radio still upstairs?"

"Of course, Mademoiselle."

She ascended. The radio's chrome and glass glistened

in the darkness. She turned on the light and waited for a while at the window to see whether a police car would pass. She saw nothing. Slowly, she undressed. She considered whether she ought to hang her allies, the dresses, around her overnight; but she did not do so. The time for those aids was past, she thought. However, she left the lamp on and took sleeping tablets.

She awoke as though she were being hurled out of something. Through the curtains, the sun's rays stabbed at the wan electric bulb. The telephone shrilled. The police, she thought, and lifted the receiver.

It was Clerfayt. "We've just arrived in Brescia!"

"Brescia!" She shook off the remnants of a dream already flying into oblivion. "You've come through!"

"In sixth place." Clerfayt laughed.

"Sixth. That's wonderful."

"It doesn't mean a thing. I'm coming back tomorrow. I'll get some sleep now. Torriani is already fast asleep in the chair next to me."

"Yes, sleep. It's good you called."

"Will you go to the Riviera with me?"

"Yes, darling."

"Wait for me."

"Yes, darling."

"Don't go away before I come."

Where would I go? she thought. To Brescia? "I'll wait for you," she said.

After noon, she walked along the rue de Seine. The street was the same as always. She searched the columns of the newspapers. She found nothing. That a human being had died was too small a matter for a newspaper item.

XIX

"I bought the house long before the war," Clerfayt said. "In those days, you could buy half the Riviera for a song. I've never spent any time here, only bought a few things and stored them in the place. As you see, it's built in the most ghastly style, but the stucco ornamentation could be knocked off and the whole place modernized and decently furnished."

Lillian laughed. "Why? Do you really want to live here?"

"Why not?"

She looked out of the dim room into the darkening garden with its gravel paths. The sea could not be seen from here. "Perhaps when you're sixty-five," she said. "No sooner. After a hard-working life in Toulouse. Then you can lead the life of a good French pensioner here, with an occasional dinner in the Hôtel de Paris and an outing to the casino on Sundays."

"The garden is big and there's a lot could be done with the house," Clerfayt replied, undeterred. "I have the money for it. The Mille Miglia proved quite remunerative. I hope I'll add to the building fund with the race in

Monaco. Why does it seem to you so impossible to live here? Where else would you like to live?"

"I don't know, Clerfayt."

"Come now, people know such things. At least they have a general idea."

"I don't," Lillian said, with a touch of panic. "Nowhere. To want to live anywhere is always to want to die somewhere."

"The climate here in the winter is a hundred times better than in Paris."

"In the winter!" Lillian picked up the words as if she were saying Sirius and Styx and Eternity.

"Winter comes faster than you think. We would have to start the remodeling soon if we wanted to be finished by winter."

Lillian looked around the gloomy room. I don't want to be a captive here, she thought. "Don't you have to work in Toulouse in the winter?" she asked.

"I can do that also. I only want to settle you somewhere during the winter where the climate is best for you."

What do I care about the climate, Lillian thought. In desperation, she said: "The sanatorium has the best climate."

Clerfayt looked at her. "Ought you to go back there?"

She did not answer.

"Would you like to go back there?" he asked.

"What do you want me to answer to that? Am I not here?"

"Have you asked a doctor? Have you ever asked a doctor down here?"

"This is nothing I need to ask a doctor about."

He looked mistrustfully at her. "We'll go together and see a doctor. I'll find the best doctor in France for you, and we'll ask him."

Lillian did not reply. So we're going through that, too! she thought. Earlier, Clerfayt had asked her every so often whether she had been going to the doctor, but he had been satisfied with her assurances that she was. This was different. It fitted right in with the house, the future, love, solicitude, with all the fine names for things she had to brush aside because they only made dying harder. The next logical step would be for him to try to pack her off to a hospital.

A bird began singing shrilly outside the window. "Let's go out," Clerfayt said suddenly. "This fancy chandelier gives the damnedest light. But all that can be changed."

Outside, the evening leaned against the stucco house walls, with their fake Moorish ornamentation. Lillian took a deep breath. She felt as if she had escaped. "The truth is that you don't want to live with me, Lillian," Clerfayt said. "I know it."

"But I am living with you," she replied miserably.

"You're living with me like someone who won't be there tomorrow."

"Didn't you want it that way?"

"Maybe—but now I don't want it that way any longer. Have you ever wanted to live differently with me?"

"No," she said softly. "But not with anyone else either, Clerfayt."

"Why not?"

She remained defiantly silent. Why is he asking these foolish questions? she thought. "We've talked about it often enough," she said at last. "Why go into it again?"

"A relationship can change. Is love something so contemptible?"

She shook her head.

He looked at her. "Never in my life have I really wanted anything very intensely for myself. Now I do. I want you."

"But you have me."

"Not enough."

He wants to tie me down and lock me in, she thought, and he is proud of it and calls it marriage and tenderness and love, and refuses to understand that the thing he is proud of is what is driving me away. Full of hatred, she looked at the little villa with its gravel paths. Did I run away from the mountains to end up here? she thought. Here or in Toulouse or in Brescia? What has become of the adventure? What has become of Clerfayt? What has changed him? Why don't we laugh it off? What else is there left for me to do?

"We can at least try it," Clerfayt said. "If it doesn't work out, we'll sell the house."

I have no more time to try things out, Lillian thought. And I have no time for experiments with domestic bliss. I must leave. I also have no more time for such conversations. I've known all that up at the sanatorium, and I fled from there, too.

She grew calm. She still did not know what she would do, but that she could do something made everything less unbearable. She did not fear unhappiness; she had lived too long with it and by it. She also did not fear happiness, as did so many of those who thought they were seeking it. What she feared was the prison of mediocrity.

That evening there were fireworks over the sea. The night was clear and a great vault, and since the horizon was formed by sky and sea, the rockets rose and fell as if they were being shot off into infinity and plunging each time beyond the earth into a space that was no longer space because it seemed to have no limits. Lillian recalled the last fireworks she had seen, at the ski lodge. That had been the evening before her departure. Was she not again on the eve of a departure? The decisions of my life seem to take place amid fireworks, she thought. But had not everything that had happened been essentially that—fireworks that were now beginning to fade and turn to ashes and cinders? She looked around. Not yet, she thought anxiously, not yet, not now! Was there not always, before the end, at least one last great flare in which everything was squandered on a grand finale?

"We haven't gambled yet," Clerfayt said. "Have you ever done that? At the casino, I mean."

"No."

"Then you have to see what it's like. It's kind of fun. Besides, the innocent always bring luck. Shall we drive over? Or are you tired? It's already two o'clock."

"Early in the morning! Who would be tired then?"

They drove slowly through the sparkling night. "At last it's warm," Lillian said, leaning back.

"We can stay here until it's summer in Paris also."

She leaned against him. "Why don't people live forever, Clerfayt? Without death?"

He put his arm around her shoulders. "Yes, why not? Why do we grow old? Why can't we all live as if we were thirty, until we're eighty, and then die quickly?"

She laughed softly. "I'm far from thirty yet."

"That's true," Clerfayt said. Somewhat taken aback, he released her. "I keep forgetting that. I have the feeling that you've grown at least five years older in three months —you've changed so much. You've grown five years more beautiful. And ten years more dangerous."

They played in the big salons first; then, when these emptied, in the smaller ones, where the stakes were higher. Clerfayt began to win. He played *trente et quarante* at first, and then went to a roulette table where the maximum was higher than at the others. "Keep standing behind me," he said to Lillian. "You're bringing me luck."

Clerfayt played the twelves, the twenty-twos, and the nines. He gradually lost until he had only enough chips to bet the maximum once more. He placed it on red. Red won. He took in half the winnings and left the rest on red. Red won again. He let the maximum stand. Red won twice more. The chips were heaped up in front of Clerfayt now. Other players in the salon began to watch. The table was now crowded. Lillian spotted Prince Fiola, her dancing partner at the party in Sicily. He, too, came over to the table. He smiled at her and bet on black. Red won again. At the next turn, black was covered with maximum bets from all sides, and players thronged around the table three rows deep. Almost all were betting against Clerfayt. Only a withered old woman in an evening dress of blue chiffon continued to join him in betting on red.

The room was very quiet. The ball rattled. The old woman sneezed. Red won again.

Fiola made a sign to Clarfayt to quit; the series had to

stop, after all. Clerfayt shook his head and again left the maximum on red.

"Il est fou," someone behind Lillian said.

At the last moment, the old woman, who had already taken in her winnings, pushed everything back on to red. In the silence, she could be heard breathing violently, and then holding her breath. She was trying to suppress another fit of sneezing. Her hand lay like a claw on the green cloth. Beside it, she had a small green tortoise as a mascot.

Red once again. The old woman's sneeze exploded. *"Formidable,"* the woman behind Lillian said. "Who is that?"

There was scarcely any betting on numbers now. The rumor of the unprecedented run on red had spread through the casino. A battery of large chips accumulated in heaped-up rows on black. Red had come seven times; the color had to change. Clerfayt was the only one to stick to red. In her excitement, the old woman at the last moment bet the tortoise. Before she could change it, a whisper ran through the hall; red had won again.

"Madame, we cannot duplicate your tortoise," the croupier said, and pushed the creature with its wise, ancient head back across the table to its owner.

"But what about my winnings!" the old crone croaked.

"Excuse me, Madame, but you neither placed your bet nor announced it."

"But you could see I wanted to bet. That's good enough."

"You must either bet or announce your bet before the ball falls."

The old woman threw an embittered glance around. *"Faites vos jeux,"* the croupier called mechanically.

Clerfayt again bet on red. Irritably, the old woman placed her stake on black. All the others likewise chose black. Fiola bet on the six and black.

Red came again. Now Clerfayt took in his winnings. He pushed a number of chips over to the croupier and stood up. "You really have brought me luck," he said to Lillian, and lingered until the ball lay still again. Black had won. "You see," he said. "Sometimes there is something like a sixth sense."

She smiled. If only you had it in matters of love! she thought.

Fiola came over to them. "Congratulations. Quitting at the right time is the great art in life." He turned to Lillian. "Don't you agree?"

"I don't know. I've had no practice in it."

He laughed. "I don't believe that. You vanished from Sicily and left behind a good deal of confusion in a good many minds. You arrived in Rome and were gone like a flash of lightning. In Venice, too, nobody could find you, I've been told."

They went to the bar to celebrate Clerfayt's luck. "With what I've won, I think I have enough to have the house redone right now," he exulted.

"You can lose it again tomorrow."

"Would you like that?" he asked mistrustfully.

"Of course not."

"I'm through playing," he declared. "We'll keep it all. I'll even have a swimming pool built into the garden for you."

"I don't need one. I don't swim—you know that perfectly well."

He threw her a quick glance. "I know. Are you tired?"

"No."

"A series of nine reds is almost a miracle," Fiola said. "Only once in my life have I seen a longer series. Black twelve times. That was before the war. In those days, there were tables with a much higher maximum than they have in the *cercle privé* today. The man who played the series broke the bank. He bet on black and then on thirteen. The thirteen came six times in twelve coups. It was a sensation. Everybody was betting with him, so that he ruined the bank twice in a night. The man was a Russian. What was his name again? Volkov, or something like that. Yes, that was it, Volkov."

"Volkov?" Lillian asked incredulously. "Not Boris Volkov?"

"Right, Boris Volkov! Did you know him?"

Lillian shook her head. Not that way, she thought. She saw that Clerfayt was observing her.

"I wish I knew what became of the fellow," Fiola said. "There was a man who created a sensation here! One of the last gamblers in the great tradition. A first-class marksman besides. He was here with Maria Andersen at the time. You may have heard of her. One of the most beautiful women in Europe. She was killed in an air raid in Milan." He turned to Clerfayt. "Haven't you ever heard of Volkov?"

"Never," Clerfayt said.

"Strange! He drove in a few races at the time, too. As an amateur of course. I've rarely seen anyone who could stand so much alcohol. Probably he wrecked himself with it; he certainly gave the impression that he was out to do that."

Clerfayt's expression had darkened. He signaled to the waiter to bring another bottle. "Are you going to play any more tonight?" Fiola asked him. "You'd better not."

"Why not? Series come in series. Who knows, there may be another run of black thirteen times."

"A great mistake to go back to the table," Fiola said to Lillian. "That's a law as old as the world."

Lillian looked in Clerfayt's direction. This time he had not asked her to come along to bring him luck, and she knew why. How childish he is, she thought tenderly. And how blind in his jealousy! Has he forgotten that it is never the other man, but always and only oneself, who does the wrecking?

"On the other hand, you ought to play," Fiola said. "This is your first time here. Would you like to play for me? Come!"

They went to another table. Fiola began placing stakes, and after a few minutes, Lillian, too, changed a few bills of her own into jettons. She cautiously staked small sums; money was more than a possession to her, it was a fragment of life. She did not ever want to be dependent upon her uncle's grudging help.

She began to win almost at once. "That's the child's

hand," said Fiola, who was losing. "This is your night! Do you mind if I go along with you?"

"You'll regret it."

"Not in gambling. Just follow your hunches."

For a time, Lillian placed her bets on red and black, then the second *douzaine,* and finally on numbers. Twice she won on zero. "Nothingness loves you," Fiola said.

The old woman with the tortoise appeared. She sat down opposite Lillian, with an angry face. Between stakes, she whispered with the turtle. On her yellow hand a diamond of great beauty rotated loosely. Her neck was as wrinkled as that of the tortoise, and Lillian saw the resemblance between the two. They also had the same kind of almost lidless eyes which showed no whites.

Lillian was now playing alternately black and thirteen. When she looked up after a while, she saw that Clerfayt was standing across the table, watching her play. Without thinking of it, she had followed the same betting pattern as Boris Volkov, and she saw that Clerfayt had noticed it. Rebelliously, she continued to bet on thirteen. After six coups it came. "Enough," she said, and raked her jettons into her bag. She had won, but did not know how much.

"Do you want to go on soon?" Fiola asked. "This is your night—that's plain. It will never come again!"

"The night is over. If we were to draw the curtains at the windows, the pale morning would turn us all into ghosts. Good night, Fiola. Go on playing."

When she stepped out with Clerfayt, she saw the Riviera as it must have been before the tourists had discovered it. The sky gleamed a brassy yellow and blue while it waited for the sun; the sea was white on the horizon, and translucent as aquamarine. A few fishing boats stood out at sea with yellow and red sails. The beach was quiet; no cars were moving on any of the streets. The wind smelled of lobster and of sea.

Lillian did not understand where the quarrel had blown up from. She heard Clerfayt, but it was some time before she understood what he was so worked up about. "What can I do?" she heard him saying. "I have to fight against a shadow, against someone I can't grasp, someone who isn't here and is therefore all the more here, who is trans-figured because he isn't here, who has the great advantage of being absent, which gives him a thousand points to his credit, while I'm here and you see me as I am, as I am now, beside myself, unjust if you will, petty, silly, and against all that, stands the glorious ideal image which can't do anything wrong because it does nothing, and I can't do anything against the memory of someone dead!"

Exhausted, Lillian leaned her head back.

"Isn't it so?" Clerfayt demanded, pounding his fist on the steering wheel. "Tell me whether it isn't so! I've sensed it all along. That's why you've been evading me. That's the reason you won't marry me. You want to go back. That's it! You want to go back!"

Lillian raised her head. What was this? She looked at Clerfayt. "What's that you're saying?"

"Isn't it true? Haven't you been thinking that, even now?"

"I was only thinking how awfully stupid the cleverest people can be. Don't drive me away by force."

"*I* drive you away? I'm doing everything I can to hold you."

"Do you think this is the way to hold me? Good Lord!"

Lillian let her head sink back again. "You don't have to be jealous. Boris would not even want me if I went back."

"That hasn't anything to do with it. You'd like to go back."

"Don't drive me back. Oh God, have you been struck blind?"

"Yes," Clerfayt said, "probably. Probably," he repeated. "But I can't do anything about it, now. That's how it is."

They drove in silence along the Corniche toward Antibes. A donkey cart was coming toward them. On its seat sat a teenage girl, singing. Lillian looked at the girl with sear-ing envy. She thought of the old tortoise-woman at the casino who had years of life ahead of her, and she saw the laughing girl, and then she thought of herself, and suddenly there came again one of those moments in which everything became incomprehensible and no tricks helped at all; the misery overwhelmed her and everything within her cried out in impotent rebellion: Why? Why me? What have I done that I am the one to be struck down?

With blinded eyes, she looked out into the magical landscape. The strong fragrance of flowers wafted across the road. "Why are you crying?" Clerfayt demanded irritably. "You don't have any reason to cry."

"I suppose I don't."

"You're unfaithful to me with a shadow," he said bitterly. "And you cry."

Yes, she thought, but the shadow's name is not Boris. Shall I let him know what its name is? But then he will lock me up in a hospital and put guards in front of the door, so that I am tended to death behind frosted-glass windows, surrounded by the smell of disinfectants, good will, and the insipid stench of human refuse.

She looked at Clerfayt's face. No, she thought, not the prison of this love. Protest against it is useless. There's only flight. The fireworks are over; there is no sense poking around in the ashes.

The car drove into the hotel yard. An Englishman in a terry robe was already going down to the beach to swim. Clerfayt helped Lillian out of the car without looking at her. "You won't be seeing much more of me," he said. "Tomorrow, training starts."

He was exaggerating. The race was through the city, and training for it was virtually impossible. The streets could only be blocked off for the race itself; otherwise the drivers had to limit themselves chiefly to driving the route and memorizing the way they planned to shift.

As if gazing down a long corridor, Lillian saw what remained, what could still possibly happen between them. It was a corridor that narrowed steadily, and did not have an exit. She could not walk along it. Others, who had more time, probably could do it. Not she. And in love, there was no turning back. You could never begin afresh; what had happened remained in your blood. Clerfayt could never again be as he had been with her. He could be that way with any other woman, but not with her. What they had had could no more be recalled than time, and no sacrifice, no readiness, no amount of good will would suffice. That was the sad, the inexorable law. Lillian knew it, and for that reason she wanted to leave. The remnant of her life was her whole life—but in Clerfayt's life it was only a small part. It therefore depended entirely on her, not on Clerfayt. The scales were too uneven; what would be only an episode in his life, although he did not believe it now, was the end for her. She could not throw it away; she knew that now. She felt no regret; she had too little time even for that. But she felt a clarity that resembled the morning's clarity. And with this clarity the last mists of misunderstanding vanished. She felt the small, sharp joy of decision. And—strangely—with the decision her tenderness returned—for she was now out of danger.

"Nothing of what you've been saying is true, Clerfayt," she said in a changed voice. "Nothing whatsoever! Forget it. It isn't true. None of it."

She saw his face brightening. "You'll stay with me?" he asked quickly.

"Yes," she said. She wanted no more quarrels in their last days.

"You finally see what I want."

"Yes," she replied, smiling.

"You'll marry me?"

He did not sense her hesitation. "Yes," she said. That, too, did not matter now.

He stared at her. "When?"

"Whenever you say. In autumn."

He was silent for a moment. "At last!" he said then. "At last! You'll never regret it, Lillian."

"I know that."

At one stroke he was transformed. "You're tired! You must be dead tired. You have to get to bed. Come, I'll take you up."

"And what about you?"

"I'll have myself a morning dip, like the Englishman,

then drive over the course until the traffic starts. It's just a matter of routine; I know the route." He stood at her door. "What an idiot I am! I lost more than half my winnings. Out of sheer temper."

"I won."

Lillian tossed her bag, filled with jettons, on the table. "I haven't counted them."

"We'll win again tomorrow. Are you going to see a doctor?"

"Yes. Now I have to sleep."

"Of course. Straight through till evening. Then we'll have something to eat and go to sleep again. I love you beyond anything."

"And I you, Clerfayt."

He closed the door gently behind him. As if leaving a sick person, she thought. It was the first time he had done that. She sat down on the bed, without an ounce of strength left.

The window was open. She saw him going down to the beach. After the race, she thought. I must pack and leave after the race, when he has to go to Rome. Just these few days more, she thought. She did not know where she would go. Nor did it matter. But she had to leave.

XX

The course was only about two miles long, but it led through the streets of Monte Carlo, right through the middle of the city, along the shore, over the mountain on which the casino stood, and back. In many places it was barely wide enough for passing, and consisted almost entirely of curves, double turns, hairpin turns, and sharply angled serpentines. A hundred rounds had to be driven, nearly two hundred miles; that meant shifting, braking, giving gas, shifting, and again braking and giving gas tens of thousands of times.

"A merry-go-round," Clerfayt said laughingly to Lillian. "A sort of circus act. There isn't any stretch where you can even half let the buggy out. Where are you sitting?"

"In the stand. Tenth row on the right."

"It will be hot. Do you have a hat?"

"Yes." Lillian showed him the small straw hat she held in her hand.

"Good. This evening, we'll eat lobster and drink chilled wine in the Pavillion d'Or by the sea. And tomorrow we'll drive over to see someone I know; he's an architect, and we'll ask him to make a plan for redoing the house. So it will be bright, with big windows and lots of sunlight."

The manager called out something to Clerfayt in Italian. "It's starting," Clerfayt said, buttoning his white overalls at the neck. He took a piece of wood from his pocket, knocked it against the car and then against his hand.

"Ready?" the manager shouted.

"Ready."

Lillian kissed Clerfayt and performed the necessary spells of racing superstition. She spat lightly at the car and Clerfayt's racing outfit, and murmured the curse that was supposed to bring about the opposite; then she raised her hands with two fingers outspread toward the track and the other pits—it was the *jettatore* exorcism of the evil eye. The Italian mechanics looked at her in mute appreciation as she passed them. Behind her, she heard the manager praying: "Oh sweet blood of Jesus and you, Mother of Sorrows, help Clerfayt and Frigerio and—"

She turned around at the door of the pit. The wives of Marchetti and two other drivers had already taken up their stations with stop watches and notebooks. I ought not to leave him, she thought, raising her hand. Clerfayt laughed and saluted. He looked very young. "And all you saints, burn up the others' tires twice as fast as ours!" the manager prayed, and then shouted: "Ready for the start! Everybody out who doesn't belong here!"

Twenty cars started. In the first round, Clerfayt stayed in the eighth position; he had not had a favorable place and had been a moment too slow at the start. He hung on behind Micotti, who he knew would attack. Frigerio, Monti, and Sacchetti were ahead of them; Marchetti held the lead.

In the fourth round, Micotti, overrevving his motor, shot out on the straight stretch that rose up to the casino and passed Sacchetti. Clerfayt clung to his rear wheels; he forced the motor likewise and passed Sacchetti barely before entering the tunnel. When he came out of it, he saw Micotti's car, smoking and slowing down. He passed him and began chasing Monti. Three rounds later, on the hairpin turn by the gas tank he reached him and clung like a terrier to his rear wheels.

Ninety-two rounds and seventeen competitors to go, he thought, as he saw a second car stopping at the pit beside Micotti's. The manager signaled to him not to attack for the time being. Probably Frigerio and Marchetti, who did not like each other, were battling between themselves at the firm's expense, instead of keeping team discipline, and the manager wanted to keep Clerfayt and Meyer III in reserve, in case the lead drivers ruined their cars.

Lillian saw the pack racing past the stands at intervals of less than two minutes. You had just seen the cars, and looked aside for a moment, when they were back again, their order differing slightly, but almost as if they had never been away. It was like pushing the glass plate of a magic lantern back and forth, in and out. How can they possibly count the hundred rounds? she thought. Then she recalled the praying, sweating, cursing manager who held out signboards and flags for them to see, waving and changing his signals according to some secret code.

After forty rounds, she wanted to leave. Something told her that she ought to depart now, at once, take the train before the race was over. The prospect of watching the slight shifts in the field another sixty times seemed to her as barren a waste of time as the endless hours spent in the sanatorium, when one did nothing but watch the hands creep round the clock. She had a ticket to Zurich in her bag. She had bought it that morning, while Clerfayt was taking one last practice drive over the course. It was a ticket for the day after tomorrow. Clerfayt would then have to fly to Rome, but only for two days. The plane was leaving in the morning, the train in the evening. Like a thief, she thought, like a traitor, I am sneaking away. Just as I wanted to sneak away from Boris at the sanatorium. Then she had had that last talk with Boris anyhow, but what good had it done? The wrong words were always said; you always lied because the truth was useless cruelty; and the end was always bitterness and despair that you could do nothing about and that always made the last memory one of dispute, misunderstanding and hatred.

She looked in her bag for the ticket. For a moment, she thought she had lost it. That moment sufficed to restore her determination. In spite of the warm sunlight, she shivered. I have fever again, she thought, and listened to the crowd shouting around her. Down below, at the blue toy harbor with its white yachts, on which people stood jammed, the cars raced by, and one of the little toy autos thrust to one side and outdistanced another. "Clerfayt!" a brawny woman beside her shouted jubilantly, pounding her program against plump thighs under a linen skirt. "The son of a gun made it!" she roared in English.

An hour later, Clerfayt had worked forward to second place. Now he was coldly and mercilessly chasing Marchetti. He did not want to pass him yet—there was time enough for that until the eightieth round, even until the ninetieth. He only wanted to chase him until Marchetti became nervous, and keep a few yards behind him, always at the same distance. He did not want to take the chance of overrevving his motor again; he wanted to make Marchetti do that, and Marchetti did it once, without harming the machine. But Clerfayt sensed that he was growing nervous when he accomplished nothing by it. Now Marchetti began blocking the road and the curves; he did not want to let Clerfayt pass. Several times Clerfayt maneuvered as if he wanted to pass, without really trying it; he succeeded in making Marchetti transfer his attention to him rather than to his own driving, and so become less careful.

They had lapped the field once, and some drivers several times. The manager was sweating and holding out blackboards and flags. He signaled Clerfayt not to attack. Marchetti had belonged to their stable only for a few weeks, and it had been bad enough that he and Frigerio had battled one another; Frigerio had developed tire trouble as a result, and was now almost a minute behind Clerfayt and five other cars. Clerfayt was being chased by Monti, but Monti was not yet clinging to his wheels. He could easily shake him off on the hairpin turns, which he was taking faster than Monti.

They passed the pits again. Clerfayt saw the manager pleading with all the saints and simultaneously shaking his fist at him, commanding him not to close in on Marchetti. Marchetti had signaled furiously to him to restrain Clerfayt. Clerfayt nodded and fell back a car's length, but no more. He wanted to win this race, with or without the manager. He wanted first prize, and besides he had placed bets on himself. I need the money, he thought. For the future. The house. Life with Lillian. The bad start had delayed him, but he knew he would win; he felt very calm, in that strange state of equilibrium between concentration and relaxation in which you are confident that nothing can go wrong. It was a kind of clairvoyance which excluded all doubts, all waverings and uncertainties. He had often had it in the past, but in recent years he had often missed it. It was a rare moment of pure happiness.

He saw Marchetti's car suddenly dance, swerve diagonally, and crash with a shriek of tearing metal; he saw the black pool of oil that had run in a wide splash across the road, and the two other cars that had already smashed into one another as they hurtled drunkenly over the oil; he saw, as if in a slow-motion movie, Marchetti's car very slowly turning over and Marchetti sailing through the air and striking the ground. A hundred eyes inside him searched for a gap in the road through which he could hurl his car, but there was none; the road expanded gigantically and at the same time shrank; he felt no fear, only tried to stride sidewise rather than at right angles. At the last moment, he realized that he must release the steering wheel, but his arms were too slow; everything was already lifting; he suddenly no longer had weight, and then came the blow on his chest and the blow in his face, and from all sides the splintered world plunged down upon him; for a split second, he still saw the horrified face of the track attendant, and then an enormously powerful fist struck him from behind and there was only the dark roaring and then nothing at all.

The car that had run into him ripped a gap in the tangle, so that the others who followed were just able to pass. One after the other, they shot by, some dancing and reeling, wrenching their cars just past the wrecks, so that metal screeched against metal as though the smashed machines were groaning. The track attendant, armed with a shovel, clambered over the sandbags and strewed sand over the pool of oil, leaping back when the howl of a motor neared. Ambulance men appeared with stretchers. They pulled Marchetti to safety, lifted him, and handed him over the sandbag barricades to others. A few officials came running up with danger signals to warn the drivers; but the field had already made a round; all had passed the site of the accident and were now coming again, some throwing a quick glance at the wreckage, the others with their eyes rigidly fixed on the road.

Clerfayt's car had not only crashed into the others, but had been crashed into from behind by Monti. Monti was almost uninjured. He limped aside. Clerfayt was caught in his car, which had been squeezed up and then hurled against the sandbags. His face was smashed, and the steering wheel had crushed his chest. He was bleeding from the mouth and was unconscious. Like flies around a piece of bloody meat, the crowd gathered at the edge of the track and avidly watched the ambulance men and the mechanics, who began frantically sawing Clerfayt free. In front of him, a car was burning. Men with fire extinguishers had managed to pull the wreck away from the other cars, and were now trying to put out the blaze. Luckily, the gasoline tank had been ripped open, so that there was no explosion; but the gasoline burned and the heat grew unbearable, and there was still the chance that the fire might leap the gap. Every two minutes, the cars came tearing by again. The growl of the motors hung like a dark requiem over the city, and swelled to a deafening howl when the cars passed Clerfayt, who dangled bloodily over the scene of the accident, as if impaled on a stake, in his upended car, illuminated by the pale light of the dying fire in the bright afternoon. The race went on; it was not called off.

Lillian did not grasp it at once. The loud-speaker was not

clear; the voice in it seemed smothered and incomprehensible because of its own echoes. In his excitement, the announcer was standing too close to the microphone. She heard something about cars that had gone off the track and crashed because another car had lost its oil on the road. Then she saw the pack passing the stand. It could not be so bad, she thought, or the race would not be continuing. She looked for Clerfayt's number. She did not find it, but he might already have passed; she had not been paying too close attention. The loud-speaker was now saying rather more clearly that an accident had taken place on the quai de Plaisance; several cars had collided and some drivers had been injured, none killed; there would be more news shortly. The positions now were: Frigerio, with fifteen seconds' lead, Conti, Duval, Meyer III. . . .

Lillian strained to listen. Nothing about Clerfayt; he had been second. Nothing about Clerfayt, she thought, and heard the cars coming and leaned forward to see the Twelve, the red car with the number Twelve.

It did not come, and into the barren stillness of horror that spread through her rolled the announcer's bland voice: "Among the injured is Clerfayt; he is being taken to the hospital. It appears that he is unconscious. Monti has injuries to his knee and foot, Sacchetti—"

It cannot be, something inside Lillian thought. Not in this toy race, not in this toy city with its toy harbor and its pretty toy panorama! It must be a mistake. His car will come shooting out of the distance from somewhere in a moment, as it did that time as the Targa Florio, perhaps delayed slightly, gouged and battered, but otherwise safe and sound. But even as she thought this, she felt the hope growing hollow, collapsing, before it had become established. Unconscious, she thought, and clung to the word. What does that mean?

It could mean anything. She became aware that she had unknowingly left the stands. She was on the way to the pit; perhaps he had been taken there. He would lie on a stretcher, having done something to his shoulder as in the

Targa Florio, or to his arm, and would laugh at his hard luck.

"He's been taken to the hospital," the manager said, sweating. "Holy Mother of God, holy Christopher, why should this happen to us? Why not to the others or—what? One moment!"

He rushed away to signal. The cars shot past; so close, they looked bigger and more dangerous than from the stands, and their thunder excluded everything else. "What has happened?" Lillian cried. "Forget your damned race and tell me what has happened."

She looked around. No one met her eyes. The mechanics busied themselves with spare parts and tires and avoided looking up. When she approached one of them, he moved away. It was as though she had the plague.

The manager came back at last. "It wouldn't help Clerfayt any for me to let the race go to the devil," he said hoarsely. "He wouldn't want that, either. He'd want—"

Lillian interrupted him. "Where is he? I don't want any sermons on racing drivers' code of honor."

"In the hospital. They took him straight to the hospital."

"Why isn't anyone with him, to help him? Why not you? Why are you here?"

The manager looked at her uncomprehendingly. "How could I help him? Or anyone here? That's a job for the doctors."

Lillian swallowed. "What happened to him?" she asked softly.

"I don't know. I haven't seen him. We were all right here. We have to stay here, you know."

"Yes," Lillian said. "So that the race can go on."

"That's the way it is," the manager replied forlornly. "We're all only employees."

A mechanic came hurrying up to them. The growl of the cars was swelling. "Signorina—" the manager spread his hands and looked toward the track. "I must—"

"Is he dead?" Lillian asked.

"No, no! Unconscious. The doctors—sorry, Signorina, I must—"

The manager snatched a placard from a box and rushed out to give his signals. Lillian heard him crying: "Madonna, Madonna, oh that damned oil; why must this happen to me; damn this life of mine!" He held his placard toward someone, waved, and held one hand high, and remained standing, although the pack was already gone, staring hard at the road, unwilling to return to the pit.

Lillian slowly turned to go. "We're coming—after the race, Signorina," one of the mechanics whispered. "Right after the race."

The black canopy of noise continued to overhang the city as she rode to the hospital. She had found only one of the horse-drawn carriages decorated with flags and colored ribbons, and a funny straw hat for the horse. "It will take longer than usual, Mademoiselle," the driver explained to her. "We must make a big detour. The streets are blocked off. Because of the race, you understand—"

Lillian nodded. She sat wrapped in grief that seemed not to be grief, rather, a dull ache that had been deadened by a narcotic. Nothing functioned completely inside her, nothing but her ears and eyes, which heard the motors and saw the cars clearly, with excessive sharpness, so that she could scarcely endure it. The driver chattered and tried to point out the sights. She did not hear; she heard only the motors. Someone tried to stop the carriage and have a word with her. She did not understand what he was saying, and had the driver halt. Perhaps, she thought, it was someone with a message from Clerfayt. The man, an Italian in a white suit, with a thin black mustache, invited her to dinner. "What?" she asked uncomprehendingly. "What else?"

The man smiled. "There might be more. That would be up to you."

She did not reply. She no longer saw the man. Her eyes dropped him; he knew nothing about Clerfayt. "Go on!" she ordered the driver. "Faster."

"All these sporty types have no money," the driver opined. "You were right to give him the brush-off. Who knows, you might have had to pay for the dinner yourself in the end. Older men are more reliable."

"Faster," Lillian said.

"As you please, Mademoiselle."

It took an eternity before they stopped in front of the hospital. Lillian had made many vows in the meanwhile, vows she believed she would keep. She would not leave, she would stay, she would marry Clerfayt, if only he would live! She made these vows and let them drop like stones into a pond, without thinking about them.

"Monsieur Clerfayt is in the operating room," the nurse at the reception desk said.

"Can you tell me how badly he is hurt?"

"I'm sorry, Madame. Are you Madame Clerfayt?"

"No."

"Related?"

"What has that to do with it?"

"Nothing, Mademoiselle. Only our rules are such that after the operation only the nearest relations will be allowed to see him for a minute."

Lillian stared at the nurse. Should she say that she was Clerfayt's fiancée? How absurd that was. "Must he be operated on?" she asked.

"So it would seem; otherwise he would not be in the operating room."

Lillian stared at the nurse. The kind that can't stand me, she thought. She had experience with nurses. "May I wait?" she asked.

The nurse gestured toward a bench. "Don't you have a waiting room?" Lillian asked.

The nurse pointed to a door. Lillian went into the dreary room in which tired potted plants drooped, old magazines lay beached, and flies hummed around a ribbon of flypaper depending from the ceiling over the center table. The noise of the motors reached even into this place, like frenzied, distant drums, muted but there.

Time became sticky as the flypaper on which the flies died a slow, tortured death. Lillian fretted the worn magazines, opened and closed them, tried to read and could not, got up and went to the window and sat down again. The room smelled of anxiety, of all the anxiety that had been radiated into it. She tried to open the window, but closed it again because the growl of the motors immediately leaped in upon her. After a while, a woman came in with a baby. The baby began to cry; the woman opened her blouse and nursed it. The child smacked its lips and fell asleep. The woman smiled shyly at Lillian and buttoned her blouse.

A few minutes later, the nurse opened the door. Lillian stood up, but the nurse paid no attention to her; she nodded to the woman with the baby to come with her. Lillian sat down again. Suddenly she listened. Something had changed. She felt it at the nape of her neck. A tension had ceased; something had relaxed. It took a while before she realized that it was the stillness; the roar of the motors had stopped. The race was over.

Fifteen minutes later, she saw an open car, with the manager and two mechanics in it, draw up to the hospital and stop. The reception nurse brought them into the waiting room. They stood around, grim and downcast.

"Have you found out anything?" Lillian asked.

The manager indicated the younger mechanic. "He was there when they pulled him out."

"He was bleeding from the mouth," the mechanic said.

"From the mouth?"

"Yes, it was like a hemorrhage."

"That's impossible. He wasn't sick!"

Lillian looked at the man. What gruesome confusion was this? A hemorrhage belonged to her, not to Clerfayt. "How could he have a hemorrhage?" she asked.

"His chest was jammed against the steering wheel," the mechanic said.

Lillian slowly shook her head. "No," she said. "No!"

The manager went to the door. "I'm going to see if I can find the doctor."

Lillian heard him in violent argument with the nurse. The sound faded, and the hot silence returned, with the two mechanics breathing loudly and the flies buzzing.

The manager came back. He stood still in the doorway.

His eyes looked unnaturally white in his tanned face. He moved his lips several times before he spoke. Then he said: "Clerfayt is dead."

The mechanics stared at him. "Did they operate on him?" the younger one asked. "The doctors must have done something wrong."

"They didn't operate. He died before they could."

All three men looked at Lillian. She did not move. "Where is he?" she asked at last.

"They're preparing him."

With great effort, she said: "Have you seen him?"

The manager nodded.

"Where is he?"

"It's better if you don't see him now," the man replied. "You can see him tomorrow."

"Who says that?" Lillian asked in a voice lacking all emotion. "Who says that?" she repeated.

"The doctor. You wouldn't recognize him. It will be better if you come tomorrow. We can drive you to the hotel."

Lillian remained where she was. "Why wouldn't I recognize him?"

The manager did not answer for a while. "His face," he said at last. "It was bashed in. The steering wheel crushed his chest. The doctor thinks he didn't know a thing. It happened too fast. He lost consciousness immediately, and didn't wake up again. Do you think it doesn't hit us hard, too?" he said in a louder voice. "We knew him longer than you did!"

"Yes," Lillian replied, "you knew him longer than I did."

"I don't mean it that way. I mean, this is how it always is when someone dies—suddenly he's gone. He no longer speaks. He's just been here and then he isn't here any longer. Who can grasp it? I mean, we feel the same way. We stand here and can't grasp it. Do you understand?"

"Yes, I understand."

"Then come with us," the manager said. "We'll take you to the hotel. This is enough for today. Tomorrow you can see him."

"What would I do in the hotel?" Lillian asked.

The man shrugged. "Call a doctor. Tell him to give you a shot. A strong one, so you'll sleep through till tomorrow. Come along now. There's nothing more you can do here. He's dead. None of us can do anything any more. When a man's dead, it's over; there's nothing more to be done." He took a step forward and placed a hand on her arm. "Come! I know what it's like. *Porca miseria,* this isn't the first time for me. But damn it, it's always the first time."

XXI

She awoke from seething sleep. For a moment, she had no connection with the world; then the grief stabbed sharply through her. She sat upright in bed with a jerk, and looked around. How had she come here? Slowly, she remembered—the deadly, late afternoon, the wandering about in the small city, the early evening, the hospital, Clerfayt's alien, damaged face, the head lying somewhat askew, the hands that someone had folded as if in prayer, the doctor who had come with her. It was all not true, it was not right, it could not be so—it was not Clerfayt who should be stretched out on the hospital bed, but she, she alone, and not he; it was a horrible distortion; someone had put across a dreadful, sinister joke.

She got up and drew the curtains apart. The sun rushed in. The cloudless sky, the palms in the light and the brilliant flower beds in the hotel's garden made the death of Clerfayt seem even more incomprehensible. Me, Lillian thought, it was supposed to be me, it was destined for me, not for him! In a strange way, she felt that she had been unfaithful; she felt like someone who had been left over, whose time was long past, who was still living only by a mistake, for whom someone else had been killed, and over whom the vague, gray shadow of murder hovered, as it might over a driver so overtired that he had run over a person he could have avoided.

The telephone rang. She started and lifted it. The representative of a funeral home in Nice recommended his firm for a coffin, a plot, and a dignified burial at fair prices. In case the body was to be sent home, zinc coffins were available.

She hung up. She did not know what she ought to do. Where was Clerfayt's home? Where he had been born? Somewhere in Alsace-Lorraine? She did not know where. The telephone shrilled again. This time it was the hospital. What was to be done with the body? It had to be disposed of, by afternoon at the latest. A coffin must be ordered.

Lillian looked at the clock. It was noon. She dressed. With ringing and bustle, the demands of death were assailing her. I ought to have black clothes, she thought. A firm that delivered wreaths telephoned. Another wanted to know what Clerfayt's religion had been, in order to reserve time for the church ceremony. Or had the deceased been a free-thinker?

Lillian could still feel the effects of the strong sedative she had taken. Nothing seemed quite real. She went downstairs to ask the desk clerk for advice. A man in a dark-blue suit rose as soon as he saw her. She turned away; she could not endure the professional expression of condolence.

"Order a coffin," she said to the clerk. "Do whatever is necessary."

The clerk explained to her that the authorities had to be informed. Did she wish an autopsy? Sometimes it was necessary to determine the cause of death. What for? Because of later claims. The automobile firm could attempt to make the sponsors of the race bear the responsibility. Then there was also the insurance to consider; moreover, there were other possible complications. It was best to be prepared for everything.

It seemed simple to die—but not to be dead. Did she want Clerfayt buried at the cemetery here? "In the suicides' cemetery?" Lillian asked. "No."

268

The clerk smiled forbearingly. The suicides' cemetery was a legend, like so much else at Monte Carlo. There was a proper, beautiful cemetery here, where the citizens of Monaco were buried. Did she have Clerfayt's identification papers?

"Papers? Does he still need papers?"

The clerk was once more the soul of understanding. Of course papers were necessary. They would have to be obtained. He would also get in touch with the police.

"The police?"

In any accident, the police had to be notified at once. That had undoubtedly already been done by the firm and the race committee; but the police must also release the body. Everything was only a matter of form, of course, but it had to be done. He would attend to it all.

Lillian nodded. She suddenly wanted to get out of the hotel. She was afraid she would faint. It occurred to her that she had eaten nothing since yesterday noon, but she could not bear the thought of entering the hotel restaurant. Quickly, she left the lobby and went to the Café de Paris. She ordered coffee, and sat for a long time without drinking it. Automobiles rolled past and stopped in front of the casino; the usual sight-seeing buses came, and hordes of tourists gathered around the drivers, whom they then obediently followed into their petty-bourgeois dream of Babylon. Lillian started in alarm when a man sat down at her table. She finished her coffee and got up. She did not know what she wanted to do. She tried to tell herself that if there had been no accident, she would be alone now anyway, in Paris or on her way to Switzerland. It did not help; the hole in the ground beside her was there; it led into a bottomless abyss and could not be reasoned away. Clerfayt was dead; that was different from his not being with her.

She found a bench from which she could look at the ocean. She had the feeling that there were many urgent things she had to do; but she could not decide on any of them. Clerfayt, she thought again and again—Clerfayt, not me! What does that mean? Everything was insane. She was the one to die, not he. What ghastly irony was this?

She returned to the hotel and went to her room without speaking to anyone. At the door, she stopped. Dead air puffed into her face; everything in the room seemed to have died along with it.

She remembered that the desk clerk had asked for Clerfayt's papers. She did not know where they were, and had a horror of going to Clerfayt's room. She knew, from the sanatorium, that it was often harder to see the things the deceased had left behind than the body itself.

She saw that the key was in the lock and assumed that the maid was cleaning. That was better than being alone in the room. It encouraged her enough so that she opened the door.

An angular woman in a gray tailored suit looked up from the desk. "What do you want?"

Lillian thought she had come into the wrong room. Then she saw Clerfayt's coat on a hook. "What are you doing here?" she asked.

"I think I might rather ask you that," the woman replied. "I am Clerfayt's sister. What do you want here? Who are you?"

Lillian remained silent. Clerfayt had once told her he had a sister somewhere whom he hated and who hated him. He had not heard from her for many years, he had said. This must be she. She did not bear the slightest resemblance to Clerfayt.

"I did not know you were here," Lillian said. "Since you are, I have nothing more to do here."

"That is quite true," the woman replied frostily. "I was told that my brother had someone living here with him. Are you the person?"

"That is not any of your affair," Lillian said, turning away.

She went out and back to her room. She began to pack, but soon stopped. I cannot go away as long as he is still here, she thought. I must stay until he's put into the ground.

She went to the hospital once more. The reception nurse explained that she could not see Clerfayt again; an autopsy was being performed at the request of a member of the family. Afterward, the body was to be sealed into a zinc coffin and sent back home.

In front of the hospital, Lillian met the manager. "We're leaving this evening," he said. "Have you seen the old nag with the big teeth? The sister? She's having him cut up. She wants to file suit against the firm and the sponsors of the race for compensation on account of negligence. She's been to the police already. You know our director. She went to see him, too. He's a guy who can stand up to anybody, but I'm telling you, he was looking pretty green after a half hour with that woman. She's demanding a lifetime pension. Claims that Clerfayt was her sole support. We're all leaving. You'd better leave, too. It's all over."

"Yes," Lillian replied. "It's all over."

She walked aimlessly about the streets; she sat at tables and had something to drink; and in the evening she returned to the hotel. She was now very tired. The doctor had left a sedative for her. She did not need to take it; she fell asleep at once. The telephone woke her. Clerfayt's sister was calling. She said she urgently had to talk to her; would Lillian come over to her room.

"If you have anything to say to me, do it now," Lillian said.

"It can't be done over the telephone."

"Then we'll meet in the lobby at noon."

"That's too late."

"Not for me," Lillian said, and hung up.

She looked at the clock. It was shortly before nine. She had slept for fifteen hours and was still tired. She went into the bathroom and was close to falling asleep in the bath when someone pounded violently on the door of the room. She came out of the tub and put on her wrapper. Before she could open the door, Clerfayt's sister came charging in.

"Is your name Miss Dunkerque?" the woman asked. She was still in her gray tailored suit.

"We can talk at twelve o'clock, in the lobby," Lillian replied. "Not now, and not here."

"It comes to the same thing. Now that I'm here I—"

"You have forced your way in," Lillian interrupted. "Shall I call the management to help me?"

"I cannot wait here until twelve. My train is leaving before that. Do you want my brother's remains to sit in the blinding sun on the platform until it suits your ladyship to talk with me?"

Lillian looked at the narrow black cross the woman wore on a chain around her neck. This female will stop at nothing to get her way, she thought.

"I have here," the sister went on, "a copy of a legal paper that I found among my brother's documents. No doubt you have the original. It has to do with the assignment to you of a house on the Riviera."

"To me?"

"You do not know about it?"

Lillian looked at the paper in the rawboned hand, on which there were two wedding rings. A widow, then—no wonder.

"Show me the paper," Lillian said.

The sister hesitated. "Haven't you seen it?"

Lillian did not answer. She heard the water still running in the tub, and went to turn it off. "Was that what you so urgently wanted to talk to me about?" she asked when she returned.

"I wanted to make it clear that the family would not recognize this transfer. We will contest it."

"Contest it, then. And now please, let me alone."

The woman stood her ground. "It would be simpler, and save you embarrassing questions, if you make a statement to the effect that you relinquish this bequest, which my brother certainly did not make except under some pressure."

Lillian stared at her. "Haven't you already drawn up such a statement?"

"I have. You have only to sign it. Here! I'm glad to see you have some understanding."

Lillian took the paper and tore it to bits. "Get out now. I've had enough of you."

The woman did not lose her composure. She scrutinized Lillian sharply. "You said you knew nothing about this legacy?"

Lillian went to the door and opened it. "That is for you to find out."

"I certainly will. Justice is on our side. There happens to be a crucial difference between proper blood relations and some little adventuress who——"

On the table stood a bowl of violets that Clerfayt had brought two days ago. Lillian picked it up without knowing that she was doing so, and pitched the flowers into the bony face. She wanted only one thing—to silence that harsh, unbearable voice. The flowers were already withered and clung to the sister's hair and shoulders.

The woman wiped the water from her eyes. "You'll pay for that!" she snapped.

"I know," Lillian replied. "Send me the bill for the hairdresser, and no doubt for the suit, and probably for your shoes, your undergarments, and the shock to your feelings. And now get out!"

The sister departed. Lillian looked at the glass bowl still in her hand. She had not known that she was capable of such acts of violence. Thank God I didn't throw the bowl, too, she thought, and suddenly began to laugh, and could not stop, and then the tears started, and with the tears came, at last, release from her rigidity.

The clerk stopped her in the lobby. "An embarrassing matter, Madame."

"What is it now?"

"You instructed me to order a coffin and a cemetery plot. As soon as Monsieur Clerfayt's sister arrived, she likewise ordered a coffin to be charged to the automobile company and had it delivered. Now yours is superfluous."

"Can't you send it back?"

"The firm's representative says the coffin was specially ordered. He says he can take it back as a favor, but not at the same price."

Lillian looked helplessly at the clerk. A grotesque image rose to her mind—of herself going back to some sanatorium in the mountains with an empty coffin, while

Clerfayt's sister carried off Clerfayt's dissected remains in a second coffin, for a family interment.

"I suggested to the lady that she take your coffin for Monsieur Clerfayt," the clerk said. "But she did not want to. The lady has her own ideas about things. She is also having her hotel expenses charged to the automobile company. Full board, of course, and last night two bottles of Château Lafite 1929. The best wine we have. The funeral home would take the coffin back at half-price."

"All right," Lillian replied. "And make up my bill. I'm leaving this evening."

"Very good. Then there's the matter of the plot. I've already paid the requisite amount. They always want such payment in advance. It's difficult to do anything today. This is Saturday. There'll be nobody at the office until Monday."

"Doesn't anybody die here on Saturdays and Sundays?"

"Oh yes. But in those cases arrangements are made on Monday."

"Put what you paid on my bill."

"Would you want to keep the plot then?" the clerk asked incredulously.

"I don't know; I don't want to talk any more about it. Put down what you paid. Put it all down. But I don't want to hear another word about it! Not another word! Can't you understand that?"

"Very well, Madame."

Lillian returned to her room. The telephone rang. She did not answer it. She packed the rest of her things. In her bag, she found the ticket to Zurich. The train was leaving this very evening.

The telephone rang again. When it fell silent, she was seized by a panicky terror. It seemed to her that more had died than Clerfayt—that everything she had known had died. Boris, too, she thought. Who knew what had happened to Boris? Perhaps he, too, was already dead, and no one had informed her because no one knew her address or had had the courage to tell her.

She reached for the telephone, but let her hand sink

again. She could not call him. Not now. He would think she was calling because Clerfayt was dead. He would never be able to believe that she had made up her mind to leave Clerfayt. She would never be able to tell him either.

She sat still until the dusk crept grayly into the room. The windows were open. She heard the crackling of the palm leaves outside like the gossip of malicious neighbors. The clerk had told her that Clerfayt's sister had left at noon; it was time now for her to be leaving, too.

She stood up, but hesitated again. She could not go before she knew whether Boris was still alive. It was unnecessary to telephone him directly. She could call the house and ask for him, giving some other name; then if the girl went to call him, she would know that he was all right, and could hang up before he answered.

She gave the number. It was a long while before the operator called back. There was no answer. She asked for the number once more, asked that it be made an urgent call.

She heard footsteps outside on the gravel paths of the hotel garden. It reminded her of Clerfayt's garden. A wave of hopeless tenderness flooded her. He had left his house to her, without saying anything about it. She did not want to have it. It would stand empty and slowly weathering, with its awful stucco ornaments—unless Clerfayt's sister, armed with the double morality of bourgeois justice, got hold of it.

The telephone shrilled. Lillian heard the high-strung French voices of the operators. She forgot her whole strategy. "Boris!" she cried. "Are you there?"

"Who is there?" a woman's voice asked.

Lillian hesitated a second; then she gave her name. In two hours, she would be leaving the Riviera, and nobody would know where she was bound. It would be ridiculous not to speak to Boris once more.

"Who is there?" the voice repeated.

She gave her name again.

"Who?"

"Lillian Dunkerque."

"Mr. Volkov is not here," the voice replied through the humming and crackling of the line.

"Who is this? Mrs. Escher?"

"No, Mrs. Bliss. Mrs. Escher is no longer here. Mr. Volkov also is not here. I am sorry—"

"Wait!" Lillian cried. "Where is he?"

The noise in the telephone swelled. "Left—" Lillian made out.

"Where is he?" she repeated.

"Mr. Volkov has left."

"Left? For where?"

"I don't know."

Lillian held her breath. "Has anything happened to him?" she asked finally.

"I don't know, Madame. He's left. I can't tell you where. I'm sorry—"

The connection was broken. The excited French operators twittered. Lillian put down the receiver. Left—she knew what that meant in the language of the sanatorium and the private houses that boarded patients. It was what was said when someone had died. It could mean nothing else—where would he have gone to? And his old landlady was no longer there either.

For a while, she sat quite still. At last she stood up and went downstairs. She paid her bill and tucked her ticket into her pocket. "Send my things to the station," she said.

"Already?" the clerk asked in surprise. "Your train does not leave for two hours. It is too soon."

"Now," she said. "It is not too soon."

XXII

She sat on a bench in front of the little railroad station. The first lights of early evening were burning, stressing the barren dreariness of the building. Tanned tourists bustled past her, making for a train to Marseilles.

An American sat down beside her and launched into a monologue on the fact that in Europe you could not get a decent steak or a tolerable hamburger. Even the frankfurters were better in Wisconsin, he said.

Lillian sat without thought, in a state of such utter exhaustion that she no longer knew whether it was grief, emptiness, or resignation.

She saw the dog without recognizing it. The animal was running in long arcs over the square, sniffing at women here and there. It paused and then rushed toward her. The American sprang to his feet. "Mad dog!" he shouted. "Police! Shoot it."

The German shepherd dog ran past him and leaped up at Lillian, putting its forepaws on her shoulders and almost knocking her off the bench; it licked her hands and tried to lick her face, and whined and howled and barked until a circle of astonished people gathered around them.

"Wolf," she said incredulously. "What are you doing here?"

The dog abruptly abandoned her and shot off toward the crowd, which quickly made a path for it. It ran up to a man who was striding rapidly toward them, and then returned to Lillian.

She had stood up. "Boris!" she said.

"So we've found you at last," Volkov said. "The clerk at the hotel told me you were already at the station. Just about in time, I guess. Who knows where I would have had to look for you later."

"You're alive," Lillian said. "I telephoned you. Someone told me you'd left. I thought . . ."

"That was Mrs. Bliss. The new landlady. Mrs. Escher has remarried." Volkov gripped the dog's collar. "I read about the accident in the newspapers; that's why I came. I didn't know what hotel you were at, or I would have telephoned."

"You're alive!" she said again.

"And you're alive, Dusha. Everything else is unimportant."

She looked at him. She understood at once what he meant—that everything else, all offended egotism, all wounded pride, had been swept away by this last consolation: that the person you loved was not dead, was still living, still breathing, no matter what his feelings were or what had happened. Neither weakness nor pity had prompted Boris to come, but rather the lightning-flash of this ultimate knowledge—the only insight that was left to him, and the only one that always remained in the end, that canceled out everything else, and that, almost always, you became aware of too late.

"Yes, Boris," she said. "Everything else in unimportant."

He looked at her baggage. "When does your train leave?"

"In an hour. Let it go."

"Where were you going to go?"

"Anywhere. To Zurich. It doesn't matter, Boris."

"Then let us leave here. Move into another hotel. I've

reserved a room in Antibes. In the Hôtel du Cap. We can get another room. Shall I have the baggage sent there?"

Lillian shook her head. "Leave it here," she said with sudden resolution. "The train is going in an hour. Let's take it. I don't want to stay anywhere around here. And you must get back."

"I don't have to get back," Volkov said.

She looked at him. "Are you cured?"

"Not that. But I don't have to go back. I can go with you wherever you like, Lillian. As long as you wish."

"But—"

"I understood you when you left," Volkov said. "My God, how I understood that you wanted to get away."

"Then why didn't you come with me?"

Volkov did not answer at once. He did not want to remind her of what she had said. "Would you have gone with me?" he asked at last.

"No, Boris," she replied. "That's true. At the time, I wouldn't have."

"You didn't want to take the disease with you. You wanted to escape it."

"I no longer know. Perhaps it was so. It's so long ago."

"Do you really want to leave tonight?"

"Yes."

"Have you a berth?"

"Yes, Boris."

"You look as though you needed something to eat. Come to the café over there. And I will see whether I can still get a ticket."

They crossed to the café. He ordered eggs, ham, and coffee for her. "I'm going back to the station," he said. "Stay here. Don't run away."

"I'm not running away any more. Why does everyone think that?"

Boris smiled. "It isn't the worst thought in the world, Dusha. When a man thinks that, it means that he wants you to stay."

She looked at him. Her lips quivered. "I don't want to cry," she said.

"You're only exhausted. Eat something. I bet this is your first meal today."

She raised her head. "Do I look so bad?"

"No, Dusha. And even if you look tired, you always snap back after a few hours' sleep. That's how you are. Have you forgotten that?"

"Yes," she said. "I've forgotten a great deal. And not forgotten some things."

She began eating, but broke off to take out her mirror. She studied herself very closely, face, eyes, blue shadows. What had the doctor in Nice said? Before summer, and perhaps sooner, if you go on with your present life. Summer—it was already summer here, but in the mountains the summer came late. She studied her face once more, then took out powder and lipstick.

Volkov returned. "I have a ticket. The train is not sold out."

"Do you have a berth?"

"Not yet, but perhaps one will be free later. I don't especially need one; I slept all the way here." He stroked the dog, who had stayed at Lillian's side. "You'll have to go into the baggage car for the time being, Wolf, but we'll smuggle you out again later."

"I can take him into my compartment."

Boris nodded. "Conductors on French trains are always understanding. When we get to Zurich, we'll consider what you want to do."

"I want to go back," Lillian said.

"Back? Where?" Volkov asked cautiously.

She was silent for a moment. "I was on the way back," she said finally. "Believe it or not."

"Why shouldn't I believe it?"

"Why should you?"

"I once did almost exactly what you have done, Dusha. Many years ago. Later I went back, too."

Lillian shredded a piece of bread on to her plate. "It's no use if someone tells you, is it?"

"None whatsoever. We have to find out for ourselves. Otherwise we'd always think we had missed the most important thing. Do you have some idea where you want to go from Zurich?"

"To some sanatorium. They won't take me back at Bella Vista."

"Of course they'll take you. But are you certain that you want to go back? You're exhausted right now and need rest. That can change."

"I want to go back."

"On account of Clerfayt?" Volkov asked.

"Clerfayt has nothing to do with it. I was all ready to go back before it happened."

"Why?"

"For many reasons. I don't know all of them now. They were so important that I've forgotten them."

"If you want to stay down here—you won't have to be alone. I can stay, too."

Lillian shook her head. "No, Boris. I've had enough. I want to go back. But perhaps you have the feeling you would like to stay here? It's ben so long since you were out in the world."

Volkov smiled. "I already know it quite well—"

She nodded. "So I've heard. I know it, too, now."

In Zurich, Volkov telephoned the sanatorium. "Is she still alive?" the Dalai Lama asked grudgingly. "All right, as far as I'm concerned she can return."

Lillian remained a week at the Hotel Dolder in Zurich. She stayed in bed a good deal. Suddenly she felt very tired. The fever came every evening. Volkov called a doctor. "She should have gone to the hospital long ago," the doctor told him. "Leave her here."

"But she doesn't want to stay here. She wants to go back to the mountains."

The doctor shrugged. "As you like. But at least take an ambulance."

Volkov promised, but he knew that he would not take one. His respect for life did not go so far; he knew only too well that too much solicitude could kill a patient just as easily as too little. To treat Lillian as if she were dying would be worse than to risk the ride by car.

She looked brightly at him when he returned from his talk with the doctor. Since the disease had been manifesting itself more openly, she had grown cheerful—as if the vague feeling of guilt she had felt over Clerfayt's death were thereby wiped out. Grief for someone else, she thought with a trace of irony, became more bearable when you knew that you yourself did not have long to live. Even her feeling of rebellion against the disease had evaporated since Clerfayt's death. No one escaped, neither the sick nor the healthy; and that made for a paradoxical compensation. "Poor Boris," she said. "What did the doctor tell you? That I won't survive the trip?"

"Nothing of the sort."

"I will survive it," Lillian said, with gentle mockery. "Just because he said I wouldn't."

Volkov looked at her in surprise. "That's true, Dusha. I feel that, too."

"All right. Then give me some vodka," Lillian said. She held out her glass to him.

"What swindlers we are, Boris, with our little tricks. But what else can we do? Since we have the fear, we may as well make something of it. Fireworks, or a mirage, or some little snowflake of wisdom that soon melts."

They drove up to the mountains on a very mild, warm day. Halfway up the pass, they met a car on a hairpin turn. It stopped to let them by. "Hollmann!" Lillian cried. "Why, it's Hollmann!"

The man in the other car looked up from the road. "Lillian! And Boris! But . . ."

Behind him, an impatient Italian blew his horn; he was driving a little Fiat and imagining that he was the racer Nuvolari. "I'll park the car," Hollmann called. "Wait for me."

He drove on a short distance, let the Italian pass, and came back on foot. "What's up, Hollmann?" Lillian asked. "Where are you going?"

"I told you I was cured, didn't I?"

"And the car?"

"Borrowed. It seemed so silly to go by train. Now that I've been hired again!"

"Hired? By whom?"

"By our old firm. They telephoned me yesterday. They need someone now." Hollmann was silent for a moment. Then he said, "They have Torriani already, of course; now they want to have a try with me, too. If all goes well, I'll be driving in the smaller races soon. Then the big ones. Keep your fingers crossed for me! How nice to have seen you again, Lillian!"

Lillian waved to him. They saw him once more, from a higher curve, driving down the road like a blue insect to take Clerfayt's place, as Clerfayt had taken the place of another, and as another would some day take Hollmann's. Lillian waved at him. They had not spoken of Clerfayt.

She died six weeks later, on a bright summer afternoon so still that the landscape seemed to be holding its breath. She died quickly and surprisingly and alone. Boris had gone down to the village for a short time. When he returned, he found her dead on her bed. Her face was distorted; she had suffocated during a hemorrhage, and her hands were close to her throat; but a short while afterward her features smoothed and her face became more beautiful than Boris had seen it in a long time. He believed also that she had been happy, insofar as any human being can ever be called happy.

John Updike

☐ THE CENTAUR (100)	22922-X	1.75
☐ COUPLES (50)	C2935	1.95
☐ A MONTH OF SUNDAYS (50)	C2701	1.95
☐ THE MUSIC SCHOOL (100)	23279-4	1.75
☐ THE POORHOUSE FAIR (100)	23314-6	1.50
☐ RABBIT REDUX (75)	23247-6	1.95
☐ RABBIT, RUN (75)	23182-8	1.75
☐ PIGEON FEATHERS (100)	Q749	1.50

BESTSELLERS

☐	BEGGAR ON HORSEBACK—Thorpe	23091-0	1.50
☐	THE TURQUOISE—Seton	23088-0	1.95
☐	STRANGER AT WILDINGS—Brent	23085-6	1.95
	(Pub. in England as Kirkby's Changeling)		
☐	MAKING ENDS MEET—Howar	23084-8	1.95
☐	THE LYNMARA LEGACY—Gaskin	23060-0	1.95
☐	THE TIME OF THE DRAGON—Eden	23059-7	1.95
☐	THE GOLDEN RENDEZVOUS—MacLean	23055-4	1.75
☐	TESTAMENT—Morrell	23033-3	1.95
☐	CAN YOU WAIT TIL FRIDAY?—	23022-8	1.75
	Olson, M.D.		
☐	HARRY'S GAME—Seymour	23019-8	1.95
☐	TRADING UP—Lea	23014-7	1.95
☐	CAPTAINS AND THE KINGS—Caldwell	23069-4	2.25
☐	"I AIN'T WELL—BUT I SURE AM	23007-4	1.75
	BETTER"—Lair		
☐	THE GOLDEN PANTHER—Thorpe	23006-6	1.50
☐	IN THE BEGINNING—Potok	22980-7	1.95
☐	DRUM—Onstott	22920-3	1.95
☐	LORD OF THE FAR ISLAND—Holt	22874-6	1.95
☐	DEVIL WATER—Seton	22888-6	1.95
☐	CSARDAS—Pearson	22885-1	1.95
☐	CIRCUS—MacLean	22875-4	1.95
☐	WINNING THROUGH INTIMIDATION—	22836-3	1.95
	Ringer		
☐	THE POWER OF POSITIVE THINKING—	22819-3	1.75
	Peale		
☐	VOYAGE OF THE DAMNED—	22449-X	1.75
	Thomas & Witts		
☐	THINK AND GROW RICH—Hill	X2812	1.75
☐	EDEN—Ellis	X2772	1.75

Buy them at your local bookstores or use this handy coupon for ordering:

FAWCETT PUBLICATIONS, P.O. Box 1014, Greenwich Conn. 06830

Please send me the books I have checked above. Orders for less than 5 books must include 60c for the first book and 25c for each additional book to cover mailing and handling. Orders of 5 or more books postage is Free. I enclose $_____ in check or money order.

Mr/Mrs/Miss_____

Address_____

City_____ State/Zip_____

Please allow 4 to 5 weeks for delivery. This offer expires 6/78.   A-14

Taylor Caldwell

☐	NEVER VICTORIOUS, NEVER DEFEATED	08435-9	1.95
☐	TENDER VICTORY	08298-4	1.50
☐	THIS SIDE OF INNOCENCE	08434-0	1.75
☐	YOUR SINS AND MINE	00331-6	1.25
☐	THE ARM AND THE DARKNESS	C2627	1.95
☐	CAPTAINS AND THE KINGS	23069-4	2.25
☐	DIALOGUES WITH THE DEVIL	G2768	1.50
☐	THE FINAL HOUR	C2579	1.95
☐	GLORY AND THE LIGHTNING	C2562	1.95
☐	GRANDMOTHER AND THE PRIESTS	C2664	1.95
☐	GREAT LION OF GOD	C2445	1.95
☐	THE LATE CLARA BEAME	23157-7	1.50
☐	MAGGIE—HER MARRIAGE	23119-4	1.50
☐	NO ONE HEARS BUT HIM	Q2507	1.50
☐	ON GROWING UP TOUGH	23082-1	1.50
☐	A PILLAR OF IRON	C2418	1.95
☐	THE ROMANCE OF ATLANTIS	X2748	1.75
☐	TESTIMONY OF TWO MEN	C2416	1.95
☐	WICKED ANGEL	Q2740	1.50
☒	TO LOOK AND PASS	X3491	1.75

Buy them at your local bookstores or use this handy coupon for ordering:

Dorothy Eden

Ms. Eden's novels have enthralled millions of readers for many years. Here is your chance to order any or all of her bestselling titles direct by mail.

☐ AN AFTERNOON WALK	23072-4	1.75
☐ DARKWATER	23153-4	1.75
☐ THE HOUSE ON HAY HILL	X2839	1.75
☐ LADY OF MALLOW	23167-4	1.75
☐ THE MARRIAGE CHEST	23032-5	1.50
☐ MELBURY SQUARE	22973-4	1.75
☐ THE MILLIONAIRE'S DAUGHTER	23186-0	1.95
☐ NEVER CALL IT LOVING	23143-7	1.95
☐ RAVENSCROFT	22998-X	1.50
☐ THE SHADOW WIFE	22802-9	1.50
☐ SIEGE IN THE SUN	Q2736	1.50
☐ SLEEP IN THE WOODS	23075-9	1.75
☐ SPEAK TO ME OF LOVE	22735-9	1.75
☐ THE TIME OF THE DRAGON	23059-7	1.95
☐ THE VINES OF YARRABEE	23184-4	1.95
☐ WAITING FOR WILLA	23187-9	1.50
☐ WINTERWOOD	23185-2	1.75

Buy them at your local bookstores or use this handy coupon for ordering:

FAWCETT PUBLICATIONS, P.O. Box 1014, Greenwich Conn. 06830

Please send me the books I have checked above. Orders for less than 5 books must include 60c for the first book and 25c for each additional book to cover mailing and handling. Orders of 5 or more books postage is Free. I enclose $_____ in check or money order.

Mr/Mrs/Miss_____

Address_____

City_____ State/Zip_____

Please allow 4 to 5 weeks for delivery. This offer expires 6/78.　　A-5

Joyce Carol Oates

☐	THE ASSASINS	23000-7	2.25
☐	BY THE NORTH GATE	P2302	1.25
☐	DO WITH ME WHAT YOU WILL	22294-2	1.95
☐	EXPENSIVE PEOPLE	23154-2	1.75
☐	A GARDEN OF EARTHLY DELIGHTS	23194-1	1.75
☐	THE GODDESS AND OTHER WOMEN	C2774	1.95
☐	MARRIAGES AND INFIDELITIES	23047-3	1.95
☐	THEM	22745-6	1.95
☐	UPON THE SWEEPING FLOOD	P2463	1.25
☐	THE WHEEL OF LOVE	C2923	1.95
☐	WITH SHUDDERING FALL	X2930	1.75
☐	WONDERLAND	22951-3	1.95
☐	LOVE AND ITS DERANGEMENTS	30811-1	1.75
☐	WHERE ARE YOU GOING,	30795-6	1.75
☐	WHERE HAVE YOU BEEN?		

Buy them at your local bookstores or use this handy coupon for ordering: